A CRYPTIC CONFESSION

Down at my feet, a thin sheet of paper must have escaped the old leatherbound book of handwritten recipes I'd been examining. I retrieved it and laid it flat on the butcher-block table. It was written in Latin. Wes bent over it and started reading aloud. It was just like Wes to be fluent in a dead language.

"... with grave suspicions that the purpose was to eliminate our most Reverend Father ... Hey, Mad, this isn't a recipe. It seems to be ..." He read on quickly to himself, and then looked up, startled. "It's signed by a Brother Ugo. And I believe he's confessing ... to murder."

"Just when things were looking up," Wesley muttered. "Just when we were going to create the hippest party the pope has ever been thrown, you have to go finding a little old confession to murder."

"It's probably nothing," I said, tucking the page into a drawer. "It's so old anyway, it can't have anything to do with us."

"Oh baby," Wes said, smiling despite himself, "from your lips to God's ears."

Other Madeline Bean Catering Mysteries by
Jerrilyn Farmer
from Avon Twilight

SYMPATHY FOR THE DEVIL

IMMACULATE RECEPTION

A MADELINE BEAN CATERING MYSTERY

Jerrilyn Farmer

This is a work of fiction. Names, characters, places, and incidents either are the product of the author's imagination or are used fictitiously. Any resemblance to actual events, locales, organizations, or persons, living or dead, is entirely coincidental and beyond the intent of either the author or the publisher.

AVON BOOKS, INC.
1350 Avenue of the Americas
New York, New York 10019

Inside cover author photo by Ronna Kovner
Published by arrangement with the author
Library of Congress Catalog Card Number: 98-90924
ISBN: 0-380-79597-3
www.avonbooks.com/twilight

First Avon Twilight Printing: April 1999

Printed in the U.S.A.

WCD 10 9 8 7 6 5 4 3 2

For my husband, Chris Farmer

Chapter 1

The way the sun filtered through the lace curtains, softening the light as it danced upon the Formica-topped table, was beautiful. The sound of Xav's voice, low, yet full of enthusiasm as he casually talked of traveling to Rome next month, was beautiful. The taste of freshly baked johnnycakes, the warm cornbread simple and moist and sweet, was beautiful. I smiled at Xav and then turned my face quickly away so that he wouldn't see my eyes.

"This recipe came from Baltimore," Xav said. "I think we might want to mention something about the history of the johnnycake. What do you think?"

I think I'm not as ready to work with the man I had planned to marry as I had thought.

Xavier Jones had been that one—the one you only find once in a lifetime, if you're lucky to find such a one at all. We'd met at the Culinary Institute in San Francisco ten years ago. Xavier had been simply the most gifted student they'd ever had. He soared above our class and promised to be the future star chef, admired and followed and envied by us all. When Xav and I fell in love, our future seemed to be guaranteed. Together we'd create a wonderful restaurant and inn. People would make it their destination, like the auberge-hotels in France. I'd decorate and manage and help cook, while Xavier would create his incredible dishes and delight and astound the culinary establishment. In the world of fine food and wine, we'd rule. That was the dream. That was the plan. That didn't happen.

"Did you know that back in colonial America, Jesuits would ride their horses on a circuit of towns in Maryland to see what the people needed and how they could help? They traveled with 'journey cakes' . . ."

"Which is where we get the name 'johnnycakes'?"

"Exactly. This old recipe for corn bread could be baked very quickly and these johnnycakes were sturdy enough to carry in their backpacks."

"I don't know if we need to emphasize the 'sturdiness' of the cakes, do you?"

Xavier laughed as he looked into my eyes. "You're so delicate. Why not boast about their sturdiness? Hard times required sturdy food."

We were working together on a project for charity. It was to be a cookbook that featured many historical recipes. When Xavier called me, I had been happy to hear from him. We were very civilized. We'd remained friends all these years. Of course, maintaining a casual friendship with an ex-fiancé had not seemed difficult when we'd been living three thousand miles apart. In fact, since we broke up we'd only spoken on the telephone a few times and exchanged cards now and then. I'd been curious to see him. In all those years he could have gained weight, lost hair, gone stupid.

I looked at him now, as he stood at the sink cleaning up from our afternoon of marathon johnnycake baking. His body was absolutely adorable, fit and on the thin side. His dark blond hair was thick and straight as I'd remembered, with a lighter streak that hung in a tuft over one eye. And there was not a stupid bone in his body.

Xavier turned and surveyed the tidied up kitchen. "Would it be okay if we leave the research materials here?" Xavier had brought over several crates of ancient recipe books, which were now neatly stacked in a corner of my commercial kitchen. See, the reality of my last ten years is that I haven't married. I never even opened a restaurant, let alone an inn. For the past seven years I've been running Madeline Bean Catering with my partner Wesley Westcott, my best friend. I guess one of life's lessons has taught me to think better of mixing my professional goals with my romantic ones.

"Just leave the crates where they are. I want to read through some of the recipes, anyway."

Xav moved over to the table and picked up his jacket. I stood up.

"I knew it would be great to see you again," he said. "I've been thinking about you. A lot."

What could I say? I had that sense that there are way too many feelings swirling around. Like it hurts to blink. Like your throat gets stiff. Maybe a mixture of anger and hopefulness and forlorn attraction, but the anger wins.

He was looking at me with such a sweet and loving expression. It just made my heart hurt with a long-familiar pain. I hadn't felt anything like this pain in years and years. What the hell!

"Madeline, would it be all right if I said a blessing on your beautiful home?"

Oh, yeah. I forgot to mention. My former fiancé? He's a Jesuit brother.

Chapter 2

"I love the name 'Mad Bean.' I mean, it's funny."

Wesley Westcott sat at a stool pulled up to the tall butcher-block table that occupied the center of my kitchen. Wes and I sold our previous catering firm a few months ago and we were now starting up a new one. Since there had been an unfortunate event at our last big party—well, all right, the host was murdered—our old business had spiraled downward. Don't get me wrong, the Hollywood crowd we cater to is into horror. Only it turns out they prefer their dead bodies on screen, not off.

Then, in a twist of fate that leaves me smiling still, our company was bought for millions just when we were about to go under. How did this amazing windfall occur? Wes insists I'm lucky. Lucky, yeah. I'm afraid you don't have to know me very long to get the irony.

It's odd how things work out. Making gobs of money was never my primary objective, but now that I am getting acquainted with having gobs, I am finding I do like the feeling. Finally, for once in my life, I am not worrying about *How much?* and *Do we have enough?* Maybe Wes is right and my luck is changing. It's just that I'm forever on the lookout for the yang that's around the corner, waiting to yank down my happy little yin.

"Mad Bean Events?" I was not pleased that Wes wanted to name our new events-planning firm using my nickname. After the fiasco with the poisoning at Madeline Bean Catering, it seemed prudent to go a little lower profile. "Don't you think the connection to our unfortunate past . . ."

"Heck, no! Not only were we blameless, but you helped solve the crime. Let's ride on the publicity. This town forgets the details, but not . . ." Wes prompted me, waiting for my acquiescence.

". . . the star," I said, shaking my head at him. L.A. has its own colorful rules, written and unwritten. Like birdwatching, Wesley and I had taken to identifying each oddly plumed one we happened to stumble across. A newly spotted rule was not to be ignored. So in that spirit, I guessed I would have no recourse but to christen our new business . . . Mad Bean.

"Mad Bean . . . hmm . . ." Wes picked up a pencil and started sketching in his notebook. He was drafting our new logo, trying this type style and that. I peeked over his shoulder and smiled. Wes had many talents.

We'd met eight years ago. He had been a grad student at Berkeley and I was starting out working as pastry chef at a very trendy restaurant there. We had become instant friends, like it had been meant to be and we got it. Eventually, we decided to try our luck down south. We moved to Los Angeles with the aim of starting small, specializing in parties that provided original ideas and knockout food, but our dream was to design major galas and give them a creative twist. Wit, we hope, might find us a niche. In time, we developed a reputation for the outrageous, like the full rodeo we staged for a famous T.V. cowboy's third wedding. It was an awesome sight as the bridesmaids were carried in on the backs of white horses who'd been dyed lavender. To match the bride's color scheme, the pooper-scoopers had been decorated with sunflowers tied on with raffia.

Our recent windfall meant we could concentrate on the lavish, technically challenging, food-oriented events we'd always dreamed of. My mood was lifting. After eleven years of cooking full time, I was finally going to "start" at the top.

"By the way, what are all those books and things?" Wes

asked. He was coloring in his improvised logos with a set of markers, but he glanced over to the crates of recipe books that Xav had left behind.

Over the years I'd been in and out of several relationships. As far as I knew, Wes had not been involved with a woman in the time I'd known him. We didn't discuss his love life, but mine was always open for debate.

Wes's general opinion was that I neither selected men who were bad enough to be an obvious flight from commitment, nor good enough to keep. My feeling was, you can only choose from what comes swimming by and some days it's just chum.

At the time that Wes and I became buds, I'd just finished cooking school. It was after Xav had left me and disappeared. Although Wes had seen pictures, the two of them had never met. I guess the time had come to tell Wesley that Xavier was back and I'd started seeing him.

Wes reminded me, "Those books, where'd they come from?"

I looked at the stack of cookbooks in the corner and answered him. "Oh, those," I said, stalling. "Just some old recipes."

"Anything good?"

Wes was like a terrier. He'd hunt this rabbit down. Best to be up front.

"Funny thing," I began. As I spoke I walked over to the crates, shuffling the old papers and leather-bound volumes around. "I got a call the other day from Xavier Jones. You remember, I've told you about him. Xavier was my old . . . uh . . . friend."

Wes put down the colored markers and regarded me. "*Father* Xavier?"

"Actually, he's a brother, but anyway, he asked if I could help with a fundraising project he was putting together. He has plans to publish a little book on the secrets of Jesuit cooking. He's made requests to the heads of all these Jesuit kitchens as well as other Catholic institutions and he's collected some incredibly old recipes. Look."

I felt the binding on a heavy old leather notebook. I opened it and noticed that the recipes had been written by hand in a beautiful script. Some of the old recipes had dates that indicated the loose pages had been gathered into the notebook over two hundred years ago.

"Yes. I'm sure they're amazing, Madeline." Wesley stared at me. "But what about the good brother?"

"He's fine."

"He's fine," Wesley said, parroting my nonchalant tone. "And how are you?"

"I'm fine, too. We're all just fine." I smiled to make it so. "Anyway, he had a pretty stunning suggestion."

Wesley, at upwards of six feet three or four, stood up. His perfect posture, his thin frame, his thick brown crewcut all seemed to be at attention. "Oh, my God," Wes said in a stunned tone. "He's leaving the church."

If the conclusion was irresistible enough, Wes could be counted on to jump.

"God, no! Can we please leave the past back in the past?"

"Can we?" Wes asked me kindly. He was a good friend. He would not be fooled into thinking his best pal had no feelings on this touchy subject. I just wasn't ready to look at them, yet.

"Aren't you in the least interested in what Xavier wants us to do?"

"Us?"

"You, me, Holly . . ." I ticked us off on three fingers. Including our assistant, Holly, we were what remained of Madeline Bean Catering.

"You mean Mad Bean Events?" He asked, perking up.

I ignored the figurative elbow that was being jabbed into my ribs. "If you insist. The reason that Brother Xavier Jones is in Los Angeles is to help the city coordinate planning for an unbelievably special event. Xavier asked us to oversee L.A.'s official . . ."

Wes was looking at me with attention. The sadist in me made me string it out. "Sit down Wesley," I instructed.

Intrigued, Wes sat back down on his stool.

I can be mean, so I waited a bit and then, with great dignity, said, "We're going to throw a party for the pope."

"Oh, lordie."

"Well, just about. Yes."

"But I had no idea! You mean here? In L.A.? I haven't heard a thing about the pope coming."

"It's not been announced, yet. But Xav is in town to do advance work."

"I'm blown away," Wes said.

I was content. I could count the times I'd shocked the man on one hand. With four fingers missing.

"So, what do you think?"

"Feed the pontiff? Are you kidding? No sweat. What's the count?"

"Two thousand for breakfast," I said. "I didn't think it would be a problem."

It was good to be getting back to work. We both loved the creativity and problem solving involved in planning parties.

"Mad, this is too cool. I mean, the pope will be eating our food. And a whole bunch of saintly types, as well."

"Calm down. This is a city-sponsored party. I'm sure a good number of local politicians will be in the mix."

"How on earth did we get this gig? Don't we have to be blessed or something?"

There's an element of good luck and good timing to everything. One week ago, Xavier called me. It was the first time we'd spoken in almost four years. He had a couple of favors to ask, he said. That got my heart pumping. But then, of course, it turned out to have nothing to do with us. Of course not. Silly to have jumped.

His first request was easy: could I help him do some work on his Jesuit cookbook project?

So. We would finally see each other again, I thought, as I said yes, sure, fine.

Then he told me the real reason he was in L.A.—the secret reason.

He said the city needed someone to take over a very special party. They needed a firm that would work well amidst the mind-numbing realities of city bureaucracy as well as the equally labyrinthine levels of decision-making within the Archdiocese of Los Angeles and then be willing to submit every idea to Rome for overall approval. Not to mention set up a kitchen under the glare of the LAPD and U.S. Secret Service. The city's original choice to handle the event planning didn't work out. Now, time was short and they needed a miracle.

The event was to be truly awe-inspiring, and such a lavish party would usually have a skyrocket budget to match. But to honor the pope, I was told most of the supplies and services were being donated by generous benefactors. I'd heard that Mayor Burke, who was a serious contributor to Catholic charities and causes, was personally underwriting the cost of insurance for the gala. There were other wealthy friends of the church involved, as well.

No detail was being left to chance. Security was incredibly tight. I was asked not to let anyone know of the pope's visit, not even my partner, until they'd cleared him and the job was truly ours.

On the morning I presented our bid, I was asked to see the mayor. After the city's recent false start, he was taking it upon himself to approve the event planner.

The charming man did not try to grill me, but instead joked around and flattered me for three minutes. Then, he graciously ushered me to his outer office to wait among a roomful of hopeful visitors.

"Victor," the mayor called out to a very elderly man, perhaps the only one in the room not trying to catch the mayor's eye. "We are so grateful to you. Let me wrap up a little business and I'll be right with you."

Across the room, an overweight Latino man, dressed in ultra baggy jeans and an oversize T-shirt, made his presence felt. His dark complexion was marred by scars. As he sat, waiting, he kept hitting the fist of one hand into the palm of the other, like he was toughening up for the ring. I felt he wanted to get my attention, but I carefully looked the other way, back towards Victor and his companion.

Since I had to wait, too, I sat in a black leather chair next to the mayor's buddy.

I tried to guess his age. Maybe ninety? Victor had a perfectly bald head and the benign expression of a happy gnome. He wore an expensive suit, heavy gold cufflinks, and, actually, too much Calvin Klein for Men cologne. I tried to guess what he might have been before retirement. Attorney, I thought.

Next to Victor sat a young woman with a radical cropped haircut. It went from black at the root to flaming red at the tip. I was amazed at how perfectly the spikes stood at attention. This gal must spend a bundle on gel. A small gold hoop delicately pierced her left nostril.

How could I not eavesdrop on such an unlikely pair?

"You are always giving," she chided him, with affection.

Wife? Even in L.A. this would be considered bizarre. While young wives were a recognized status symbol, this one stretched the boundaries of even that Hollywood fatcat privilege.

"Why not?" he asked, amused.

"Let someone else give, for a change," she said, although it sounded more like teasing than a serious complaint.

I stole another glance in her direction. Way too young for a daughter.

"The good Lord has given me much," said Victor quietly. "I can only do the same, Beatrice."

"Then let the mayor give you his award. Why shouldn't people know how generous my great-grandpa is?"

Aha. I felt better about the whole relationship and relaxed. That shows how weird things can get here sometimes. You never really know.

The young man across the room stood up and stretched, exposing a not very pretty gut beneath his oversize tee. I felt his brown eyes on me and kept my gaze down. Who were these people who waited to speak to the mayor? And was security nearby?

"I do not do this for awards, cara . . ." I heard Victor saying, but then the secretary called me and I rose.

"Miss Bean," the woman said when I approached her desk. "The mayor would like to thank you for coming down here on such short notice. Mr. Zoda," she called.

I had been dismissed.

As I turned to go, I caught the eye of the young Latino man. He did not return my casual smile. I still believed that pretty much every male within city limits was looking to score. But—addendum to the rule—not necessarily with me.

By the time I drove home, Xavier had already left a message. We were approved by church and state, as it were. We had been granted the most thrilling contract to be had by a caterer since the grand opening of the Getty Museum.

I told the entire tale to Wesley and he loved it. To one another, we were better than Oprah.

"Xavier made it happen," I said.

"You know what they say in this town," Wes said admiringly. "It's not about talent, it's about contacts."

Another of our oddball L.A. rules flew by and I smiled.

"I offered to do the event at cost, of course."

"Which we can manage," Wes said with a gleam in his eye, "because we're newly well to do. Oh, I always suspected that money was in some way connected with happiness."

"Not happiness. Freedom."

"Yes, and now we're free to feed the *pope*. Wow. This is a great way to kick off Mad Bean Events."

"Now there are a few hundred details they need to settle. And the pope's schedule is not nailed down. But assuming there are no pressing miracles, come hell or high water, we're feeding His Holiness."

"Madeline, I'm actually feeling a lot more conciliatory toward this ex-boyfriend of yours. I may not beat him up."

That got a laugh out of me. Wes is the last one you'd

ever imagine fighting anyone. It's me who likes to punch it out, when I'm at the gym, anyway. But his loyalty to our friendship is awesome.

"Your enemies are my enemies." He smiled back at me.

"Xavier Jones is not my enemy." I sighed.

"He broke your heart, didn't he?" Wes was suddenly serious.

"Everyone gets their heart broken. Besides, that was years ago."

"Yeah. But hearts take a long time to heal." He looked me over and then asked, "Despite everything that happened and all those years, when you saw him again, you must have felt . . . something?"

"What are you talking about? He's taken a vow of celibacy. He's practically a priest."

"Hey, watch out. You dropped a page."

Down at my feet, a thin sheet of paper must have escaped the old book of recipes I'd been examining. I retrieved it and laid it flat on the butcher-block table. It was written in Latin. I picked up a word here and there. Wes bent over it and started reading aloud. It was just like Wes to be fluent in a dead language.

" '. . . with grave suspicions that the purpose was to eliminate our most Reverend Father . . .' Hey, Mad, this isn't a recipe. It seems to be . . ." he read on quickly to himself and then looked up, startled.

"What? What is it?"

"It's signed by a Brother Ugo. And I believe he's *confessing*."

"Like confessing his sins to a priest?" I asked.

"No. Like confessing to *murdering* a priest."

I stared at Wesley. "Could this be a joke?"

"This is not Catholic humor."

"Does he happen to mention which priest?"

Wes read it through again. "It's only one page from what looks like a personal diary. It goes on, but we don't have . . ."

As Wes spoke, I quickly turned the old cookbook upside

down and shook it gently. No other pages slipped out. I put the heavy leather binder on the counter and flipped through the recipes. All were bound in place. There were no other loose diary pages.

I looked at the paper again.

"Well, it can't be *that* old. Look. It's written on plain paper, not parchment."

Wes turned the document over. "I believe it's acid-free paper," he said, feeling the surface, "but that doesn't mean it's contemporary. The Jesuit order observes the Rule of Economy and hasn't used parchment, which is much more expensive, in their casual documents since, I'd hazard a guess . . . the fourteenth century."

"You mean this confession might be seven hundred years old?"

I looked at the neat black ink and the even rows across the sheet.

"It's so odd," I said, puzzled. "A confession . . ."

"Yes."

"Of murder."

"Yes."

"I wonder what it's all about?"

"Just when things were looking up," Wesley muttered. "Just when we were about to launch Mad Bean Events with the hippest party the pope has ever been thrown, you have to go finding a little old confession to murder."

"It's probably nothing," I said, tucking the page into a drawer. "It's so old anyway, it can't have anything to do with us."

"Oh, baby," Wes said, smiling despite himself, "from your lips to God's ears."

Chapter 3

"You mean the *pope* pope, or some other pope?" Holly asked, her mind apparently blown senseless.

"You know the one," I said. "Rome, big hat, loved by millions."

"Is this cool or what?" Holly asked.

"Cold," I said.

"Freezing," agreed Wes.

Holly giggled as she pulled her sweater tight around her long thin arms. As our first and only full-time employee, Holly has been with us almost from the start. She assists at parties, helps keep the administration details of our business in order, and brings her own creative zing to our close-knit little team.

"Do you think the pope likes Mexican?" Holly asked, deep in thought.

"He loves all people," admonished Wesley. "And, my word, Mexico is predominantly Catholic."

"No, junior!" Holly snorted. "Mexican as in *food*. Honestly!" She stood up and stretched. Holly is a tall one, nearly six feet without benefit of heels, and she seems to keep her astonishingly thin figure intact despite eating like a mastodon. Today she wore a pair of faded bell-bottom blue jeans with a cropped white T-shirt that came well short of covering her navel. Over that she wore a thin black sweater, because despite her devotion to her own wacky sense of fashion, this girl was always cold.

"Oh, *Mexican*," Wes said, thinking. "I like that. What do you think, Madeline?"

"Interesting," I agreed.

"I'll start gathering recipes," Wes volunteered, heading upstairs where I have a library of cookbooks and files of menus.

"And I'll get my notes about the requirements," I offered as I walked to my downstairs office.

"Maybe we should pack a basket of baked goodies for the Popemobile," Holly suggested, as she followed me through the house. "Papal food to go."

My old white stucco Spanish hugs the Hollywood Hills. Modest in size, it mixes graceful strokes of wrought iron with Art Deco flourishes and is topped with its original red tiles, typical of the homes built in the twenties in Southern California.

But lovely as I find my house to be, you'd never mistake it for the suburbs. My nearest neighbor is a retaining wall that separates my backyard from the full blast of the Hollywood Freeway, eight lanes of congestion built in the fifties smack through the center of historic Whitley Heights.

I've lived here for the past five years and converted the lower level of the house for work. The remodeled kitchen has been outfitted for commercial-size food preparation, while I use the former dining room, complete with chandelier and French doors that open onto a back courtyard, as my office. On my desk, I found the notes Xavier had written out with the requirements for the pope's event. Across the room, on the wall over Wesley's desk, a black and white photo of my home's original owner stands guard.

The house had been built by a silent film star, huge at the time, a comic famous for his "googley" eyes. Down from his silver frame, old Ben Turpin gave me his trademark "look" as I checked the notes.

Standing there, on the polished hardwood floor, I felt the creative vibrations of my home's former inhabitant. And, despite the urban snarl and freeway noise so nearby, the atmosphere around Whitley Heights was downright romantic. Throughout the years, it attracted the cross-eyed, oddest and spunkiest to reside in these hills.

Wesley joined Holly and me in the office. We hunkered down in comfortable chairs, me behind my desk with Wesley and Hol opposite. A few hours blurred by as we came up with and rejected dozens of breakfast extravaganza scenarios. The sun was setting and we devised a plan to get creative and cook up some of our more interesting ideas right then and there.

We turned on lights as we moved through the darkening hallways on our way to the kitchen. After hours of talking about morning food, we had worked up major cravings for eggs and cured meats and pastries. As each of us found a spot of counter space upon which to work, we fell into a companionable silence and began gathering our ingredients.

When I'd been baking earlier, I did up several lovely fresh whole wheat loaves. There was something about their humble farmhouse simplicity that started me thinking. I was inspired to create an equally rustic dish in which the bread could star. I began by cutting each loaf into thick slices, which I planned to toast. As I prepared the grill, I shot a look over at the others.

Wesley was elbow-deep in the flour bin while Holly was chopping tomatoes. They had their heads together.

"What are you two talking about?" I asked.

"You," Holly answered promptly. "I just asked Wes who you had to sleep with to get us this pope gig." She was baiting me, of course. And her approach was so shameless that even Wes stopped the Cuisinart to hear how I'd answer her.

I shook my head at them sternly. I gave off a "Hey, this time you've gone too far!" scowl. They weren't fooled for a minute.

"So tell me all about this Xavier character," Holly asked, not to be deterred. "Were you really going to marry him?"

"First of all, I haven't even seen the man for over eight

years.'' I turned the bread slices over and brushed them with melted butter.

''And . . . ?''

''It's strange, you know. I was afraid that I'd see him again and maybe I wouldn't even know him. Maybe he would look too different from my memories, like a stranger.''

''Did he?''

''He was exactly the same. Cute and sweet and really talented. He always had this genius about food and he still does. But even so, everything was different. And I'm pretty sure it's me.''

''Life goes on. One changes,'' Wes said.

''Isn't that sad?'' I looked at my friends. ''I just felt this melancholy kind of whoosh. He'd meant so much to me. And now, I'm not sure if I remember who I used to be back then.'' I had never been keen on talking over the past.

''End of innocence. Growing up. Reality. It's hell,'' Wes said.

''Why did he, you know, go south on you?'' Holly asked as she continued her work preparing what looked like salsa, and if she didn't pay closer attention, it was going to get really hot.

''Who knows?''

''How awful. Here you are one minute going to marry the boy of your dreams and then next minute he's, like, adios.''

''Holly, enough jalapeños,'' Wes suggested from his position near the deep fryer.

''Oops.'' Holly stopped mincing and paid closer attention to her work.

''So how did it end? What did he say?'' Wes asked.

''He made dinner for me. I was sitting there, chatting on about our restaurant plans or something. And then he told me to stop for a minute.''

''What did he make?'' Wes asked with interest.

''Who cares?'' Holly scowled at him. ''Mad, go on.''

* * *

I never saw it coming, of course. Simply a stupid twenty-one-year-old idiot. Xav had been experimenting with recipes for *mouclade*, a succulent dish of plump mussels in their shells swimming in garlic- and shallot-scented broth. I remember he used these small Prince Edward Island mussels. Odd what one remembers.

The little kitchen of my apartment smelled wonderful. The windows were steamy from cooking. I was sipping a white wine we'd just studied at the institute and talking about the merits of leasing a small store in Healdsburg. I'd gotten it into my head that a smart way for us to start out would be to open a gourmet market with a tiny dining room on the side.

Xav came over to where I was sitting and bent down. He kissed my forehead and said, "Madeline, stop for a minute. I have something to tell you. We need to talk."

The moment crystallized. Air became solid. My simple, presumptuous happiness was for that last moment intact.

"We always talk," I teased him. I was still the same girl, with but seconds left of that self before the end came neat and sharp and cruelly swift.

"I've made a decision, Madeline. It's time I tell you."

"What?" I asked, and then was momentarily distracted by the unmistakable sound of a guillotine blade as it silently descended.

Xav sat down on a kitchen chair across from me and took my hand. He was smiling.

"What's going on, Xav?"

"You know about my feelings for you, of course."

"You love me." I couldn't imagine what was going on, as the guillotine blade, now a whisper, kept coming.

"I'm going to finish up at the Culinary Institute next month. And then I am going to study at the seminary. Maddie, please see how important this is. If I don't listen to this voice inside of me, I might regret it. Can you understand?"

"I'm lost. What are you saying? When are we getting married?" I was struck by how reasonable and normal his voice sounded, deep and reassuring. What was he going on about?

"We have to postpone the wedding."

"Postpone it? Why?"

"Didn't you hear what I said? I'm joining the Society of Jesus, Madeline. I'm going to enter the novitiate of St. Isaac Jogues in Pennsylvania."

"But our wedding . . ."

Xav brought my hand up to his lips and kissed it gently. "I will be taking vows. You understand, don't you? This has nothing to do with you."

"We're breaking up?" I finally heard that horrible blade hit the block. "You don't want . . ."

"I love you, Madeline. Please believe me. But this is the way it has to be."

Tears collected along my lower lids. "This can't be happening. We love each other. I don't believe you want to leave me."

"I don't. I don't." He looked at me and seemed to run out of things to say.

Holly and Wes were staring at me. I flashed them a grin. "He never said why. I was pretty young. I mean, I thought I knew him. That's a laugh right there. But I learned. You never know people. Not even the ones you are closest to."

"You know me," Wes said with assurance.

"You know me," Holly echoed.

"Maybe I do," I conceded. I'd made it my business to study people and their behavior. I looked closely now, and scrutinized the signs and signals that sometimes go counter to the words. My clients were startled at how well I was able to interpret their wishes, even when they'd failed to fully articulate them. It was my hypervigilance. Let's just say I was now on guard, more or less permanently.

Wesley kept a sharp eye on the frying basket he'd dunked, sputtering and hissing, into the hot oil. Holly was expertly working a skillet, flipping freshly made flour tortillas, while I turned to peel a paper-thin slice of *prosciutto di Parma.* I placed the delectable Italian cured ham upon the toast and kept my eye on the eggs I was poaching.

I caught Holly looking at me. She had such a googley expression, she actually reminded me of my home's comic ancestor, Ben Turpin.

"What, Hol? What are you thinking in that twisted head of yours?"

"Just hear me out. I know he killed you back then, Mad. But this Brother Xavier isn't back in your life by accident. He's been brooding for a decade about the decision he made. He had to see you again," Holly insisted. "And you look gorgeous. You're successful. You're doing what you always said you'd do, making it in the food world. I don't know what you were like way back then, but today you are devastating. I bet he came back here to see if you and he still had a chance."

"Get out!" I had to laugh. "It's not like he left me for another woman, you moron. He picked God. You've been watching the soaps again, haven't you?"

"Scoff if you want. Someday 'General Hospital' is going to get the respect it deserves. It's Dickens for the nineties."

I checked my watch. It had somehow gotten to be eight-thirty in the evening.

"Breakfast's ready," Wes hollered.

We each brought our creations to the pine farm table and set out our dishes. Wes had a flair for pastry, and tonight he made tender sourdough doughnuts laced with cherries, which he had piled high on a lovely yellow platter. Holly was pouring freshly squeezed orange juice, spiked with vodka, along with her dish: creamy scrambled eggs, tucked into rolled fresh tortillas, served with a lively tomato and cilantro salsa. I finished my offering by topping the prosciutto-covered toast with the poached eggs and then drizzling them with scallion oil.

We served ourselves with generous portions of everything. As I cut into my poached egg, the green of the scallion oil swirled against the molten gold of the yolks and I sighed with pleasure. For a few minutes, the tasting and critiquing and eating took over a hundred percent of our attention. The respite from analyzing my sorry past, however, did not last long.

"But Brother Xavier's come back to you," Holly said, after thinking things over. "I find that significant in the extreme."

"Hello? Is anyone besides me on Planet Earth?"

"You guys are so trusting," Holly said. "I swear, if you watched daytime T.V. more, you would not be so out of it."

"Is there any way we could change the subject?" I asked.

"Like what's more interesting than a man of the cloth visiting his former fiancée?"

"How about the confession note?" Wes suggested, catching my eye. He was saving me. I love that guy.

"What confession?"

"We found an old document that appears to be a confession to murder written by someone calling himself Brother Ugo."

"No kidding? Who's Ugo?"

"We don't know," Wes said, picking up the tale. "But the note was written in Latin and sounded persuasively real." Wes pulled it out of his folder and smoothed the old paper on the pine table. Both of us came to look at it more closely.

"It starts in the middle of a sentence, like it's the last page of a longer document." Wes was finding his place, mumbling a few words in Latin until he found the right place. "Here. He says, '. . . I have sinned. I now know I am the one responsible but I am not allowed to talk. There are crimes so enormous that no one may ever hear them spoken of. I have taken a life. This I never intended. I am now filled with grave suspicions that the purpose was to eliminate our Reverend Father. I have forsaken my training. I should have followed Rule Six. Had I but kept the Rule, I should not be guilty of this foulest sin against our very

Father. There can be no forgiveness for such a fool as I have been.' That's it. Then it's signed 'Fra. Ugo.' Brother Ugo."

"Is this for real?" Holly wondered.

"It seems to be," said Wes. "We don't know who this guy Ugo is, of course."

"And we don't know when it was written," I added, "or where."

"And we haven't a clue about the alleged victim." Wes said. "But it's disturbing, isn't it?"

Holly sat in thought. "Can we look into it?"

"I'm not sure it's really any of our business," Wesley said.

"But maybe someone was killed," Holly suggested.

Wes shook his head. "We don't know enough. Chances are this is a very old document. We found it tucked into a notebook of recipes and some of the recipes in it go back two centuries. And it most likely came from Europe."

"So we're gonna do, like, nothing?"

"Well, I'll give the note to Xavier," I said. "It's his book of recipes. Perhaps the church will investigate."

"But you're so good at finding answers, Mad," Holly said. "You're great at murder."

"That was a one-time-only deal," Wes said with finality.

It's true, I had once met a killer. And I believed I was pretty much at my lifetime limit. "Wes is right," I said reluctantly, glancing again at the mysterious document. "I'm retired. Let's talk about something else."

"You won't talk about your former lover, the priest. You won't talk about murder in the cathedral. Honestly, Maddie, what's left to talk about?"

"Anyone think the doughnuts need more sugar?"

Chapter 4

Things were moving fast. The Vatican had released the news that the pope was going to visit Los Angeles. It would be a brief visit, with only enough time for him to perform a prayer service at Dodger Stadium, a venue that easily held sixty thousand. We'd been given the go-ahead to begin planning for the pope's breakfast, which would take place immediately before his appearance in front of the thousands. The two weeks of prep time disappeared in a dizzying jumble of meetings and approvals and protocol.

With the event three days away, I'd been shopping all morning, placing orders for ingredients, and getting our big news out by the gourmet grapevine. After this morning, suppliers and acquaintances would be spreading the word that Mad Bean was back, and she had the pope. As I danced between the stalls at the early morning produce market, I managed to put the word out that we were still hiring staff, would be interested in finding a new linens supplier, and had not yet committed to coffee beans, but time was short.

I was back home by ten-thirty and proceeded to unload my day's supply of greens into my Traulsen refrigerator. Here, in my cheerful kitchen, amid the fresh grid of white tiles and miles of butcher block counter, stood the industrial-strength restaurant supply appliances. My favorite is the brushed stainless-steel refrigerator with its glass door. The well-lit strawberries and cheeses, salamis and greens become a changeable color-splashed art piece, the focus of my white room. Late at night, during commercials on Leno, I just barefoot it across the terracotta tiles and peer inside for a snack.

This morning I was running a little late. I'd told Arlo to meet me a half an hour ago, so I rushed as I put the last of the fresh radicchio into a yellow bowl and scooted it onto a glass shelf.

"Hey."

I turned and watched Holly pour herself a cup of coffee.

"Hey," I answered. "Have you seen Arlo?"

"Upstairs. He said you were having trouble with the TV."

"You mean I have an actual live male up in my bedroom?" I squealed. I grabbed a can of Diet Coke, my caffeinated comfort drink of choice, and headed up to my room to see how Arlo was doing with my faulty cable.

We'd been seeing each other, pretty much exclusively, for over three years. Arlo Zar is very, very funny. Professionally. Arlo produces a very popular sitcom, which means he writes it, which means he's at the studio a lot. With my catering hours taking up most weekends, we managed to see one another a few times a month. Still, it was the closest I'd come to a relationship and it satisfied Arlo as well.

"Wait a minute," Holly called after me as I dashed down the hall.

"I'll be back," I said, and then climbed the sweeping staircase up to the second floor where I'd fitted out a small apartment for my personal needs. In what had been Ben Turpin's master bedroom, I'd set up a sitting room, with a slipcovered sofa facing the small fireplace decorated with its original Batchelder tiles in a matte moss green. The second bedroom was now my library/dining room, and the humble third bedroom held my humble bed.

It was fun coming home to a man fixing something. I called out to my man.

"Arlo, sweetie?" I sang out down the short hall. "Does my big macho man have his tool out?"

Arlo usually appreciated a double entendre, especially

whilst in my bedroom. What I hadn't accounted for was that Arlo was not alone. In my tiny room, in which my queen-size bed, covered with quilts, and an old dresser could barely coexist, Arlo was talking to someone. I saw right away that the someone was Xavier.

"Oh, hi." I put so much sunny spin on the "hi" that I'm sure no one could hear surprise in my voice. To say nothing of alarm.

"Xavier. Arlo. Well. I guess you two have met." What an idiot I was. They were sitting on my bed with maybe two feet separating them. They'd met.

Arlo was fiddling with a screwdriver, like he'd been working on the cable or something. He looked pretty much the way he always does. His brown curly hair needed cutting, but otherwise he was neat as a pin. He tended to be well pressed, right down to his faded jeans. He's that wiry type, the kind that doesn't carry an ounce of fat. Among his many "quirks" is that he's very particular about his food. It's been pointed out, with my passion for exotic cuisine, the absurdity that I would end up with a guy who will permit no green food to touch his plate, save iceberg, and then only when cut in a wedge and topped with Kraft Thousand Island. I've explained that it keeps me in balance.

I squeezed into the small room and, noting that the bed was crowded with two-thirds of the men I'd ever been involved with, chose instead to lean casually against the wall.

"Madeline." Xav stood up and almost bumped into me, so tightly were we pressed together. "I came by to drop off some ideas . . ."

"Please, sit," I said, interrupting. It was either that or hold my breath for the rest of our conversation. Xav hesitated for a moment and then sat.

"How'd you two end up . . ."

". . . in bed together?" Arlo smirked, looking pretty damn comfortable lounging on my bed.

"We came at the same time. Sorry I didn't call you first, Maddie," Xav explained.

"So I brought him up here to help me debug your cable

mess until you got here. I understand you two are old friends from San Francisco?''

How much background had they covered in their attempt at making small talk? See, I'd told Arlo I'd been engaged a long time ago, but nothing else.

''Been talking long?'' I asked.

''Yeah. I got the dirt. In fifteen minutes I've found out Xavier's most intimate secret.''

''Oh?'' I felt the room rock. Could we be having a mild earthquake?

Xavier was laughing. ''He didn't find me out. I confessed.''

''Shocking,'' Arlo joked. ''Your friend doesn't even own a television.''

''But I apologized, man. Give me a break.''

Yeah. They were getting on like gangbusters. Heaven help me.

''Arlo's been telling me about his work. Fascinating,'' Xavier went on, then turned on the bed and spoke to Arlo. ''Did you ever consider what a blessing it is to have such a huge audience?''

''Every time I renegotiate my contract, pal.''

''People listen to you. Your voice matters. It's a blessing. What a unique opportunity you have to put forth a positive message.''

''I could get another level out of my scripts you mean?'' Arlo suddenly got quiet. ''Jesus, that's exactly what I've been missing in this episode. Amazing.'' Arlo was buzzed. ''You know, Xavier, 'Woman's Work' is filming tomorrow night. How about you coming to see the show?''

''That would be great,'' said Xavier.

''Great,'' I said, with about fifty percent enthusiasm.

''No trouble. And bring a date,'' Arlo offered.

''A date,'' I repeated. Had Arlo missed the vital fact that Xavier was *Brother* Xavier?

Xavier smiled at me and then said to Arlo, ''Thanks. But I don't date.''

"Don't worry. I'll take care of it. We'll find you someone who's not gonna break any mirrors."

This is what comes of not filling in the troops. I was some general.

"Arlo. Brother Xavier is here for the pope's visit. Get it? *Brother* Xavier?"

"Okay, then," Arlo said, standing up quickly and leaving Xav to sit alone on my quilted bed. "Sure wish someone had mentioned that before I went into a ten-minute routine about condoms."

"Never laughed so hard," replied Xavier, smoothly, "notwithstanding the church's position on birth control."

"So," Arlo said, startled but laughing by now, "you're an actual priest? Where's the warning collar?"

"The Society of Jesus also includes those who are called brothers. We are full Jesuits but we are not ordained to the priesthood. Don't feel bad. Actually, very few people know about us."

"But you, uh, brothers can't date," Arlo said, cutting to the chase.

"We take a vow of celibacy, yes."

"Get out of town!"

"Arlo," I said.

"Hey, it's interesting. You're not priests, so what kind of stuff do you do?"

"We serve the church through our work in the community and we practice in occupations outside of what you'd call monastery life, out in the real world. We call this 'service without power.' "

"Kind of the exact opposite of the guys who run my studio." Arlo began to giggle again. "Man, so you're an honest-to-God *Jesuit.* Tell me more."

"Our order was founded by St. Ignatius of Loyola in 1534," Xavier said, smiling a little when he realized that Arlo was truly listening.

I realized for the first time how hard it must be for Xavier, choosing a life that is so foreign to the outside world.

"In the early years," Xavier went on, "Jesuit Brothers

distinguished themselves as architects, painters, musicians, builders, linguists, you name it. After 1814, most of the brothers became artisans. And since the Second Vatican Council, we've been encouraged to obtain advanced degrees."

"No shit."

Before we'd sucked the last oxygen from the tiny room I said, "Shall we go downstairs where I can offer you men something to drink?"

Arlo wanted to reconnect the cable, so I led Xavier back down to the kitchen.

"Great guy," he said.

I checked Xav's face for a reaction. Surely he'd figured out that Arlo and I were on, well, bedroom familiar terms.

"We've been seeing each other for a few years."

"I don't want you to think I'm prying into your private life, Madeline. I don't want to make you feel uncomfortable."

Then why did you come back? Aloud, I asked if he'd like some coffee.

"Thank you."

As I turned and handed him the cup I found him staring. "You lookin' at me?" We used to do that. It was a variation of a line from *Taxi Driver* and when we'd been together we had quoted it back and forth, seeing who could most convincingly recreate DeNiro's reading. Odd. I hadn't thought about that in years.

"You look great, Madeline."

"Thanks."

He sipped his coffee. I refilled my glass of Diet Coke. The seconds ticked silently by.

"When I was told to come to Los Angeles to work on the pope's visit, I knew I had to come and see you. I wanted to."

"I'm glad you did."

"It's been a long time, Madeline."

"Yeah. So what do you think?"

"I thought you'd be married by now, you know? Settled, with lots of kids."

"Yeah. That's me."

"I thought you wanted children. Didn't you?"

"I did. I do. Some day. But not now."

"It would have been easier for me if you had a lot of kids, Madeline. Then I'd know you had found happiness."

"Hey, Xavier. Kids are not the only way a woman can be happy. I never realized you were so . . ."

"No, don't say it. That's not what I really meant, anyway. Let me try to get myself out of that one. See, I just wanted to know that you were all right."

"I'm fine."

"Really?"

"Why did you dump me, Xav? Why did you ask me to marry you and talk about how our life would be and then just . . . ?"

He put down his coffee cup and stared into the small puddle he'd made in his saucer.

"It's all old news anyway, Xav. So just for curiosity's sake, why the hell did you disappear?"

"I didn't want to hurt you. You know that." He took my hand and looked at it. "I had . . ."

Into the kitchen walked Arlo. Xavier looked up and then let go of my hand. The moment was gone.

When no one spoke, Arlo jumped into the void. "Hope I didn't interrupt anything, uh, religious."

"I was just about to show Xavier something interesting. It's an old letter Wes and I found when we were looking through some recipes."

"What letter?" Xav asked.

"It's written in Latin." I went to a drawer and retrieved the document. "It seems to be a confession."

"Whose confession?" Arlo asked.

Xavier read through the Latin and looked up, perplexed. "This is truly bizarre. It seems to be a confession to murder."

"That's my Maddie," Arlo sighed. "She's getting to be a regular murder magnet."

"What does the note mean?" I asked.

"It's hard to say. Let me take it back with me. I'll show it to someone who may be able to check the name of the man who is mentioned. It's a puzzle. Why would such a remarkable document be stuck into a recipe book?"

"It was among the papers you had shipped to you from the Castel Gandalfo," I said, as puzzled as ever.

"What's that?" Arlo asked.

"That's the pope's summer residence," Xavier said, frowning. "What would an admitted murderer be doing in the pope's kitchens?"

Chapter 5

Once the guard at the gated entrance to the Warner Bros. lot checks his clipboard, hands you a parking pass, and causes the gatearm to raise up, you leave the world of the hopefuls and enter the realm of the arrived. Here, a private pastel-colored city spreads out, crisscrossed by narrow streets. Forty-four enormous sound stages, each several stories high with identical barrel-vaulted roofs, hulk in row after windowless row, with the numbers painted on their enormous peachy-pink stucco walls the only way to differentiate Stage 5 from Stage 16.

Inside these gates, cars are seldom driven; those who work within ride bikes, or golf carts, or stroll. Don't be fooled by the nonchalant attitudes, worn like faded jeans by this city's inhabitants. In the constant battles for survival of the fittest, most talented, best connected, most fanatically determined, these are the victors. Their casual smugness is understandable. If there really is such a place as Hollywood, this is it. And don't look now, but we were the ones on the inside.

It's a whole lot of fun hanging out at Warner Bros. Its 110 acres hustle with purpose. At first, you can't believe that someone has allowed you to just wander around, like Alice inside a heavily guarded Wonderland. Today, a small forest of tree limbs being touched up with green paint could be glimpsed through the open cavernous door to Stage 2. The sound of power saws buzzed like distant bees under the cloudless blue sky. At the small intersection where four soundstages met, women wearing bald caps and strapless gowns could be spotted catching a smoke outside a row of trailers.

There were some ground rules for not getting your butt kicked off the lot. First, no matter how big a fan you might be of this show or that, you have to control your impulse to squeal and/or accost celebrities. It sounds easy enough, but turn a corner, and my God! That's George Clooney shooting hoops. Stay calm. Rule two is look down. There's a large variety of stuff to trip over. Don't. Then there's rule three, noise. There are times not to make any. Generally, anytime you see a red light flashing outside a soundstage, it means they're filming inside. No one opens the soundstage door, walks, whispers. Follow those three simple guidelines and people pretty much leave you alone.

I've been coming to Warner Bros. for years now, working on various series like Arlo's show, "Woman's Work," catering meals for casts and crews. Dating the producer is a time-honored method of doing business and is referred to in these parts, admiringly, as having friends. Isn't nepotism a nasty word?

Today Holly and I were here strictly as guests. Since we sold the catering business last November, I'd naturally had to turn over my badge I.D.

I hurried Holly along as we parked behind Stage 26, pulling my Grand Wagoneer into a reserved spot, a perk for wives, lovers, whatevers of the folks who work above-the-line on hit series. In the hierarchy of television production, budgets created a caste system, dividing people according to perceived worth. Costs of employees who create, such as "talent" (by which they mean actors), producers, directors, and writers, are generally placed above-the-line on the ledgers of T.V.'s bean counters. The salaries for crew and technicians are found, somewhat symbolically, below-the-line. It boils down to this: you could be married for twenty years to the guy who pulls the camera and you park in East Kishniff. But even a casual acquaintance of the actor who plays "the nosy neighbor" gets to park on the lot.

It was six-thirty, and we were running a little late. The audience was let in at six, and folks tended to get nervous when seats are still empty fifteen minutes before cameras were scheduled to roll. But another perk for above-the-line guests was having seats in the front row thoughtfully taped off for one's late arrival.

"It feels weird to be here and not be working," Holly said.

"I know. It's the first time I've ever been on this lot and didn't know what Arlo was eating for dinner. Odd." I jumped down from the Wagoneer and locked it. Holly came to my side and hooked my arm.

"We're tourists," she giggled.

"So, where's Donald tonight?" I asked. Holly had a new "friend" and Wes and I were keeping our fingers crossed.

"He said he had plans, but he's gonna try and stop by here later." She hugged my arm and giggled again.

For the occasion of attending tonight's filming of episode ten of "Woman's Work," Holly wore a tight pair of orange bell bottoms, topped by a pink satin shirt, left unbuttoned down to the middle of her bosom. Her white-blonde hair was spiked, and creatively gelled so that the ends of her bangs came to points. I had on a tailored black linen suit. We checked each other out.

"What's under the jacket?" Holly inquired, pulling open the single button and seeing for herself. Underneath was a skimpy black lace camisole top. She smiled. "Wear it like that. Show a little skin. Give Arlo a thrill."

I buttoned up. "The man is one thrill away from a nervous breakdown on the night they do one of his scripts."

The red light was not blinking, so I opened the side door to the soundstage and we entered. In the dim working light backstage, we made our way carefully toward the front, stepping over the dozens of thick cables strewn all over the floor. Already we'd practiced rules two and three, but Holly and I were old pros. We could hear the subdued talking of the seated audience in the distance, but we were shielded from view by the artificial walls of the show's set.

Holly would not let me off the hook about my conservative wardrobe. "Worried about what your priest will say?"

"He's not actually a priest. And he's bringing another one, so behave yourself."

"We're double dating a couple of Jesuits? Jeez, no one's gonna believe me when I tell them about my night."

We came around a corner and I saw Arlo standing with some of the writers. They kind of stand out as a group. Usually they're the ones with the dark hair. Everyone else seems to be some kind of blond.

They were standing next to the crafts services table, which was loaded with goodies such as crackers with pate, Brie, and fruit, and a huge five-pound gold box of Godiva chocolates. These are the treats, kept fresh all night, upon which the movers and shakers of prime-time television can stimulate their caffeine-fueled creative momentum. Arlo came over and put his arm around me. Since I was wearing fairly high-heeled pumps I was about eye to eye with him. Holly towered over us both.

"You're here. Great. Xavier and his buddy have been here since six."

We were standing out in front of the set, off to the side, and I looked up at the rows of risers where the audience was seated. There in the front I saw Xav and a younger man with curly black hair. They weren't looking our way, but were caught up in the experience of seeing the set and the cameras and the lights and the dozens of crew members getting ready for the show.

"How ya doing?" I asked Arlo.

"He's not himself," one of the writers answered for him.

"He's not even drunk yet," said another, in mock awe.

"I did a major rewrite last night," Arlo told me.

He was forever rewriting.

"And . . ." I looked at him, expecting his usual self-criticism.

"You be the judge," Arlo said.

As Holly and I walked over to our waiting seats, she whispered to me, "Did Arlo just smile?"

I had to admit it was a first.

"Brilliant," said Brother Frank del Valle. "I laughed so hard. But it wasn't just funny, I was hit on another level as well. It must be so much fun to work on a show like this."

"I don't think I've ever heard Arlo say he was having fun, have you?" Holly asked me.

"Well . . ."

"Oh, come on. I think you must all be taking things for granted. I can't believe you know Erica Moss. She's something else," the young Jesuit said with enthusiasm.

"Dottie is a real original," I began, and then started over. "Brother Frank, we call Erica Moss by her childhood name, Dottie. Did you know that?"

"Man, how cool is this? We're getting to hear some inside stories." Brother Frank turned to Xav. "Thank you, Brother Xavier, for sharing this experience with me. And I can't believe that the writer put such a spiritual message into the story."

"It's making me rethink my decision not to watch any commercial television," Xavier agreed. "Madeline, I had no idea your friend Arlo had such a gift."

"He's got an Emmy," Holly offered.

"But this was different," I said. Not only had Arlo packed some exceptionally funny jokes into the twenty-two minutes, but he had actually gone deeper than most sitcoms attempt. I was puzzled.

"Did the lawyer see herself as a victim, too? Wasn't that a great moment?" Xavier asked, stimulated by the experience of watching Arlo's script acted out by a cast of zany characters.

Arlo joined our group just then, and seemed, well, happy.

"Arlo!" Holly grabbed him and planted a nice kiss somewhere near his mouth. "You are soooo talented!

You've got actual minister-like-types talking about actual like moral issues here. And not only that, everybody was laughing like crazy. What got into you, dude?''

''Thanks. Yeah.'' Arlo grinned. ''I guess it didn't suck.''

I looked at Holly and she looked at me.

''Arlo, you're so . . . well . . . so calm. I mean that's great. The show was terrific.'' I'd seen a lot of sitcoms from the back of the house and this episode had been truly touching. The jokes came off less bitter than Arlo's darkest but were still sharp. That's a hard line for a smart sitcom script to walk.

Xavier started explaining to Brother Frank and Holly how he and Arlo had briefly discussed the idea behind ''service without power'' yesterday, but before this evening he had never seen a humorous side to it.

The members of the audience were filtering up the stairs and out the public exits. But just then, a dark young man with a shaved head and very baggy pants came down from the bleachers and moved right past us, trying to get out through the door off the stage. Before he could get very far, a studio page intercepted and rerouted the young man back up the steps.

In the meantime, one of Arlo's assistants, a young woman named Jody Mazzoli, came up and handed a note to Arlo. He checked it and gave it to Xavier. Xavier read it and showed it to Brother Frank. And then Erica ''Dottie'' Moss, the star of the series, came up to our group.

She was in her later thirties. Those were Hollywood years. For those who reside in other parts of the world, think dog. Her deep red hair framed a heart-shaped face, complimenting her peachy complexion. She was still wearing the green leotard she'd worn in the final scene when her character, Zoë Diller, was caught in the Buddhist temple after dark.

''Mad, honey!'' she called to me, and slid her size-two hips between Arlo and Jody to grab my hand. ''You've left us, you horrible girl!'' I hadn't seen Dottie since I'd sold my company and I'd become a rich thirty-year-old retiree.

"I heard you got over *three*." Only Dottie would know the intimate terms of my contract. Only Dottie would whisper the number of millions so loud most of the audience who were departing the sound stage could hear. Actors love an audience.

Arlo changed the subject for me. "Dottie, I'd like you to meet some friends of ours. This is Xavier Jones, who's an old friend of Maddie's and his friend Frank . . ."

"del Valle," Frank helped him, furnishing his last name. "Brother Frank del Valle."

"Oh!" Dottie said, dimpling to her new fans. "You're brothers! And you don't look a thing alike. But aren't you both handsome. Mad honey used to have excellent taste in men, I see. And then, somehow, she went awry." Dottie pinched Arlo, so he'd get the joke.

Frank handed the note back to Xavier and Xav said, "Excuse me. I regret having to leave the presence of a star, but there's someone who needs to speak to me near the stage door."

"Why don't you stay with your friends and I'll find out what it's about?" Brother Frank offered. He looked around. "I just need to find the right door." He was very handsome, with big brown eyes in a dark angular face, and he looked to be in his younger twenties.

"I'll show you, my dear," Dottie offered quickly. "I believe this is the door you want back here. Why it's not so very far from my trailer. And if you're good, I'll even give you a peek inside. Bet you never saw where they keep us T.V. stars when we're changin' our clothes."

"That's okay, Dottie," Arlo piped up. "I can take him . . ."

"Oh, shucks, Arlo. Can't I entertain a fan if I want to?"

Behind us, the audience had cleared out and now the work lights had come up. Dottie, wearing her poison-green leotard and tights, led the way, followed by a somewhat amazed Brother Frank.

"I'm looking for a Bible reference here," Arlo joked to

Xavier. ''Like Veronica leading Archie to slaughter?''

Xavier and Holly laughed.

''That's the problem with your mom letting you read the comic-book version of the Old Testament,'' I said.

Arlo looked after Brother Frank. ''I hope he'll be okay.''

Xavier said, ''Before Frank joined the order, he had a lot of experience on the streets. He can take care of himself.''

''For real,'' agreed Holly. She had been talking with Brother Frank all night, during the many breaks between the scenes. ''Brother Frank grew up in South Central, where they have those serious Latino gangs. I'm pretty sure he can handle Dottie.''

Arlo was not resting easy. ''Jody,'' Arlo turned to his assistant. ''Go save the guy from our star.''

Jody left as we said goodnight to Arlo. He and the cast still had work to do. They would go over the notes he and the director had made during the filming. Any pickup shots would have to be refilmed now. All around us, cast members were saying goodbye to their guests as well.

So far, spending the night watching my current boyfriend's show with my former fiancé was going fine. Get enough people around you for insulation, and the mood can't get too introspective. Besides, Brothers Xavier and Frank had been so interested in the process of making a TV show that we'd had plenty to talk about.

Jody came rushing up to our group just as we were breaking it up.

''Arlo! You've got to come outside right away. Something's happened.''

''What is it?''

''Come out to Dottie's trailer, please!''

''Wait a minute. What's wrong with Dottie?'' When something upset your star there was a price to pay. Any producer has to take that seriously.

''Hey!'' yelled a guy from the sound crew. He was running onto the set. This was beginning to alarm us all.

''Hey!'' he yelled, more agitated than I'd ever seen a

member of a TV crew before. ‘‘Call security! I think a guy croaked.’’

‘‘Did Dottie see someone have a heart attack?’’ Arlo asked Jody.

‘‘Does someone need assistance?’’ asked Xavier, concerned.

‘‘Where’s Brother Frank?’’ I asked, feeling sick.

‘‘That young man, your friend . . .’’ Jody said to Xavier.

‘‘Is he helping the poor fellow?’’ asked Xavier kindly.

‘‘I’m sorry. He *is* the poor fellow. And I think he’s dead.’’

Chapter 6

Arlo leapt up the three steel stairs to reach the door to Dottie's trailer. The rest of us were right behind him. It was almost 10 p.m. and it was dark out. Giant lights shone down from the corners of the soundstage buildings, revealing empty backlot streets. On one side, several luxury motor homes were lined up. They're used as dressing rooms and private space for the stars who work here. Dottie's trailer was the closest to the stage door, as befitted her celestial position on "Woman's Work."

"Dottie, it's Arlo. Let me in."

The door swung back until it slapped against the side of the RV. The bright artificial light caught the figure in the doorway. It was Dottie, standing there stark naked.

"Whoops!" called out Holly, just behind me. And then, after a second, "Man, those cannot be real." Respected rumor had it that Dottie had her lower ribs removed in order to perfect a twenty-two-inch waistline, and that she'd had the area north of there augmented and everything south of there liposuctioned. This was not the time to go into it with Hol.

"Dottie, I'm afraid you have an audience here," Arlo said. "Maybe you should get yourself decent, honey."

"Good advice," Jody said to no one in particular. "Just twenty years too late."

"That's all right," Dottie said, unconcerned with her lack of attire. "Never mind. Arlo, we've got an itsy problem.'' Without appearing to hurry, Dottie grabbed a flimsy robe and slowly put it on, moving back into her RV. One by one, we followed her in, first Arlo, then me, Holly, and Jody. Xavier stood outside the trailer, looking concerned.

''Dottie, you okay?'' Arlo asked. A Jesuit may be laying dead somewhere, but in Hollywood, that's the appropriate question. How's the star?

''Now, don't get all upset on me,'' Dottie said, linking her arm around Arlo.

''We just wanted to make sure you're all right, D,'' Arlo said, soothing his leading lady.

I pushed past him and got Dottie's attention. ''Jody said a man died. Is that true? Did you see anything?''

''Over there,'' Dottie said, gesturing toward the back of her trailer. In the front room were leather-covered sofas and a small table. The tiny kitchen was just beyond. Fresh flowers were in bowls and vases, and a platter of papaya and melon was laid out on ice. I walked past Dottie and Arlo with Holly at my heels, and pulled back the curtain that separated the front room from the bedroom in the rear. The bed was covered with a white satin duvet. Lying serenely on the bed was Brother Frank, his eyes closed as if for a short nap.

''Holy . . .''

''. . . shit,'' Holly finished my thought.

Brother Frank's head was resting in a bright red stain, the back of his skull caved in. His arms were neatly crossed over his chest.

Arlo and Jody crowded in behind us.

''I told you. I came to the trailer to give Dottie her notes and then there was . . . this. I told you,'' Jody said.

''Yeah, Jody. I get it,'' Arlo said. ''Go get Brother Xavier—the guy outside. Man, I don't know what happened here, but it sucks.''

Before Xavier could see what had become of his friend, Carlos Schwartz pushed his way into the doorway of the tiny bedroom.

"This is bad, Arlo," Carlos said, his big voice booming off the low ceiling.

"It's a tragedy," whispered Dottie, squeezing in next to her manager. "He was so beautiful. Life is short."

"His was, doll, not yours. So everybody, get moving. Get this body out of here. Now. Arlo, give me a hand."

"You shouldn't move that man's body," I said, shocked.

No one gave me a second look.

I raised my voice. "Hey, guys. Really. Nothing should be touched until the police get here."

"Better take the duvet," suggested Dottie, ever the practical one.

"The what?" asked Arlo.

"The comforter. It's soaked with blood. Better take it with the body."

At that moment, Xavier was finally able to push into the bedroom at the back of Dottie's trailer. He saw his young Jesuit friend and froze. I saw pain in his eyes. Then, he moved over to the body and took Frank's hand in his. He knelt down and began to pray. As he whispered the Latin words, Carlos the manager started pulling the corners of the comforter up and flipping them over onto the body.

"Can't you give the poor man a few minutes here. He's saying some kind of prayer, for Christ's sake!" Dottie hissed at Carlos.

"We don't have no few minutes, Dot. Okay, everyone, back out. Back out!"

"Shouldn't someone rethink this?" I asked.

Carlos, a short, squat man with a significant gut and a silly salt and pepper ponytail, leaned near the bed. In an instant, he had the light body of Brother Frank, wrapped in fluffy white satin, flung over his shoulder, fireman-style.

"Hey! He's moving the body," Holly called out.

"Oh, boy. I'm not sure about this," Arlo mumbled as the body was hauled down the tight passageway towards the front of the trailer.

I turned to Dottie.

"What happened? I thought Brother Frank was supposed to meet someone by the stage door."

"No one was there, honey. So I thought he might like to see my, you know, things."

"What was Brother Frank doing in your bed?"

"Exactly the question we don't want to answer, Arlo," Carlos said as he opened the door, with the body still slung over his back, and stepped onto the steel steps. Xavier, not wanting to leave his fellow brother, quietly followed Carlos out of the RV.

"What am I going to do?" Dottie wondered.

"The media will get this, it's too hot to keep," Jody said, doing what assistants to producers do, pulling out her cell phone and tapping it.

"Jody," Arlo said, pulling her aside, "get Barbara Welsh on the phone right away. Dottie's going to need her."

Holly turned to me and asked, "Who's Welsh? Dottie's attorney?"

"Publicist," I said with a straight face.

"I need Christina," Dottie added in her chirpy drawl.

"Therapist?" Holly guessed, trying to get with it.

"Makeup artist," I answered. In time, Holly would learn that when stars like Dottie got worried, the crisis was usually more about lipliner.

"Someone's getting Christina," Jody announced with one hand over the mouthpiece of her cell phone.

"Bravo," I said.

Arlo turned to me. "You're bugged, huh?"

"Does anyone but me want to know what happened here?" I asked.

"I do," said Holly.

"Dottie has had a shock. Maybe she doesn't feel like talking about it. Carlos will take care of things when he gets back," Arlo said.

I glared at him. A wonderful young Jesuit brother was dead. Why wasn't that important here? It seemed everybody had an agenda and none included dealing with the poor man's death.

"I'm so sorry . . ." Dottie said. She started to whimper. Perhaps the situation was beginning to get too real.

"Dottie, did you kill Brother Frank?" I asked her, exasperated.

"We don't have to know," Arlo suggested to her quickly. The coward.

"Me? How could I kill him? I was in the shower," Dottie said, as if that made the whole thing clear.

"Well, that at least explains your lack of clothes," I said. Although it seemed to me there had been plenty of time from the moment she'd told Jody to get Arlo until the time we all arrived at the trailer to have covered up her assets.

"What was Brother Frank doing in your bed?" I asked again, wondering why no one else was asking.

"Was that poor boy your brother, Maddie?" Dottie asked me, her blue-gray eyes reflecting enormous, if belated, concern. "I'm so sorry for your loss."

"Actually, we'd only just met him tonight." I explained. "He was a Jesuit brother working with my friend, Brother Xavier Jones. So you must tell me what happened."

"No you don't," said Carlos, coming back into the trailer. As Dottie's manager, he naturally had to protect his franchise. As Dottie's ex-husband, he was feeling more possessive than was legally his right.

"It's okay, Car," Dottie said. "Just get me a drink, would you hon?"

"Perrier?"

"Too bubbly. My stomach's been acting up."

"Evian?"

"No. Something hot, maybe."

"Coffee?"

She made a face at Carlos. Coffee didn't appeal.

"Latte? Cappuccino? I can send out."

"Too much caffeine. How about some herbal . . ."

"Can we talk about the death of Brother Frank del Valle here?" I asked. Perhaps I'd allowed too much exasperation to creep into my voice, but I got the attention, at least, of what might be the only witness to the death of an innocent young man.

Just then, a knock came at the door. Jody answered it. A guy from studio security popped his head in the trailer.

"Sorry to disturb you, Miss D, but I just thought you should know that a couple of folks have called the gate and reported what they said was a . . . uh . . . occurrence near your trailer."

"Is that so, Gary?" Dottie was seated on a pink leather banquette-style sofa. She crossed her legs, and the slit on her robe did its thing.

The leg-crossing did not go unnoticed by Security Man Gary. He gawked and smiled. He looked to be in his upper fifties, by the gray in his hair and the padding under his belt.

"Just thought I should let you folks know, that's all."

"Thanks, Gary," Dottie drawled. "By the way, could you be a lamb and get the commissary to send me an herbal tea?"

"Sure thing, Miss D. Do you like chamomile?"

"Not tonight. I think something with fruit."

"How about black currant?"

"She hates currants," Carlos said, jeering at his rival for Dottie's thirst attentions.

"Do they have that thingie?" Dottie wondered. "With the oranges, I think."

"Orange pekoe?" asked Security Guard Gary.

"That sounds divine," squealed Dottie, smiling up at her hero.

Holly shot me a look. I whispered to her, "Lipton."

"Can we get to the point?" I asked the group, a little louder than was absolutely necessary. "What exactly happened here? Has anyone called the police?"

"I didn't," Dottie said. When I looked startled, she said defensively, "Well, I didn't want to touch anything, of course."

"I think your own cell phone would have been okay,"

I said. "What about you?" I asked the security guy.

"Why, no," Gary said, leaning against the sink in the little kitchen. He smiled at Dottie and said, "I'm investigating. Right?"

Arlo said, "Gary, maybe you'd better get that tea for Miss D. We'll handle this situation. Thanks."

When Gary left, Arlo turned to us. "Mad's right. We're going to have to call the police. Jody has cancelled the rest of the crew for this evening. She reached Brockman and he's coming over here right away. It's his studio, so they'll handle the press for now. Dottie's going to talk to the police and then go home. Can you do that for us, honey?"

"Sure, Arlo. I'd like to cooperate fully with any and all authorities. The thing is, I just don't know anything."

"Well said, Dottie." Carlos the manager grinned. "And that's what you're going to tell Barbara Walters."

Chapter 7

Holly sat on the pink leather banquette, the exact spot that Dottie had recently been occupying, with both hands on her head. She brushed her spiky bangs up, out of the way, and began massaging her forehead with her long fingers. Then she stopped, mid-rub, elbows up in the air, and looked over at me. "What gives, eh?"

Fifteen minutes of sporadic activity had seen everyone go off in different directions, eventually leaving Holly and me alone in Dottie's dressing room trailer. Holly tried to rouse me from my dizzy thoughts again. "Apparently, there was an accident. Isn't that what someone said?"

"Arlo." I finally spoke. "Arlo was the one who mentioned the word accident."

"Huh. I guess that Brother Frank guy must have fallen somehow, and, like hit his head on something and, well . . ." Holly tried to connect the dots and, missing a few vital numbers, ran out of steam.

"Holly, how does a twenty-three-year-old guy fall to his death on top of a Beautyrest?"

"Tripped?"

"Onto a very firm pillow?" Neither one of us actually wanted to smile. Gallows humor. It can be as uncontrollable as giggling at a funeral. Out of line, definitely, but sometimes also beyond control.

"Madeline," Holly spoke to me firmly.

I stifled myself.

"Maybe he fell onto the headboard?" Holly suggested.

"I don't know." We both looked towards the back of the trailer where the bed in question was just sitting there, begging to be examined.

Holly stopped massaging her temples and let her whitish wisps fall back down into her eyes. "Maybe we could take a tiny peek," Holly offered. "It's not like there haven't already been an army of people in Dottie's bedroom."

"And that's another thing," I said. "What was this religious almost-like-a-priest guy doing in Dottie's bed in the first place? Hadn't he just gone outside for a minute to meet somebody?"

"Maybe Dottie didn't know that Frank was a Jesuit brother who had taken vows of celibacy," Holly replied, getting to her feet and offering me a "you first" gesture down the passageway to the bedroom. I rose and, as directed, went first.

On the bed, the duvet had been removed, along with Frank's body, and the stripped mattress revealed no traces of the incident. There was no blood. The headboard, a swirly polished brass number, had a lot of jutting curlycues adorned with porcelain beads, but none were dented or showed any signs of blood or mayhem.

We each studied the bed.

"Even if a person fell on one of those brass hoozies, would he actually die?" Holly asked, doubtfully.

"How could he?" I answered. "Everybody bangs their head on the furniture, sometime. They don't die, for goodness sakes. They get a bump."

"That's why God invented black and blue," Holly chimed in.

"Holly." I pointed at her sternly.

"It just slipped out."

I eyed the small room. There was not much space. The queen-size bed took up two-thirds of the floor, with a tiny dressing table and full-length mirror on a brass stand in the corner.

"Those must be Dottie's awards," Holly said, reading

the framed certificates that covered one wall.

''How many times has she been nominated?'' I asked.

Holly finished counting. ''Seven times a bridesmaid, never a bride.'' Emmy had evaded our star. ''But she's got a bunch of People's Choice awards.'' Holly picked one up from the dressing table.

''Hol, maybe the police will be looking around. Try not to leave too many fingerprints.''

''Oh, yeah. Sorry,'' She put down the statuette. ''I wonder how Brother Xavier is taking this.''

''I spoke to him a few minutes ago. He said they moved Brother Frank's body to the studio infirmary,'' I said. ''Xav's doing okay, I guess. He's the calm type, you know? And then he's got this whole kind of centered thing going for him.''

''I think they call that religion, Maddie.''

''Yes. Well, it's still got to be horrible for him.'' I sighed, thinking about how painful things had suddenly become. How quickly life shifts gear. How vulnerable we all are. I felt a need to keep talking.

''Xavier hadn't known Brother Frank very long, just since he's been rooming at the rectory at St. John's while he's in town.'' I checked my watch, but didn't really register the time. ''He said he'd sit with the body until the church sends someone to take it.''

''The poor guy,'' Holly said.

''On top of everything, he's got the pope arriving in three days. I think he's worried about what the press could make of this.''

''I see his point. Young handsome Jesuit found dead in the bed of a beautiful T.V. star. This stuff keeps 'Hard Copy' on the air.''

''And the timing is so unfortunate. Xavier's mission is to make sure the pope's visit goes well. If this turns into a scandal that won't go away . . .'' I stopped in mid-thought.

''Hey, what's this?'' I had been trying to straighten the sheet that had gotten bunched up near the wall, a result of the hoisting of the body from the bed. I felt something hard.

"Is it a gun? Is it a knife?"

"The young man was neither shot nor stabbed, Holly. But it's something . . ."

"Well, you've already rearranged the sheets. How much more can it hurt to take a little peek?"

I carefully pulled back the white eyelet top sheet to get my "little peek" at what was so hard just beneath. Wedged between the bed and the wall, jumbled up in the top sheet, was a ten-inch-tall chrome-plated, spade-shaped statuette sitting atop a marble base. It was half-wrapped in a white terrycloth hand towel that was smudged with a few tiny droplets of dark red.

"Uh oh," Holly muttered. "What kind of accident was this?" We looked at each other. Holly must have been thinking the same thing I was thinking because she asked me, "Where did they take Dottie?"

"Jane Seymour's trailer." The lot was fully booked. This week, Miss Seymour was shooting a series of commercials here during the day. In this emergency, her trailer had been "borrowed" so that the star of "Woman's Work" could be comfortable while she awaited her interview with the authorities.

Dottie was gracious, as always. Ensconced in her new digs, she promptly asked for a Diet Dr. Pepper, her special gourmet diet ranch dressing and Christina, her makeup stylist. Several trips back and forth to her old dressing room were necessary before the cold drink, the creamy ranch, and cosmetics artist were found and escorted to the Jane Seymour/Dottie Moss trailer.

"So what's with Dottie? Did you think she was acting funny?" Holly said.

"She's blessed by a natural self-absorption so great I don't think much else penetrates. Most of the time I think she's fun, but if a thing doesn't center on Dottie Moss, she loses interest pretty damn fast."

"True," Holly said.

"Actually, she was acting just like her normal self,

which is interesting. You'd think if she was trying to cover something up about Brother Frank's death, she'd be much more concerned. She'd play it with loads of shock and fear. You know, some screaming would be in the picture,'' I said.

''That's right. She'd be saying just the right thing, and, assuming she had on the right kind of makeup, start cranking out loads of tears.'' How quickly Holly caught on. ''So do we think she wasn't involved?''

I shook my head, not knowing what I believed. ''She's an actress.''

''True,'' Holly agreed, and then added in a whisper, ''but not monumentally talented when you get down to it.'' When it comes to the business, everyone's a critic.

I looked at Holly and we shared a wordless thought. We moved back through the trailer and I used the toe of my shoe to nudge open the door to the tiny bathroom. The shower stall was slightly fogged. A towel draped over the sink. The space was faintly humid.

''Well,'' I said, ''it appears that Dottie did take a shower.''

''Before or after the . . . accident?'' Holly whispered.

The door of the trailer swung open and in stepped Arlo.

''Yo,'' he said to Holly. He came over and slung a tired arm around my shoulder. ''Oh, Mad.'' His crisp khaki shirt had wilted somewhat. His jeans had lost their knife crease. He began to rub his eyes behind his wire-rims.

''Has Dottie explained what happened here?'' I burst out. ''We've actually found something . . .''

''She's fine. She's okay. Dottie's a real trouper. She's done regional theatre, don't forget,'' Arlo explained.

He didn't get it.

''Arlo,'' Holly jumped in, ''Brother Frank is dead and there may have been a murder here. Don't you see?'' Her hands pulled her bangs up off her forehead and held them there.

''What murder?'' Arlo asked. ''The poor guy wanted a

tour of the backstage area and Dottie was kind enough to take him around.''

''And . . . ?'' I looked at the man, exasperated.

''And . . . and . . . something happened, some accident, and he died somehow or other. But it doesn't have anything to do with Dottie. She didn't even know the man.''

''Arlo, did Dottie even realize that Brother Frank was a Jesuit?'' Holly demanded. ''He and Brother Xavier don't wear those priest-type suits with the jazzy collars. Did Dottie think Brother Frank was just an adoring male fan?''

''Holly, I don't know.''

I noticed lines on Arlo's forehead, where his eyebrows pinched together. For once, this T.V. wonderkind looked all of his thirty-five years.

''Arlo, you look exhausted,'' I said. I wanted to do something, and nurturing Arlo was the only thing available.

''Never mind. The police are here. Couple of detectives are talking to Dottie now.''

''I wonder why they aren't over here?'' asked Holly.

''Yeah. Wouldn't they want to tape off the crime scene?'' I asked.

''What makes you so sure it wasn't an accident?'' Arlo finally asked, succumbing to our forward push of alarm.

''Maddie found a heavy blunt instrument. And it was covered in a towel. And the towel had blood stains.''

''He was bludgeoned to death?'' Arlo asked, now seriously shocked. ''With what?''

''Dottie's Cable Ace Award.''

''Oh, man. She was so proud of that one. You know, she's never won the Emmy.''

''Hollywood is rough, man,'' Holly offered.

''Guys!'' I heard my voice sound a trifle more high-pitched than normal. ''Get a grip.''

''You're right,'' Arlo said. ''So what should we be feeling? Like, sad?''

You have to either hate Arlo or just pity him that he couldn't find his feelings with a *Thomas Bros. Street Guide*.

''I feel disgustingly freaked,'' offered Holly, always

willing to lend an emotion, if one can only decipher it.

"And yet," Arlo went on, "I've been amazingly calm. It's Brother Xavier. I just went over to speak with the guy, and he had some incredible words of comfort."

"Did he?" I asked.

"He's beautiful. He's the guy who should be most upset. If I were him I'd be acting like a shit. But you know what? After all he's been through, he was concerned about me. He said that sometimes we might face a blow that seems too big to handle. But that's just the time to turn to God, you know, give him our faith, or whatever."

I had never heard Arlo talk this thoughtfully. Actually, I had never heard Arlo talk so long without leading up to a punchline.

"Brother Xavier told me," Arlo went on, "that we may never get the answers we seek. But with God's help, we can get through anything. Sometimes we just need to accept that life is a series of tests, of questions."

Never to be answered?

I looked at Arlo, who was finding peace in the very thought that was driving me crazy. I knew faith worked for many. I knew it worked for Xavier. But the only peace I'd find would be when every damn mystery was solved.

Chapter 8

The deadline panic of planning one of the most important civic events in the last decade pushed to the front of my thoughts. I had a million things to do. Even before I opened my eyes, I was making a "to do" list. The top priorities involved the final staff selection for the big event. With security sensitivity at an all-time high, we were to submit our employee list by this afternoon so that they might be screened and approved. But in between my plans and my organizing, my brain kept zinging back to Brother Frank del Valle. I was having a real hard time accepting that his death was something I would never understand. I had to tell myself the police would handle it, so I could focus on the work at hand.

I tried to keep my mind on the details to be worked out with the venue. The Otis Mayfield Pavilion, a large downtown theater that housed Broadway-size shows, was the site selected. Since the Mayfield has a fifty-foot ceiling, we suggested setting down a temporary floor on top of the theater seats, elevating the entire dining space to stage level. We selected a frosted Lucite for the flooring, which could then be illuminated by placing lights beneath it. I had to check with Wesley, since he had met with the Mayfield people last night, to see if they'd gotten approval from the fire marshal.

I showered quickly, drying off with a large white terry-cloth sheet. My hair is so thick and curly, I spend half my life waiting for it to dry. It hung down several inches below my shoulders in a clumping mat of copper corkscrews. My head was the acid test for creme rinse. If I could get my fat gap-tooth comb through the thick tangle, I was prepared to do the testimonial.

The comb-through did not result in too many pulled-out clumps, and after the strenuous workout, I shook my head, retriever-style, letting beads of water sprinkle where they might.

As I pulled on a fresh pair of jeans, I walked into my library. This was originally the middle bedroom but now has a dining table and an ingeniously rigged dumbwaiter, allowing me to prepare meals downstairs in the kitchen and then transport them easily upstairs. It also has a closet, befitting the bedroom's original use, in which I keep some of my extended wardrobe. I found a pale yellow v-neck sweater, which I pulled over my head. I was adjusting the white T-shirt underneath when I walked back into my bedroom and noticed the answering machine blinking the number "2."

The first message was from Wesley at 7:40. He must have just missed me as I stepped into the shower.

He said he'd e-mailed me a list of potential servers and cooks and barpeople. I should look them over and we could get together later to pare down our final list.

The great thing about Wes was he could be counted on to be obsessing about the exact same thing as I was. Together, I'm afraid we form a compulsive, control-freakish, manic hive that neither of us can see as in the least bit unhinged. The results can be a mixed blessing: our parties tend to be extremely well planned, while we live the slightly anxious lives of the terminally analytical.

The second message was from Xavier. It came in at 8:11.

"Hello, Madeline. I hope you are all right after last night. I didn't really get a chance to talk with you and I'm concerned about how you may be feeling about . . . well, about the death of Brother Frank del Valle. I didn't know this brother very long, just a few days, really, but still . . . My heart is heavy, you know? I'd really like to talk to you.''

Listening to Xavier's husky voice, I began to remember what it was like when we were together. We had both been notorious for leaving phone messages so long they used up all the tape in the machine. Forgotten memories fluttered over me. As he went on, he sounded somehow more like the man I remember loving, once. I even began to remember the old me.

''Anyway, I'm coming by your house to drop off the last of the parish guest lists which have been given security clearance. I was told by the FBI that this parish doesn't have a secure fax line, or whatever. I should be there by eight-thirty. Listen, if you're home, could I come in and talk? Oh, yeah, and there's something else kind of shocking I'd like to talk to you about. It's weird, but I've found out some new information about that old letter of confession you found. It doesn't make sense. Still . . . Well, see you soon, I hope.''

I looked at my watch just as the doorbell chimed from downstairs. Eight-thirty, and my hair was still wet.

''Hi,'' I said, opening the door to see Xavier standing on my doorstep, holding a large envelope.

''Hi,'' he said. ''I'm glad you're here. Did you get my message?''

I nodded as I led him through the entry hall and into the living room. This is where we hold client conferences, when necessary, and do employee interviews. It still looks a lot like a living room and I motioned Xavier to the coffee-colored leather chair. Men usually liked that chair. Maybe it was the hobnails.

''So you know,'' he continued, settling into the chair, ''that I've got the final guest list. Can you believe the amount of work it takes just to send out an invitation to this event?'' He handed the envelope to me.

I smiled at him, wondering if he was going to get to the more serious things we had to discuss.

''This is great,'' I said, referring to the paperwork. ''We're right on target with our schedule.''

Neither of us was ready to start speaking about what was troubling us most, the death of Brother Frank. Were we always so reticent about expressing our darker, most difficult feelings? Perhaps we were. I began to see things about our past relationship differently. Yes, avoiding the difficult topics was one of the things the two of us had in common.

''So, what did you find out about the confession?'' I asked, still going with the avoidance dance that had been ''our'' pattern, like ''our'' song, or ''our'' wine.

''Well, I was doing research to see if the name Brother Ugo came up in any of the computerized directories for the Society of Jesus. You know, Internet stuff. I guess I didn't get much sleep last night,'' he said, looking up at me with his shag of dark blond hair falling onto his forehead. Approach the subject slowly, I thought, and from an oblique angle. Good one.

''So I didn't do a really thorough search. Not all years are in the database. There's a fair amount of really old, historical stuff, and some modern lists, but there are whole blocks of years still missing. Even centuries.''

''But you found Brother Ugo?'' I asked, wanting in on the mystery.

''Well, I found *a* Brother Ugo. He was a Jesuit brother in the sixteenth century, in France.''

''Hmph,'' I said, thinking. That didn't scan.

''I know. It's not the Castel Gandalfo, which is near Rome, but then I really didn't think Brother Ugo's note was very likely from the pope's palace. It was a loose sheet of paper, so it must have gotten stuck in the wrong ledger somehow.''

''So who was this Brother Ugo? Did he murder someone?'' I asked, my hope for a good ending to our mystery renewed.

''Sorry. No. Not that that was ever recorded, anyhow,'' Xavier said, smiling at my disappointment that a good Jesuit brother had not committed murder.

"Who was he, did you find out?"

"Well, yes. He was a beekeeper in Avignon."

"A beekeeper?" I asked, suddenly perking up at the thought of all that venom right at the clever brother's disposal. "But did he . . . ?"

"Actually, Maddie, that's all I could find out over the net. But here's the thing. This morning, I just got a response to my inquiry about Brother Ugo from Monsignor Picca at St. Bede's the Venerable. That's a parish out near Pasadena. This monsignor is a church history buff, I've been told, and he says he may know of this Brother Ugo of ours."

"Wow! Are you going to go see him?" I asked, feeling the excitement of the chase.

"I want to. I should. But with everything that happened last night, I've still got to keep up with my mission here. The plans for the visit of His Holiness cannot be disturbed in any way. It's two days and counting."

"Don't remind me," I said, smiling at how much we still had to do.

"Remember taking that class with Chef Claude and learning to deal with the panic before an event?" Xavier joked. "Well, I may need a refresher course."

I almost snorted. Xavier was the only man you'd ever need if the world began burning. He didn't have any nerves. But I could tell he was aware of the heat.

"This Monsignor Picca," I started. Xavier looked at me. "Well, I mean Pasadena's not that far, just over the hill. Maybe I could go out there this morning and find out more about our sixteenth-century cleric. I mean, I found his note. I feel like he was calling out to me, you know? Like I owe it to him."

"Do you think you could? You must have your hands full with the big event . . ."

"I'm mostly preproduction, Xavier. And I'm on schedule." I held up the envelope that Xav had come to deliver.

I walked him to the front door and we stopped there for a moment.

"The thing that happened last night," Xav said, finally bringing up the horror neither of us could comprehend. "I have been to chapel, of course. And I prayed, Maddie. But I am unsure of what else I can do to be of service. Perhaps I will go visit Brother Frank's family."

"You are so giving," I said, admiring the way he had of putting others' needs always ahead of his own. Not my needs, of course, but everyone else's.

"There's nothing to be done about Brother Frank except wait and pray," Xav said, but his voice was a lot less than confident. "If only this could be settled before the pope arrives. If he could be spared . . . Ah, enough of my complaining."

"I'll call you later," he said. And then standing there, he looked me directly in the eyes. We stood there like that for a while. "Thanks, Maddie." And then he was gone down my steps.

I'd find out the secrets behind the Latin confession of old Brother Ugo. And maybe look into the death of Brother Frank del Valle, as well. I was feeling empowered, a dangerous state of being if ever there was one.

Chapter 9

"I am helping a friend look into a matter," I explained to the young male voice on the other end of the phone. "Monsignor Picca knows of a Jesuit from long ago, a Brother Ugo, I believe."

"How extraordinary," the secretary replied, with enthusiasm. "We are most interested in the past. You know the monsignor is a respected historian, although unpublished as of yet, with a special interest in the history of our church. If you could make it to our offices before nine-thirty, I'm sure the monsignor would be happy to give you five minutes."

It was almost nine now but if I rushed, I might make it. He gave me directions to a large Catholic church in an exclusive community northeast of the Hollywood Hills.

I was not dressed for church. Off came the comfortable casual clothes. I popped into my "living room," the original master bedroom and the closet that contained what passed for my dress-up wardrobe. The only thing that was suitable was a sleeveless navy linen dress. Did I even own a pair of pantyhose? The trouble with dressing up in "nice" clothes once a millennium was accessories. I finally found a pair in my bedroom dresser and then I had to remind myself to slow down. It would be just my luck to rip them.

With no time to tame the beast known to normal women as hair, I pulled the lot back into a low ponytail, grabbed my purse, and ran.

I was still uncontrollably absorbed with thoughts of Brother Frank. I kept running over again and again the events, innocent in themselves, which had somehow led to death. At least this mission to unravel the mystery of Brother Ugo's bizarre confession might take my mind off that painful subject for a while.

I was driving against traffic, counter-rush-wise. While most of the cars in Los Angeles were pointing their headlights towards downtown and destinations west, I was breezing my way up the uncrowded side of the 2 Freeway. The air, a crisp sixty-two degrees, would warm up as the day wore on, rewarding the tail end of January with some of Southern California's best weather.

La Canada–Flintridge was one of the least publicized wealthy neighborhoods around L.A., like Brentwood used to be, once upon a time, before some of its neighbors brought in a bit too much publicity. Still, one couldn't beat the community of La Canada for keeping itself quiet. Most people in Southern California had barely heard of it, and those who had didn't have much of a clue as to where you'd find it.

La Canada is nestled in the foothills of the Angeles Crest Mountains, just on the other side of the Rose Bowl from Pasadena. I found St. Bede's on Foothill Boulevard without much trouble.

Unlike the great cathedrals and majestic Gothic churches that inspire even nonbelievers to give religion a shot, the buildings at St. Bede's were designed in that style of fifties architecture that made you wonder what in the world architects were up to back in the fifties. Blond cinderblock does not a believer make. The complex included a small Catholic day school, along with the sanctuary and rectory. I parked my old Grand Wagoneer in the lot near an office building and entered the lobby. The sign on the main floor directed me to Monsignor Picca's office. It appeared that he was the priest in charge of this parish. I found myself wondering at the modesty of the length of my dress. All right, I decided, if I didn't sit.

The young priest seated at a desk rose when I entered the small office.

"You must be . . ." he faltered, looking for some note on his desk.

"Madeline Bean. I hoped I might speak with Monsignor Picca." I checked my watch. Nine-thirty-three. Not too bad.

"Just one moment, Miss Bean." He sidestepped the narrow passage behind the desk and silently opened the panel door that connected to a larger office.

A few minutes later he reappeared and motioned me to come in.

"Monsignor Picca, this young lady has been sent by Brother Xavier to inquire about the matter of Brother Ugo. Her name is Madeline Bean." Then the assistant slipped out the door, closing it behind himself.

"Come in, sit down," called out the monsignor in a hearty, hoarse voice. "My dear young Marilyn, is it?" He sat behind a large blond wood desk with a highly polished surface. Not one object was placed upon the desktop.

"Madeline Bean," I offered.

The monsignor wore glasses with thick lenses in round silver frames. They were unspeakably hip, although I was sure the style must have gone in and out of style, and back in again, with the monsignor none the wiser.

He looked to be at least eighty, with a thinning cloud of white hair circling his wide scalp. His nose, perhaps strong and commanding in his youth, could now only be truthfully described as huge. There was something to his voice, some accent I couldn't immediately place.

"I must go over to the school in a few minutes time, but I understand you wanted to see me." He took a moment to look me up and down, adjusting his glasses to fit more properly. "I was expecting to speak with a young man, was I not? A Jesuit priest, I believe, or no, it was a good brother, wasn't it? At any rate, a member of the Society of Jesus had put out an inquiry into a most puzzling, a most baffling matter."

"Brother Xavier Jones and I found an old note. It was

signed by a Brother Ugo. We were curious, you see. It seemed to be a confession but there was no date."

"My, my." I believe his thick lenses masked the startling shrewdness in his faded brown eyes. Those specs assuredly came in handy in his work.

"And your connection to this would be . . . ?" he asked me kindly.

"Brother Xavier and I have been working together. We're involved with the plans for the visit of . . . His Holiness." I hoped I was saying it right. Not being Catholic, I had planned on figuring out all the protocol issues before the event. "I am catering the large breakfast reception to welcome His . . . um . . . Holiness to Los Angeles."

"How wonderful! Of course, you must be busy."

"And Xavier is an old friend. I mean, Brother Xavier. Jones." Sometimes I need to stop talking. I could see why people loved to talk to their priest. This man's eyes were so kind.

"You have come on a busy day, so I imagine the information you are gathering may be important to you. The story of the Jesuit brother baker, Ugo," he said, smiling slightly. "You cannot guess at the memories that name brings back to me. When I received the archdiocese bulletin and saw the note about the search for a Brother Ugo posted among other business, I knew at once that it had to be my Brother Ugo."

"Your Brother Ugo? But I understood that Brother Ugo was a French beekeeper from sixteenth-century France."

"Oh, dear. How extraordinary. But you see, the Jesuit brother I knew was also called Ugo. And he was a master baker."

The note we found was stuck in a book of recipes. Bread recipes.

"And where did you meet your Brother Ugo, Monsignor? Here in California?"

"Oh, my no! This is a subject that takes me back to another time, my dear, and another continent.

"Are you, by any chance, familiar with my work? It is

an interest of mine to study the turbulent history of our century. I am intent on clearly presenting the facts so that in the future, historians and scholars will be able to understand how our dear Roman Catholic Church has struggled and how she has prospered in the hearts of the world."

"Why, no, I hadn't realized . . ."

"It has been my privilege to witness unique events. I believe God wants me to record them. And so I busy myself with my studies and with my journals. There is not too much time, you see."

It must be hard to be filled with such purpose and strength of mind, but watch age make away with your physical abilities. I noticed the cane that rested against the side of his desk. And then I noticed a beautiful gray tiger-striped cat, coming from behind the desk to check me out.

"Stan," the monsignor called, chiding his feline companion, "you know the rules, my friend. Leave the guests alone."

"I don't mind," I said and reached down to pet Stan.

"You have cats?" he asked, and his tone seemed to warm up.

"I'm afraid I travel too much to make a good home for a cat."

"You'll settle down one day," Monsignor Picca predicted.

"Does this historical research you do have something to do with Brother Ugo?"

"I was assigned to work in Rome during World War Two. There are not many of us left now who remember that time."

It was almost fifty-five years since the war ended. Kids of twenty during WWII were grandpas of seventy-five at least. "Are you writing about that time?"

"Just gathering research," he said, spreading his hands. Seeing an opening, Stan jumped up on Monsignor Picca's lap. "Sometimes a small group of us likes to gather and reminisce. Sometimes a cache of documents is discovered and we review them."

"Who is involved?"

"Only a few, now. But we each have a special subject we research. One of my associates is a treasure buff. As you may know, there were rumors for years that the Nazis sold off art treasures in the west. Only recently have artworks been discovered residing right here in museums in America. Can you imagine?"

He told me about several Picassos that had been stolen by the Nazis and then sold off because Hitler considered Picasso a lesser artist. Many museums were now embarrassed, trying to explain how these stolen artworks now resided in their own collections.

I didn't see how this could have anything to do with Brother Ugo the baker, but it was hard to keep this sweet man on the subject without seeming rude.

"You see," he went on, stroking Stan's neck, happy to talk all morning, "my friend is keeping a record of stolen and missing artwork. It's like a detective story. Do you ever read detective stories?"

"I love Agatha Christie," I said.

"As do I," he said. "I enjoy hearing about my old friend's latest discoveries and suspicions. He is retired, you see. He has the time. And he has a special fascination with the famous Treasure Room of Catherine the Great."

"Monsignor, I know I cannot take up too much of your time."

"Yes, of course," he said, catching himself. "You are here to learn about Ugo."

"If you have any information, we'd be grateful."

He opened a drawer, and the shift in weight must have made his lap a less restful spot. Stan took his leave, dropping silently down behind the large desk.

"I have a file," the monsignor was explaining, as he opened another drawer.

I noticed Stan peeking around from behind the desk, eyeing my lap.

As Monsignor Picca searched, he began talking again of lost Nazi treasure.

Up came Stan, light on his feet, but heavy when he landed. How it was that I found myself sitting in an office in a Catholic church in La Canada, listening to an elderly priest talk about Nazi mysteries with a gray-striped cat on my lap, I was finding it hard to say, but sometimes we are meant to take the meandering path.

The elderly priest brought a manila folder out of the bottom drawer. With a twinkle, he teased me. "Ah, but you want to know about a baker." His shrewd eyes searched my face. "You said you found a note?"

"I brought a copy. It's in Latin."

"May I see it?" the monsignor asked.

I handed the Xerox copy of the confession note across his large spotless desk. The room was silent as he slipped his glasses down almost to the tip of his nose to better catch the spidery script.

"We had no idea, of course, if this letter was real, or when it had been written. Brother Xavier thought . . ."

"Yes. Yes. Real, I have no doubt it is. But as for the crime . . ." The longer I listened to his voice, the more I noticed an almost undetectable musicality in his manner of speaking. Perhaps a trace of an accent. I found myself scratching Stan's neck where he liked it.

Then he smiled at me and asked, "Would you like to hear the story of this confession?"

"Of course. Can you tell it to me?"

"It goes back many years, my dear Madeline. So long ago that I was startled, I must tell you, when I heard the name of Brother Ugo the baker. How did you young people find his note?"

"It was stuck in an old book of recipes that dated back several hundred years," I said.

"Really? But this story does not take us back that far. I am an old man, but not quite that old." He let out several dry hacking coughs, which, combined with the grin, signified laughter.

"This story comes from a time that was very difficult for those of us who lived in Europe," Monsignor Picca went on. "In the very late thirties, our dear Rome was surrounded by the Nazis. You remember your history, of course. The Vatican had won the right to become its own sovereign nation only a few years earlier, in nineteen-twenty-nine. It was a glorious achievement, but one that was politically unstable back in those troubled times. With the terrible unrest in so many of the neighbor countries, the rising Nazi powers in Germany attempted to exert pressure everywhere, even on Rome."

"Were you there, Monsignor?"

"Yes, yes. I was assigned to work in the Vatican as an underchancellor to one of Pope Pius XI's own advisors. It was an exciting time, yes. There was a lot for a young man to learn about the world. I was studious and I made friends. The opportunity to serve God and His Holiness, Pope Pius XI, was a great gift, you see? I was born quite near to Rome, of course, and my family was very proud of me, as is natural. And they liked me to be close by."

"Not like today, I guess," I said, thinking of the culture differences he must have encountered coming to Los Angeles and leaving the life of the Vatican behind. This must have seemed like the furthest corner of the universe to a young priest from Rome.

"True. But then my sister came to live near me in Los Angeles shortly after I was assigned to this area, and that was forty years ago. With my sister and her family and my loving parishioners, we have been happy here." He smiled. "But the Brother Ugo you are researching is from that time I spent in Rome, or more accurately, just outside of Rome in the summer residence of our pope. Brother Ugo was a master baker there, and he served there until his death."

"Did you know him personally?"

"Brother Ugo? I remember the man. Short and round, he was. But with a sweet heart, and a gift for baking, of course. Alas, we didn't have many opportunities to get to know each other. I was busy with my studies and my duties, but I do remember a time I was asked to help look into a very sad matter when Brother Ugo died."

My heart began beating faster. "Was there a problem?"

He looked at me with watery brown eyes, magnified through his lenses.

"There were . . . questions. I'm afraid we never had any satisfactory answers. But it was wartime, you remember. And there were rumors that swirled, my dear, like dust at your feet. It was a difficult time. Even for the Vatican. Especially for the Vatican." He shook his head at his memories. "I remember only that poor Brother Ugo's death had been unexpected. If there was anything more to it, I never found a bit of evidence.

"I was young at the time. I'd thought of Brother Ugo as an old man, but he must have only been in his late fifties, not an age we expect a healthy man to die. And so, the sad rumors. Some said he had poisoned himself, but that was malicious. A man of God would no sooner kill himself than kill another man."

I thought that one over. "Brother Ugo left this confession . . ."

"That is what I wanted to see." Monsignor Picca pushed his glasses down his rather long nose and reread the Latin in front of him. "I collect documents, you see. If this document was written by Brother Ugo it might aid in my research."

"In what way?"

"My child, Brother Ugo was the mildest man imaginable. He spent his days baking heavenly breads and meditating in chapel. He never hurt a fly. Poor man.

"However, I believe there was a stunning plot at work during the late thirties that threatened the very existence of the church, and now . . ." He reread the document.

"May I keep this for further study? I'd like to check it against my journals from the time."

"Of course. We have a copy," I said, still unsure of what we were really talking about.

"I should like to study the matter further. I still have many papers from that time. I keep everything. My dear sister is always asking me to go through my things and organize them, and every time I promise her that I will.'' He smiled at me. ''When I retire, I tell her.'' And again, the monsignor let out his jolly hacks and grins.

Just then, there was a light tap on the door.

''Come in,'' yelled the monsignor in his hearty, hoarse voice.

The door was opened by the assistant. Two young children stood silently in the doorway. Stan the cat came out from hiding and began to rub his furry spine against the leg of the boy.

''Have you been sent to fetch me?'' Monsignor Picca asked them, beaming at their astonished faces.

Neither the plaid-skirted girl nor the blue-sweatered boy could muster a word.

''I'll be right with you, children,'' the old man called out to them. And then he turned to me.

''This is unfinished business, and for a thorough man it is hard to put an unfinished thing down. You are like that too, I can see.''

I was always surprised when anyone could see anything about me. I felt opaque, and yet what he said was quite true.

''I like to solve puzzles,'' I admitted.

''As do I. You see? We are quite alike.''

I regarded the two of us and smiled.

''Not on the outside, perhaps. But then there are other parts.''

''Not many look that deeply, Father,'' I said.

''God does,'' he said.

Good point.

''Since you and I are kindred spirits who do not stop until a puzzle is solved,'' the monsignor continued, ''I shall look into my records and report to you. Perhaps I can find the poor fellow's full Christian name, at the very least. May I phone you later?''

''Of course.'' I stood and handed him my business card. ''Thank you for giving up so much of your time.''

''Not at all.'' He also stood and moved to the door.

The two silent children each took a hand and began to pull him along.

"My escorts." The monsignor let out some more jolly dry barks and the children giggled.

"It was a pleasure to meet you, Madeline Bean," he said, shaking gently free of the little girl's hand to take my own.

"I'll check with my sister Claudia. She has many of my old things at her house. I'll go tonight. Would that help?"

"That would be wonderful. Thanks to you, I believe we may have actually discovered the identity of our Brother Ugo. But I must admit, I'm no closer to understanding what this confession is all about. Who is it that Brother Ugo confessed to killing?"

"It is disturbing," Monsignor Picca said, his lightly accented voice suddenly serious. "But this old jagged piece may fit into a startling puzzle."

I could tell that until the elderly priest solved this puzzle on his own, he did not appear inclined to reveal more.

I let go of his gnarled hand, and the very young lady in the St. Bede's school uniform grabbed the prize. Off they went, the two seven-year-old guides leading their elderly friend off to school.

The clear hard glare of winter sunshine greeted me as I stepped outside. The haze that comes with springtime was still a ways off. I reached in my bag to find my sunglasses as I walked across the blacktop of the church parking lot and nearly walked smack into a pickup truck that had lurched into reverse a half a step ahead of me. Although I was not in danger, the driver slammed on his brakes with exaggerated urgency.

The driver's window slid down, and I expected to see an apologetic face poke out.

"My fault," I called out to the driver. "I wasn't watching where . . ."

"Stupid bitch!" the man at the wheel shouted.

The calm dignity of the large cross of St. Bede's stood silent witness.

Stunned, I moved back a step so I could see the face behind the venom. A man with a red complexion and hair that looked unnaturally dark.

Halfway out of his parking space, he threw the truck into park with another lurch and opened the door.

"I'm sorry," I said, wondering if I had crossed paths with a lunatic. I quickly glanced around hoping to spot nearby churchfolk to help me out.

"Sorry, is she?" the man shouted back to the truck as he came toward me.

The birds of La Canada were singing this morning, and even though a middle-aged man was about to deck a nice young woman, they kept up their tuneful racket come what may.

"Have we had a misunderstanding?" I asked, looking directly into his small dark eyes. No matter what I said, the red-faced man was clearly getting himself even more worked up.

"No misunderstanding, sweetheart," he said, seething. He walked right up to me and put one of his beefy hands on my shoulder. My purse strap slipped down my arm.

"Hey! Keep your hands off me." I jerked my shoulder and backed away from him.

"Shut up," another voice said. His companion was tall and beefy, with dark fuzz around a saucer-size bald spot. He had come out of the passenger side of the truck.

I was being mugged in a church parking lot in a suburb so quiet, half of L.A. didn't even know where it was.

"I don't have anything you want in my purse," I shouted, hoping to attract attention by raising my voice.

"Grab her," the first man instructed.

The big bald guy moved behind me and wrenched one hand around my waist and the other one over my mouth. I smelled pickles on his fingers and felt like vomiting. My heart pounded and my head began to ache with panic.

"Here's some advice," the first man said. "If you're

smart you'll take it. Drop all your business for the next coupla months. Got that?"

I was wearing heels. I lifted my knee. Without hesitating I jabbed down with all my strength on the inside knob of baldy's anklebone. The hand over my mouth loosened. His other hand almost let me go, but then he snatched at my dress. I spun away. He caught a handful of waistline fabric and like a yo-yo, I could only get so far away before he yanked me back.

"Stop screwing around!" the first man yelled at his partner. Then to me, "You don't want to get hurt, just lay off your plans for the pope's party. That's not something for you. You got that? Lay off the pope's visit."

I stopped, stunned, trying to let it sink in.

"This is about . . . *catering*?" I yelled at him and he turned away and moved towards his truck. "You're *kidding*, right?"

The guy who was holding me let go and hopped back into the truck.

"Who are you?" I yelled at them. "Are you crazy, attacking someone at a church?"

The truck, which had been left halfway out of its space, was thrown roughly into gear and backed the rest of the way out. Pulling up, it shot out to the street and made a right.

My heartbeat was coming back on-line.

"LUNATICS!" I shouted. "IDIOTS! BASTARDS!" But they had peeled out of the lot and were heading onto Foothill Boulevard by the time my brain had thought up that stunning retort.

I picked up my purse from the pavement and slapped at my clothing to straighten myself out as a group of young men walked past me, eyeing the sinner whom they had certainly heard swearing outside of a church.

Chapter 10

"Are we going to see Donald's movie?" I asked Wes, as he walked into my entry hall, looking tall and handsome in a spotless linen blazer over a spotless white T-shirt.

"Sort of," Wes said, wiping the nondirt from the soles of his immaculate canvas sneakers on the little rug at the door.

"Dinner first?" I threw on my short black leather jacket and grabbed my shoulder bag.

"Something like that." Wes stole a quick look at himself in the entry mirror. I looked into the mirror, too. Standing just in front of Wes, about a head shorter, we were both able to make last minute adjustments, he brushing a hand straight back through his short cropped hair, I tucking a few errant tendrils into the clasp at my neck.

We were at the point in the upcoming event where most of the prep work was done. And before our load-in began in twenty-four hours, we had a slight lull. None of us could rest, so we decided to go out and help Donald celebrate.

"Is Donald nervous?" I asked.

"You could say that." Wes smiled at me in the mirror.

Donald Lake was Holly's most recent boyfriend. They'd been seeing each other for a couple of months. If a guy hung around more than one night, it was usually a relationship for Holly. If he was still there into a new season, the relationship was heavy. Donald was tiptoeing close to that serious ground.

Before we knew him, Donald had written a screenplay while working days driving a delivery truck for a florist. He left the script along with a showy spring flower arrangement in front of the home of one of the youngest and hippest of agents at the International Creative Management talent agency. Tonight, three and a half years later, *Gasp!* was opening in movie theaters across the country and Donald Lake's big debut was upon us.

"My car or yours?" I asked Wesley, as I held open the front door of my house to let him leave first.

"Well, here's the thing . . ." Wes said, leading me out.

Odd. Parked down on the street in front of my garage door was, of all things, a van.

"The thing is . . ." Wes continued, "Donald wants to drive around."

"Where?"

"It's a *thing,* Maddie. Opening night, you know?"

"With us?"

"Well, I don't think there was room in the producer's van, so . . ."

Hollywood economics are harsh. Movies cost incredible amounts of money to make so they have to earn incredible amounts of money just to break even. Opening night is a big deal in Hollywood. If the box office doesn't start out hot on the opening weekend, it's all over; the accountants know the movie is a flop.

This all-or-nothing fever can get the people most involved totally nuts. Not content to stay home, the stars and producers now drive around and visit theaters on opening night, hoping to get a "feel" for how well the picture is doing. The producer will rent a van and invite the stars and the director to drive from theater to theater, hoping to hear the audience cheering.

In the case of *Gasp!* our first-time screenwriter wasn't invited to join in their ritual paranoia. But things could change. If the picture did well this time out, Donald might find himself in the big shot's Chrysler in the future.

"Donald rented it," Wes said, as we stepped up to the

new Town & Country. ''Holly asked me to be the designated driver so Donald could get drunk.''

I smiled. ''To celebrate?''

''Or blot it out. Either way.''

I stared at the large silver beast at the curb. ''I am *so* not a van person,'' I commented.

Wes gave me the eye. ''Force yourself, Madonna.''

I climbed aboard the suburban capsule and settled into what I believe was called a captain's chair. Hmm. Comfy. I found Wes had a can of Diet Coke awaiting each of us, taking up only two of what had to be about fourteen cup holders. My Wagoneer doesn't have cup holders. I felt a small pang of envy.

''My meeting with the orchid people went late, so I came straight over,'' Wes explained. ''We need to go back to my place to pick up Holly and Donald.'' Wes pulled out into the clear evening. ''Talk to me, woman. What's been happening?''

For a few moments all I could do was let out a rather pathetic, ''Arggg.'' With the death of Brother Frank still a mystery, there had been some serious suggestions that the pope's visit should be postponed, but things seemed to have settled down by late afternoon. I filled Wesley in.

''How could someone get onto a secure studio lot, enter a star's dressing room, and kill somebody? It's impossible. It had to be an accident,'' Wes pondered.

''Unless Brother Frank invented a new way to accidentally bash himself on the head with an acting trophy, I think not.''

''And why Brother Frank? It makes absolutely no sense,'' Wes said. ''Unless . . .'' He seemed to get lost in the thought. ''Holly said his cousins belong to a gang. Think that could be related?''

''Wes, he was killed in Dottie's dressing room, not on the corner of Western and Sunset.''

''Which brings up the question of all questions. You think Dottie did it?''

''No. I don't. She's so . . . so . . . loopy.''

"Right. She may be getting desperate, but I don't think she's reached the point where she's murdering men who won't sleep with her."

We'd been through this many times. This is where one of us said, well, the police will investigate. And the other one said, yeah, unconvincingly.

"What's really odd, Madeline, is the news coverage. There is none. Nobody's got this story."

"You noticed that too?" I asked, glancing across the van at Wesley. Perched in the co-pilot captain's chair you get this super high-up view of the world. Pretty cool.

"A man is killed at a Hollywood studio. That is usually considered news. Man, Dottie has lucked out."

"Perhaps it's the studio."

"Keeping things quiet?"

"It happened in their private kingdom," I said. "They're in control. They have their own security. When the police were notified, I bet it was done at a very high level, with lots of secrecy."

"Just think what other crimes could be committed on the lot, with no one the wiser."

"No kidding," I said.

"It's suspicious," Wes said. "You know when the cops get involved nothing stays quiet for long. Reporters hang out at the station and these kinds of stories leak. Someone's controlling this. Someone with more clout than the studio."

It dawned on me. "Maybe it's the church," I said. "They've got to be sensitive about a Jesuit killed by an unknown assailant. And Brother Frank del Valle had ties to gangs."

"Yes. And then the pope is coming . . ."

Wes turned the van up Vine and drove past the cylindrical Capital Records building, whose kitsch architecture resembled a stack of records. The red light at the tip of its roof antenna blinked on and off. Every twenty seconds the light blinked out the word "Hollywood" in Morse code. In case, I don't know, some sailor got lost?

"Let's get crazy for a minute," I offered. "The mayor of our city goes to . . . what church?"

Wes smiled.

"And didn't I hear that the mayor got married again?" I asked.

"I hear you. He needs a favor, you think, to get his last marriage annulled so this new wife will be kosher."

"Exactly. In the doing-a-big-favor-for-the-pontiff department, how would keeping this whole mess out of the glare of the world's press rank?"

Wes said quietly, "Up there." We were waiting out a red light at Melrose and Wes turned his head to look at me.

"Let me just get this straight," he said. "You think the mayor is conspiring with the Catholic church and a major Hollywood studio and a famous redhead to cover up the death of a young Jesuit."

"Only in a nice way," I said. "See, everybody is happy in this scenario."

"So what you're saying," Wes said with escalating sarcasm, "is this could just be a win-win-win-win situation." He shook his head.

"What a world, what a world," I muttered, quoting a melting witch.

"So, who is going to go to bat for poor Brother Frank?" Wes asked, full of concern. Then it hit him. He should not be giving me any ideas. I hated to melt. I preferred drying off and fighting. He spun on a dime and mock-begged, "Please don't say us."

"Hey, we're just speculatin', pardner. And anyway, we've got a movie to see."

We pulled up to a large duplex in Hancock Park, which had been built in the twenties. The archways and red tile half-roofs and arched windows had been restored to pristine condition. Hidden fixtures spotlighted the building, illuminating the white stucco against the blackened night. Both the top unit and the bottom were huge apartments, their romantic Spanish architectural flourishes sheltered behind enormous ferns and lush tropical landscaping. Wes owned the place and lived in the home upstairs. His tenants downstairs had recently moved out so he was taking this opportunity to refurbish the unit. In the meantime, Holly was staying there. She was constantly in need of a new place to live.

We knocked and Holly answered, beaming.

"Come in, come in," she beckoned. The unit was mostly empty. The living room held no furniture, but the newly refinished hardwood floors gleamed.

"You guys ready?" I asked.

"I am." Holly was dressed in a pair of off-white jeans and a cream and khaki silk bandana that she'd twisted in the front and wore as a kind of strapless bikini top. To keep warm, she'd added a milk-chocolate–colored suede jacket.

"Don't you want shoes?" I asked.

She looked down at her bare feet, with the tiny gold ring on one toe, and said, "Nah. I'm fine."

"Where's Donald?" Wes asked.

"I think he's puking."

"Aw. Already?" I asked, walking down the arched hallway and shouting, "Donald! Let's go! There'll be plenty of time for puking later. Hey, the night is young."

"I'm just going to get a bowl for the back of the van," Holly whispered. "You know, just in case."

Donald showed up in the hall. He was six feet tall or so, exactly as tall as Holly and that made me wonder if her new shoeless look had a hidden agenda.

"Hey, Donald, you ready?" I asked. He gave me a shy smile. Donald had this country boy face with such deep dimples they formed parallel lines down each cheek. His squinty eyes were bright blue. He gave me a brotherly peck on the cheek. I like guys who were raised in close families. Holly had found a nice one, for a change.

"Let's raise hell," Donald suggested, in such a soft, good-boy voice, we all got the joke.

Off we trooped to the van. Wesley held me back a moment for a private word.

"This is the cool part of not working every damn Friday night of our lives."

Chef work and catering do a number on one's social life.

I was getting into the mood to have fun, and for the first time in several days, I felt like I might actually have some.

On the way to Westwood, our first official stop, Donald filled us in on *Gasp!*

"See, they had Tom Cruise in it originally."

"Tom Cruise!" Holly's eyes lit up. "Oh, man! How'd they lose Tom Cruise?"

"Schedule conflicts, I think," Donald said, his arm around Holly in the middle seat of the van.

"Tom Cruise. Man!" Holly said. She was taking the loss pretty hard.

"Well, he's not actually anything like the character of Bennett, sweetie," Donald told her. "This script really features the womens' parts. So if Tom Cruise had done it, they'd a' changed every damn scene to put him in there more."

"Yeah," Holly said. Her missed chance to be going with a guy who wrote a script for Tom Cruise was a painful loss. But she was recovering.

"So what happened then?" Wes asked Donald.

"Well, after Cruise fell out, it went to Leonardo DiCaprio."

"Wow," I said. This sounded like a big production.

"But he got too hot or something. Maybe it was a money thing."

"Jeez. You lost Tom Cruise and Leo?" Holly was bummed.

"Then someone thought David Schwimmer might do it, but his people turned it down."

"Cruise to DiCaprio to Schwimmer? I'm surprised they didn't try adapting it for Whoopi Goldberg," I whispered to Wes.

"But I love Morgan Freeman," Donald said, defending the star of his very first movie.

"He's great," Wes said, over his shoulder, and we all agreed.

As Wes pulled up to a corner in Westwood, he announced, "This is it, folks."

Dozens of people were standing near the box office of the Westwood Theater. And it got better.

"Open your eyes, Donald," I suggested.

We all stared. People were lined up all the way down the block, waiting to see Donald's movie.

"Oh, man!" Wes said, starting to get excited. "It goes on to the next block."

We drove past the line as it snaked down the street.

"I need a drink," Donald called out.

"I've got the puke pot in the back, honey!" Holly offered, giggling.

The van slowly cruised the line of Friday night daters, all waiting, bless their little hearts, to see *Gasp!*

"Holy moley! It's three blocks long. The damn line goes all the way . . ." Holly was bouncing in her seat. Boing! Boing!

"Now I do feel sick," Donald muttered.

Holly rolled down her electric window and yelled to the waiting crowd, now queuing up four blocks from the theater, "*Fuck* Tom Cruise, baby!"

"Holly, behave yourself," I said, as I yanked her back into the van by the back of her bandeau top.

I turned to the ashen-faced Donald and directed, "Puke pot."

And, "Park," I commanded Wesley, on a roll.

Wes pulled in one of those Westwood parking lots that cost a thousand dollars. In the company of Donald Lake and his four-block line, such concerns were really beneath us.

We walked past the crowds on a Hollywood contact high. Donald approached the young uniformed geek at the door. After a few words back and forth the very nice geek motioned to us to come on in.

Donald dimpled at us. "It's cool. The guy said we could just hang out in the lobby and watch from the back of the theater." We entered ahead of the pack.

"We need Milk Duds," Holly announced. "For luck."

Just then, the line that had been waiting outside to see

Gasp! was let in. As the crowd of people rushed into the theater, they began to swarm the concession counter. Holly and I jumped in line quickly while Wesley and Donald went on toward the theater.

"Where's Arlo?" Holly asked me.

"Working." Arlo always worked. For the past three years we'd both had outrageous schedules with demanding jobs. Since I'd semiretired, I had noticed that we had become somewhat off-balance, timewise.

"Isn't Donald cute?" Holly asked.

Lucky Donald. It was not possible to strike out, chickwise, on a night when your very own *movie* was opening very, very big. I hoped Donald appreciated his unique position.

"Adorable," I agreed, happy to see Holly so happy. Her luck with men had been, up until this one, dismal.

My phone rang. Out from my deep dark shoulder bag I retrieved my cell phone and punched "start" just in time.

As our line moved up, bringing us closer to the glassed-in jujubes, I mashed a hand against my free ear in an attempt to block out the noise.

"Oh, hi. What's up? Is anything wrong?"

Holly had moved up to the counter and was ordering her lucky Milk Duds. She turned and asked if I wanted anything.

"It's Xavier and I can barely hear him," I told her quickly, and then added, "Can you get me a Diet Coke, please?" as I moved away from the noisy crowd.

"Can you hear me now, Madeline?" Xavier asked me again on the other end of the cell phone.

"It's a little better. "

"I just wanted to talk to someone."

"Okay," I said.

"I mean, I wanted to talk to you."

"Would you like to meet us?" I offered. "We're kind of driving around, checking out lines."

"I can't. I just wanted to find out how things went this morning with the monsignor."

"Fine. I didn't learn that much. But it seems like our Ugo wasn't as old as we'd thought."

"Really?" Xavier asked, interested. "You know, it's funny. I'd wanted to reread the confession, but I couldn't find it. Did I leave my copy at your place?"

"I don't think so. We made two copies, right? You took the original and I took one for me and one for the monsignor."

"That's what I thought, too. Huh. I guess I'm getting confused with all the paperwork that's been going across my desk now that the pope is about to arrive. And then, I heard some news from the police."

"What happened?" I asked.

"They've arrested someone. It turns out it was a gang member who killed Brother Frank del Valle."

I could hear Xavier sigh.

"That's horrible. Are they sure?"

"The young man confessed, I believe. But this has to be just between you and me. We have to keep this whole incident very quiet."

"I may have to tell Wesley. And Arlo. Is that okay?"

"I trust your judgement, Madeline. It's a relief, in a way. Now that they've made an arrest, I hope everything will begin to settle down. Anyhow, I thought you'd feel better to know that the man responsible for Brother Frank's death has been arrested."

"Do they know why he did it?"

"Did you ask why? It's a tragedy that boys feel they need to belong to gangs in the first place. That is what Brother Frank thought. That's why he had wanted to help. I believe his cousins are still involved in gang life, which had been a deep concern of his."

"It's so sad, Xavier."

"Yes. But at least with this swift arrest we can all begin to heal. And, now, of course our plans can move forward."

"You mean about the pope's visit?"

"He arrives tomorrow night."

Holly walked up to me, her face beaming, handed over

an enormous cup of Diet Coke, and whispered loudly, "The movie's about to begin."

I got off the line with Xavier and we rushed to the theater, which was now seriously packed. Donald and Wes were standing at the back, with Donald pacing a nervous dance.

"Milk Duds, honeybear," Holly sang as she waved the box in front of Donald's face.

"I couldn't eat anything, Holly," he said, "Thanks, but . . ."

"*Lucky* Milk Duds," Holly continued singing, with an excited smile, as she manically raised and lowered her colorless eyebrows beneath her white-blonde bangs.

Finally, she broke through Donald's trance. As the last coming attraction trailer faded to black, Donald lunged for a lucky *anything* as his first movie began to play.

Chapter 11

2424 PICO is a trendy restaurant that's slightly off the beaten path. Tonight it was jam-packed with hip young things making the scene. It goes without saying everyone was wearing black. For several years now the fashion people have been telling us that brown is the new black. But don't let them fool you; black is the new black.

We were starving. After catching about ten minutes of *Gasp!* in three different Westside cinemas, we had to eat. Holly and Donald picked the restaurant. The food here is ambitious, and the service is sometimes independent, but the crowd is fabulous, a mix of lovely young Brits looking to be discovered and the I'm-not-famous-yet-but-wait-until-next-year types.

We brought our glow of success with us. Holly headed straight for the ladies room as Donald met up with some of his pals at the bar. Pretty soon the room started receiving free drinks. Even though many groups had been waiting an hour or longer for their reservations, the atmosphere in the place got remarkably cheerful. Does any town love a winner more than ours?

I pulled Wesley over to a quiet corner and told him about my conversation with Xavier, or ''Bro'' as Wes had begun calling him.

''The police have arrested some gangbanger,'' I reported. I nursed my drink, full of thoughts. The world has recently rediscovered martinis but I've always had a thing for them.

I tasted the hot vodka of the moment, Belvedere. Sipping, I pondered the meaning of this sudden end to the silent investigation of Brother Frank's death.

"Does Bro believe the police have the right man?" Wes asked.

A sudden pang caught me unawares, almost bringing tears. I would always be confused about what Xavier thought. I had known him, once. I had. But now I doubted.

Look at our past. Like, one day he's going to marry a person and the next day he's taking vows of celibacy—how strange was that? Wes waited patiently, watching me.

"Wes," I said carefully, "do you think Xavier is gay?"

"Of course not."

"Of course not," I said.

The way in which Wes could handle the zigs and zags of my typical conversation rivaled Unser at Indy, with not so much as a squeal of his mental wheels.

"How could he leave you?" Wes said, switching to this new subject. "That's the big question, isn't it?"

"The truth is, I could never understand his kind of faith," I said, quietly. "That's why I'll never understand how he could have left. There's never been anything wrong with Xavier. I'm the one who's missing something. I mean, what a relief to put everything into God's hands."

"Men are bastards, eh?"

I gave him a fond look and went back to my drink.

Wes patted my hand and, with the detour into Mad Bean's self-pity over, zigzagged back to our previous topic. "This notion that a gang member did it—somehow broke onto a very secure studio lot, entered the dressing room of a T.V. star, tracked down a monk, picked up a statuette, and committed murder—that incongruity isn't alarming anyone but you and me. So maybe we should just leave it alone for tonight."

"Agreed." I finished my drink.

Holly returned from her visit to the restroom, full of news.

"Parker Posey was in the bathroom with me!" she announced, gushing. "I peed in the stall next to Parker Posey!"

"My, what exciting lives we lead," Wes said, deadpan.

Holly turned to me and added, "She's so cool. So where's my Donald?" She swiveled toward the bar and spotted him. "There he is!"

"Wesley," I said after she'd fluttered off in Donald's direction, "lighten up. Give Hol a break. This is her first real boyfriend in a long time."

"And I believe this is the first one who has ever been able to pay his own Visa bill," Wes said.

"Even better," I agreed.

"Didn't Marlo Thomas used to call her boyfriend 'my Donald'? You know, on 'That Girl'?"

"I thought that was Ivana Trump?" I teased him.

"That was '*the* Donald,' " Wes corrected, and then belatedly got that I was having a bit of fun with him.

"Okay." Wes grinned. "A moratorium," he offered, holding his tonic water on the rocks in the air.

"I will drink to that," I said, although my martini glass was low on actual drink.

"Me, too," added Holly, now back with us and raising a banana daiquiri up over her head.

"Lake, party of four," called out the hostess.

"Can that be us?" Holly asked, checking her watch. "We've only just been here ten minutes."

"Donald's a star," Wes reminded her.

"*My* Donald?" Holly squealed.

Trying not to laugh, I grabbed Wes by the arm and followed the pretty hostess as she slinked her way to the back of the room, showing us to a pleasant table. Donald left his admirers at the bar and joined us. I was pleased to see the waitress who followed him was carrying a tray with fresh drinks.

"Who was that girl you were just talking to?" Holly asked as we were getting seated.

"Claire Danes," Donald said. "She was congratulating

me. Can you believe that? I can't figure out how all these people already know that *Gasp!* is a hit. It's only ten o'clock. Weird."

"In the old days they had tom-toms, my boy," Wes said. "But nowadays we've got something better."

"Buzz," Holly explained to her darling Donald.

How can there be secrets? Hollywood is the ultimate beehive. *Everything* that happens is confided to a nutritionist, faxed to a studio accountant, bragged by competitive nannies in another language, sweated over with a personal trainer, name-dropped in preschool parking lots, ranted bitterly to a therapist, confessed to the dentist between the gargle and spit, chuckled over by valet parkers, approved by the pet groomer, blurted out during a shrill custody battle outside Toys 'R Us, and leaked to the tabloids. So, of course, everyone knows everything before everyone else. Buzz.

Donald beamed at us. "So tell me what's been going on. Holly says you guys are going to do a big party for the pope. That's huge."

"Donald, you're so new at this Hollywood thing it hurts," Wes chided. "You are never supposed to talk about anyone other than yourself. It's the law here."

"The teasing ban," I reminded Wes.

"He can't help himself," Holly explained, and then turned to her Donald. "Ignore him, sweetkins."

"Man, I think it's incredible that the pope is coming to Los Angeles. This town is in need of serious redemption," Donald said.

"Madeline's making His Holiness some of her famous homemade granola, just to fortify him to face L.A. That should handle it," Holly joked.

Seeing as Donald and I were almost smashed, we decided to let Wesley be our designated menu handler, as well as driver, and he told the waitperson what we were all to have. He, or she, had a partially shaved head and multiple piercings. I was struck by the realization that Holly's fashion adventures, bare feet now shod in thick-soled Doc Martens in a bow to restaurant health codes, were rather tame.

The waiter took our menus back, but not before he asked for Donald's autograph. Yes, we were enjoying ourselves, basking in the heat reflected from Holly's Donald. In the land of dreams, almost everyone is an aspiring something. If it's not actor, it's director; if not director, it's stand-up comic. Take someone for drinks in L.A. and by the third Amstel Light they're telling you about this script they wrote and if their cousin's hairstylist gets it to Loni Andersen they might get it optioned. There are literally thousands of Subaru salesmen and English teachers, not to mention yoga instructors and airport shuttle drivers, who have a script or two in their drawers that could be the next *Titanic* if someone would give it a shot.

This enormous yearning to be discovered is almost palpable. Of all the fairy tales Hollywood itself believes in, the frog who is really a prince must be our favorite. That made Donald's victory the sweetest kind. He was the proverbial unknown talent, a guy who came from nowhere, who had no relatives or friends in high places, a goddamned lucky son-of-a-frog who had been kissed by fate.

Talent is important here. Connections are important. Hard work and perseverance and paying dues are important. But nothing is as venerated here as much as luck because anyone could get lucky, right? This is a town that worships that kind of luck.

I, myself, yearned for luck at times, but I was also very interested in the work and so I was kind of frustrated that we hadn't actually seen any of Donald's film.

"I'd like to know more about your script," I said to Donald as things began to settle down at our table. "What inspired you to write *Gasp!*?"

"I found these great old true stories and I got hooked," Donald answered, happy to be talking about his work. "I wrote the entire script in my old Valley Village apartment. I was doing some research for my masters and I found these old European diaries. I was struck by how different the world seemed then. It was only fifty-five years ago, but it could have been centuries. Real low-tech, you know? But with all the crap that was going down during World War Two, there were also fantastic acts of personal bravery.

"Think of it—people being dispossessed, flung from their normal lives, facing enormous threats—it moved men to acts of passion and compassion. Not everyone was a sinner; not everyone was a saint. But almost everyone was tested, see? And some of the stories were naturally cinematic. I started getting excited about writing a screenplay that captured what I was feeling. I mean, what do you do? Do you risk everything to help, or do you close your eyes and become part of hell?

"I started with the Nazis rounding up Jews. Then I added a young couple on the run. Once I got to work writing, it took me less than a month to finish the script."

"You are so deep," Holly said, hooking her leg around Donald's under the table.

"So where did the alien motherships come in?" asked Wes, tentatively.

"Later."

We waited while another round of drinks was delivered compliments of a table of agents this time.

"Yeah. I got the script out there but nobody wanted to do a picture about Nazis." Donald looked at us like, can you believe that? "Nuts, huh? But then they said they could see it as a sci-fi epic if I changed a few things and that seemed pretty funny to me. So I holed up for an entire weekend and rewrote it. Just to crack up my roommate, you know? Only it was good. It really worked."

"So it's a Nazi story played in outer space," I said.

"It's about this man who's trying to get out of Europe before the Nazis catch up with him and throw him in a concentration camp. He's on the run and he hides out in Italy using some false papers. While he's in hiding, he meets a woman with a young son and they, you know, fall in love hard. This part was a true story, by the way. I'm not making up anything. But then, the borders start closing up tight. You remember at the start of *Casablanca,* how there were some people who bought travel visas on the black market and got phony passports? They had to get out of Europe, somehow, and they were desperate. And that sneaky bastard who had the stolen documents was planning to sell them to the highest bidder if the Nazis didn't catch him first. Remember *'Reeky, you must hide these letters of transit! Please, Reeky!'* ''

I watched Donald as he did his Peter Lorre impression and laughed and talked about his story. Perhaps he would hang onto his natural enthusiasm. Unfortunately, it was not always so. The ride Donald was on too often took a detour through the dream grinder. But not always.

''Anyway, there's all this suspense and then they escape and then they get caught,'' Donald continued.

''Don't tell me the end,'' I said.

''I won't. But there's the basic moral issue of who betrayed whom? Of what is moral in an unspeakably immoral time in history? Of how far would you go to save yourself or someone you loved?''

''But played out on Alpha Centuri,'' Holly added.

Donald laughed. ''I know I'll be criticized. So what? I don't have a problem with popular culture. Maybe the story loses some of its resonance, taking it out of Europe. What can I say? It's only a movie.''

''I can't wait to see it,'' I said.

''I think the producer left in a lot of the good stuff, so I have no complaints. And, you know? It actually works to have this story placed in the future. It says that we can't get comfortable thinking this is a horror story from the past and nothing like this could ever happen again. It's a clarion warning that we must guard against this future or pay an unspeakable price.''

Where had Holly found this guy? He *was* deep.

The food was brought to our table. Although the descriptions in the menu had been so darn *California* it had given

Holly and me the giggles, there was nothing wrong with the presentation. Wes had ordered me the lobster ravioli, which was prepared with spinach greens and a coconut milk and saffron sauce. My kind of thing. For Holly, he selected Chilean sea bass with mango salsa and dried fig sauce. She appeared to be happy with it, although Holly was always happy with food, no matter what. Wes ordered himself the honey-pomegranate-glazed game hen with apricot- and pistachio-studded cous cous, and for Donald he chose the tenderloin of beef with garlic mashed potatoes and a Cabernet sauce. It all looked amazing and we dove in.

As I surveyed the restaurant I noticed the hostess taking a telephone call, jotting down a note, and then delivering it to a silver-haired man at a nearby table. His had to be the only gray hair in the establishment, I thought, and then, as I watched him look at the note and pass it along to the young man seated next to him, suddenly I remembered something.

"Holly," I said, perhaps a little too urgently.

"Mad," she answered, equally urgent. We had reached our martini and daiquiri limits.

"No, really, Holly," I tried again, and put my hand on her bare arm to get her attention.

"What?" she said, "Want to try my fig sauce?"

"Holly, when we were at the studio, Arlo's assistant Jody brought a note."

"Yes, so?" she asked, trying to follow me.

"So, wasn't the note addressed to *Xavier*? Isn't that what Jody said? Think, Holly."

"I didn't pay attention, Maddie. I . . . Wait a minute. Was that the note he gave to Brother Frank?"

"Yes!"

"What's this about?" Donald put down his fork and looked at Holly.

"Oh, Donald. It's about what happened last night, when this poor sweet Jesuit guy died. I didn't want to upset you on your big day."

"You mean someone died at the studio last night?" Donald asked in alarm.

"Well, yes," Holly said, looking at me. We had agreed not to discuss it with too many people, but I would have thought she'd surely have told Donald.

"That's weird," Donald said. "I was on the lot last night and never heard a thing."

"You were?" I asked, as we all three turned to stare at Donald.

"I got there late. I couldn't find anyone."

"We were out back by the trailers," Holly explained.

"Didn't you see Arlo roaming around?" I asked, curious that we hadn't gotten a message that Donald was looking for Holly.

"Nah. The soundstage was practically deserted. Only person I saw was some woman who had been in the audience for the show and come back to try to find her purse she left behind. She was just looking for it when I got there. I asked her where everyone was, but of course she didn't know anything. She said she'd been waiting outside by the audience entrance to the stage, hoping someone would let her in. And then some guy told her to just pull open the door, it wasn't locked."

I looked up. "A man standing around one of the stage doors told her this?" I asked, thinking about the note and the meeting that never happened.

"Honest, Maddie, I don't know," Donald said, becoming alarmed by the urgency in my voice. "The woman was around forty, but pretty, you know? Hispanic, I think. She just started complaining to me about waiting a long time to get back in, trying to be polite and not break rules, needing to find her purse . . . like that."

"And the man she saw by the stage door?"

"She said he was very rude. Or mean. Something like that. And, oh yeah, she said he was bald. Like 'The bald guy just yelled at me to open the door.' And, you know, I just said, 'Well, that's strange, 'cause mostly the people who work at the studio are real nice.' You know, small talk."

When Holly gets excited she pulls on her clothing, and now she was tugging her strapless scarf top up with both hands. "But what does it all mean?"

I'd been drinking too much to get my mind around all these new thoughts. A note had come for Xavier. Brother Frank took it and went to meet someone by the back door of the soundstage—someone who never showed up. Dottie got the great idea to give a Jesuit brother a bedroom tour. And now a menacing man was spotted near a different entrance to the soundstage.

I shook my head, but instead of clearing it, I felt dizzy. How did all this fit with the arrest of a gangbanger? I thought back to last night. I seemed to recall, dimly, seeing a young man with a shaved head in the audience, but my brain could no longer be relied on for clear memories.

My cell phone rang. I was lucky to hear it over all the chatter and clinking and music in the crowded restaurant.

"Maddie?"

"Yes?" Add the level of background noise to my martini-induced brain-haze and I was having a hard time putting a face to the female voice on the phone.

"It's me. I've got to see you right away. Where are you?"

"2424 PICO." My voice was coming out a notch too loud. I made a mental note to speak more normally. "The restaurant," I whispered.

"You got a table on a Friday!" The voice sounded impressed.

I racked my Belvedere-enhanced brain. She knew me by name. She had my private number. She was . . .

"Can you come up to the house?" she asked.

"Who is it?" Wes whispered.

"Someone," I whispered back.

"I hear a man's voice," the woman on the phone continued. That voice! I almost had it . . . "You're not cheatin' on old Arlo, are ya', honey?"

It was Dottie! Now what in heaven's name was she calling me about this late?

"Dottie," I said loudly, as one is wont to do when one wants to make it perfectly clear she may be drunk on trendy vodka, but she certainly knows who she is talking to most of the time. "I am with Wes and Holly and Holly's friend, Donald Lake."

"The young director?" Dottie asked, interested.

"Writer," I said. "We're checking out his new movie, *Gasp!*"

"You always stay *tres courant*," Dottie gushed. "I love meeting your friends. Don't forget to bring that nice young Donald Lake over to see me sometime or I won't forgive you. Hey, I know. How about now? We'll celebrate. I've got Dom, baby."

I rode a giddy wave as I thought, *must keep Dottie away from Holly's Donald.*

Whether Dottie thought "networking" with Donald would be a great chance to enhance her career or her master bedroom, I couldn't tell.

"He's not your type, trust me."

Dottie considered that for a moment. "*Oh.* Gay."

I didn't think it necessary to correct her.

"Then you come over, Maddie. I need to talk to you now. It's super urgent, honey, or I wouldn't bother you."

I chuckled over that one. "I don't have my car tonight. How 'bout next week?"

"Don't worry about transportation, silly. I'll have Carlos pick you up." And before I could protest further I heard her muffled shout to Carlos to go on and get me, pronto.

We talked for another minute and when I disconnected, three pairs of eyes were staring at me. I looked at my dinner companions and sighed.

"Dottie Moss is sending Carlos here, now, to pick me up and take me to her house."

"We're still going to drive around some more," Holly complained. "And this time we're going to really sit down and watch the movie, Maddie," she added, knowing exactly how to tempt me.

"Damn," I complained. "I don't want to see Dottie tonight. I wish I'd told her that. When I drink just an itsy amount, sometimes I . . . I'm so . . ."

"Weak?" Wes offered.

"Easy to manipulate," Holly said, matter-of-factly.

"Sweet-natured," Donald suggested, in a vote of kindness.

"Screwed," I finished.

"What's happening at Dottie's house this evening that's so damned important, I wonder?" Holly asked.

"She said she wants to talk about what really happened in her trailer last night when Brother Frank was murdered."

All three of them stared at me.

"That is just so weird," Donald said, shaking his head. "Of all people, why on earth would she think of talking to you, Madeline?"

All three of us stared at him.

"Maddie's got a rep," Holly told him. "She's good at this stuff."

"Stop that," I chided, feeling like my head all of a sudden weighed ten thousand pounds.

"Old news," I told them. As I put my sloshed head down upon my arms I instantly realized how good it might feel to fall asleep.

"Hot tea, here," Wes called out to a passing waiter.

"English Breakfast," Holly added.

"Better make that 'to go,' " suggested Donald.

I looked up to see the bulldog form of Carlos Schwartz, wearing a tall Texan cowboy hat, sidle up to the table.

"Thanks for coming on such short notice, Maddie," Carlos said, trying to hold my chair for me.

I stood up. My brain cleared a level. Holly and Wes and I hug when we say goodbye, so they stood up, too. Donald was family by now and did the same.

"Dottie will not be denied," I said, grabbing my bag.

"You got that right," Carlos agreed. "She respects you is the truth. I can talk 'til I'm blue in the face," the stout guy said as we walked towards the door, ''but does she listen?''

''What exactly is the problem, Carlos?''

''You gotta convince her not to tell what she knows about that priest's murder to 'Entertainment Tonight.' ''

Chapter 12

I'd been to Miss Erica ''Dottie'' Moss's house several times before. She lived in a big spread-out ranch-style house on one of the few flat lots in Bel Air. It was designed in the fifties by an architect popular for producing western-themed dwellings of gigantic proportions.

The footprint of the house looked like a giant wagon wheel. You entered by a front door placed in the hub. The enormous hexagonal room made for a dramatic entry. Its ceiling vaulted upward over two stories to a wooden tower. Hallways ran off from the hexagon like six spokes, leading to separate bedroom wings, an office wing, and a kitchen/scullery/maids wing, as well as spokes that led to a Texas-size living room and dining room. Dottie called it The Ranch.

Carlos pulled Dottie's black Mercedes station wagon into her circular drive, the quiet now interrupted by a muffled pitter-patter as the luxury shock absorbers cushioned most of the jogging one would expect driving over the rough faux-cobblestones. The property was blazing with lights, showing off a lush landscape that had been designed within an inch of its life. There were paved walkways and rustic benches. There were about two dozen cement animals, many with ribbons around their necks. A humped bridge crossed a pond where the tall grass looked professionally freeform.

On the ten-minute drive up the canyon past million-dollar bungalows, Carlos had made an adept attempt at small talk. He mentioned the syndication deal that was being negotiated for the reruns of Dottie's series, knowing that I might have an interest since Arlo is involved in the negotiations. He commented on how good it was to see me when I wasn't cooking. Carlos was a bull, but he couldn't have survived so well in this rarified Bel Air china shop if he hadn't learned a lesson or two in tap-dancing between the aisles.

He had been pitching for Dottie since they were kids together near Amarillo and his supporting role seemed to define him. Even after they divorced ten years ago, there had never been the slightest question of Dottie getting a new manager. They were a team. It struck me that they were a family business, of sorts. They were Dottie Moss.

Carlos hopped out of the Mercedes and bounded around to get my door before I'd unfastened the shoulder belt and grabbed my purse up from the floor. For a big guy, he could really move.

"Here we go," he said, as he held my door open.

"Thanks." As I stepped out into the bright glare that spotlighted the home's exterior, I smoothed the back of my long black knit dress, feeling suddenly like I was on stage.

Carlos unlocked the front door with his key and as we stepped across large Mexican terra cotta tiles into the entry, he tossed his cowboy hat onto a chair, exposing a hairline which had not only retreated, but long ago surrendered. His graying ponytail tried its best to compensate, but it just looked as if his hair was making a run for it and it was working its way down his back.

"D!" Carlos yelled out to the empty hall. He shrugged and turned to me. "I better go find her."

He shifted that big gut of his over his jeans, unbuttoned the top button, and then flipped his keys onto the center table. The Gucci key ring skidded across the rustic wooden surface and then tinked as it hit crystal. A three-foot-tall Waterford vase anchored an arrangement of branches and orchids, which extended another five feet higher under the vaulted tower.

As I waited, I checked out the dozens of photos, which hung on the walls. Dottie and Somebody Famous filled every frame.

When she had been a simple country singer, wearing thin silk jeans and skimpy fringed tops, her signature red hair had been big, real big. I smiled as I looked at shots from fifteen years earlier showing that big-haired Dottie hugging an equally big-haired Dolly Parton. As the years went by, Dottie Moss's hair got smaller and tamer, until she hit pay dirt doing an unexpectedly wonderful job in a hit comedy movie. *The Camera* made her crossover from Texas singer to Hollywood star complete.

She had played a country girl who goes to New York to be a fashion model. She winds up being made over by a millionaire and trying to fit into his high society life. That surprise blockbuster led to other film roles, although none ever matched *The Camera* for success. Eventually, Dottie did what most actresses in their thirties do as they see younger women getting the first look at the best movie scripts. She settled for a sitcom.

Carlos was behind all of these decisions as he tells everyone who will listen. Carlos knew it was time for Dottie to get out of Nashville. Carlos knew Dottie had to get the part in *The Camera* and he bombarded the producer's office for months until they gave her a screen test. Carlos knew it was time to look for a series. Carlos knew Dottie had to play a professional woman and he pushed hard to get her the lead role in "Woman's Work," a show about a lady lawyer in Chicago.

And so a Hollywood career is propelled along—by an ex-husband with a knack for marketing and skin so thick that he can be told "no" a dozen times and still happily pick up the phone and speed-dial it for rejection number thirteen.

As I found a small photo showing Dottie standing in

front of Westminster Abbey smiling with Boy George, I heard her coming down one of the halls.

"Darlin'! Carlos got you here so darn fast, I hardly had time to change my clothes. Sorry about that," she said. Dottie, in her white lace unitard, linked her arm in mine and steered me toward the living room.

I remembered the decor. Taxi yellow plaid criss-crossed over four big sofas and many assorted ottomans, benches, and wing chairs. The pine plank floor was covered here and there with white area rugs while the low tables, slapped with a coat of rustic green paint, held gargantuan arrangements of sunflowers and peonies. This lady alone must put her florist's kids through private school.

"Sit, kitten." She waved me to a plaid sofa and walked with her natural grace to the bar. "Whatcha havin'?"

She selected a doubles glass of cut crystal, eyed it against the lamp light for spots, and then dropped a few ice cubes into it.

"Diet Coke."

"That's your thing, isn't it? I remember. Well, how about drinkin' with me tonight? You like vodka?" Dottie held up a bottle.

"I'm falling asleep, Dottie." Perhaps I'd have been a more gracious guest if I hadn't been ambushed into coming over. It was my own fault I gave in to her summons so easily. On a good day, it is hard for me to say no to people. On a night when I'm halfway to wasted, it's that much harder. And at any time of day or night, toast or stone cold sober, it is notoriously hard to say no to a celebrity. And then, of course, my curiosity was always getting the best of me.

"Okay, sugarbean," she said, smiling like she was used to grouchy girlfriends, "I'll wake you up."

Dottie gracefully carried a small silver tray from the bar to the green coffee table and sat beside me, with one slim leg tucked under her. She handed me the heavy glass of ice and Diet Coke and then lifted her own glass, filled with bourbon.

"Here's to us, hey?" She took a big gulp of bourbon and didn't flinch as it went down.

I set my drink on the tray. "Dottie, what's the story? Did you talk to the police last night?"

"When those sexy ol' policemen came to question me they were very polite. Kinda like their mamas had raised them proper." She winked at me and took another long hit of bourbon. "But when all was said and done, I don't think those officers never asked me any questions. Now don't that beat all?"

"It does." Again, I could only wonder why the investigation was so cursory. "What really happened last night?"

"When I stepped out of the shower? Oh, God, I know I'll go to hell for this." She crossed herself with the hand that held the bourbon glass.

I waited.

"See, I was drippin' wet, and so I peeked into the bedroom, looking for a towel . . ."

I imagined the scene back in Dottie's luxury trailer as it must have been the night before and tried to recall the Bible story about the sacrificial goat. There was Brother Frank, taking a look around Dottie's room, studying momentos and photos while the star is in the shower. Just what had she planned to do to the man? A little ambush, perhaps, with the wet and naked star appearing from the bathroom sans robe and definitely sans modesty. I imagined the surprise with which Brother Frank would have had to deal with that amazing event.

"Dottie, what were you thinking?" I'd found celebrities usually don't mind us regular folks being shocked by their outrageous ways. They don't expect us to have their spunk.

She smiled apologetically. And then she giggled. She giggled until she cried. Wiping a tear from her cheek, she drained the last of the bourbon.

"Dottie?"

Waving the empty glass in a large circular gesture, she

said softly, "I've been goin' at the bourbon for a little while."

I took the glass out of her hand and set it down on the tray. "Dottie, do you want to tell me what went on with Brother Frank?"

"How in the blazes was I supposed to know that cute young guy was a Catholic priest?" she whispered at me, aghast and subdued. "He didn't have on any collar. He didn't look like no priest I'd ever met. He was just such a sweet guy. Kinda star-struck. I offered to show him around and he was so . . . like . . . respectful." She looked up at me as if for agreement. "You know what I mean?"

She hit the heel of her hand against her temple once, twice, three times.

"Of course he was respectful," she grimaced. "He was a goddamned *Catholic priest!*" She was getting louder and louder.

"Calm down, Dottie," I said. "Look. How could you know, right?"

"How could I know?" she asked me, seizing on the point. "It wasn't like anyone told me or nothin'. Hell, he was just a fan, I thought. That guy he was supposed to meet never showed up, so I figured I'd take him into my dressing room and show him around. It's only natural that some chemistry is gonna develop. I mean, I'm a regular gal and he's a regular guy."

"Well . . ." She was in such a state, I didn't want to be the one to remind her that Frank was actually more like a "regular guy" who had taken vows of celibacy.

"So I suggested we relax. Why not? I mean, we were getting along just fine."

"And?"

"I was kind of surprised when he didn't pick up on it."

Oh my goodness. Poor Brother Frank.

"I guess I was a moron, all right? But I swear, as Jesus is my witness, he never ever said nothing about being a Jesuit or whatever it is. What did I know? I figured he needed a little more time to figure out just how lucky he was going to be. Let's face it, more than one man has been dazzled around me. Sometimes they just don't realize I'm a flesh and blood woman, like anyone else, know what I mean?''

I'm afraid I did.

''I mean, when it comes to civilians, some of them can get pretty scared when they are in the presence of a superstar. They kinda freeze. I've seen it plenty of times. Some guys can get so darn nervous they have trouble getting it up, even. So I figured this guy just needed a little time to, like, pull himself together.''

''What did you say to him?''

''I don't know. Something like, 'You just get yourself comfortable, sugar lump, while I get fresh.' Nothing embarrassin' thank the Lord!''

I had never seen her embarrassed. This might be a first.

''So that was it,'' she said, bouncing up a little unsteadily and walking back toward the bar. ''Nothin' too bad, I don't think.'' She refilled her glass.

''And you really heard nothing at all while you were in the shower?''

''Nothing, yeah.'' It was taking most of her concentration to fill the glass without spilling any bourbon. I was getting more and more sober while Dottie Moss got aggressively less so.

''Well, now wait,'' Dottie rambled on. ''I heard arguing. But I really think the voices were coming from outside.''

''You heard arguing?'' My patience was shot. ''Dottie! Could it have been Brother Frank?''

''Well.'' She put down her drink before it ever made it to her lips and thought. Then she looked up at me and asked, ''Dollface, do you want another Diet Coke, or are you all set there?''

Her hostess gene kicked in just as we were getting somewhere. Hell and damnation.

''Dottie, think. What about the voices you heard arguing? Could it possibly have been Brother Frank arguing with someone?''

"Those trailers have pretty thin walls, you know? And of course I had on some music . . ." She thought hard. "Supertramp, I think."

"Okay, Dottie. Go on."

"And there were voices. I always seem to pick up on some conversation or other that's going on outside my windows. I complain. You should hear me complain to Arlo. But I mean! I'm an artist. I need to be concentratin' on my lines. I complain, but does it do any good?"

"No. Because you heard voices last night, didn't you. They were arguing, you said."

"Damn right. Loud voices. I remember. I was singin' along to Supertramp and the shower was gone full blazes. I mean that's one perk I insisted on and I got. The shower in my unit is first class all the way. But then I heard a man kinda shouting. And then another man was talking. That much I do know. But whether they were inside or outside, I couldn't tell you."

"Oh."

"Don't get so down about it, precious. It couldn't have been inside the trailer. No one was there except Frank."

Dottie was either too swacked to get the importance of what she was saying or she was in denial so deep she didn't have the nerve to face it.

"How long were you in the shower?"

"Just a few minutes." Dottie came back to the sofa and sat down on the cushion beside me.

"And when you came out . . ." I prompted.

"I was wet. I told you. I just needed a towel."

Neither she nor I felt like mentioning that there were plenty of towels already stocked in the tiny bathroom.

"What happened then?"

"I was as naked as the Lord made me, and I was headed down the tiny little hallway back to the bedroom when I heard someone knock at the door and then turn the handle, you know, to come on in. I turned around to see who it was and that little girl of Arlo's, what's her name, Jody, was in before you could say lickety-split."

"Did you know what had happened to Brother Frank?" I asked. Trying to get Dottie to focus in her present state of intoxication was getting harder.

"Of course not! Do you honestly think I'd be planning to entertain a . . . a . . . corpse in the all-together?" she sputtered. "I should think not!"

"No. Right. So when did you find the body?"

"I didn't, sweetie. I never did see the poor dear man. Jody was going on about the show. She said I had to be back on stage to get notes."

I was growing more impatient. "But what about Frank?"

"I mentioned I had a gentleman caller. Jody thought he'd better go. So she just sashayed back down the hall to tell him our time was up."

"That's when Jody first saw the body," I finished.

"And the girl was not cool. Oh, my, no. She let out a holler and I got quite upset. Everybody knows I've got delicate nerves. So I just reminded her to please keep her voice down. But she didn't. No, ma'am.

"She shouted at me not to go back into my bedroom. Can you imagine? It was the darnedest thing! I knew she was a good girl and she wouldn't go on upsetting my nerves with all that hollering if there hadn't a been a damn good reason. She told me, 'Dottie, don't do nothin' 'til I get back!' So I just followed her advice to the letter. I backed myself up and found something in one of the cupboards to soothe me down."

"You never saw the body? You didn't wonder what had happened to your gentleman caller?"

Dottie met my eyes with her steadiest stare. "I take direction," she said with fierce pride. "You may ask Mr. Martin Scorsese if that ain't God's honest truth. I'm a professional, miss. I knew better than to fool around."

"So you . . ."

". . . sat still and waited," she said proudly. "Oh. And sipped my drink in a ladylike manner."

Well, hell's bells.

"And then we all came storming in," I said, finishing

up her story from the point that I entered it along with a half dozen others.

"Exactly."

"And you never got dressed because Jody told you not to do a thing and, well, you . . . ," I said with a dead serious face, ". . . take . . . direction."

Listening to Dottie's ever-drunker account of the night Brother Frank visited her trailer did seem to make sense, if one could accept the logic of an ego-saturated pretzel. At this point in the evening, I could.

"I think the men you heard arguing were inside your trailer, Dottie."

"You do?" Her eyes were wide but I could tell she'd come to the same conclusion.

"Yes. What were they arguing about?"

"I haven't the foggiest idea of a notion," Dottie said. "I wish I did."

"Are you sure the only voices you heard were male?"

"That I know. Honey, I know the sound of men fightin' and I would know it in my sleep or under the shower."

I sighed. It was late and I was tired. We had come to the end of the tale with almost no clues or insights.

"Dottie, I've got to go and see if I can figure some of these things out."

"You were very clever, weren't you, about Bruno Huntley, that rascal?"

"Not really clever," I protested.

"Bullflowers!" Dottie breathed eighty proof carbon dioxide on my face. "But the problem is that you are much too intoxipated to drife."

"I'm better now," I told her.

"Spend the night here," she offered with her legendary generosity. "We'll have a pajama party."

"At any other time I'd jump at the chance," I told her, "but right now I have to get back home."

Standing, I was happy to find that I was, indeed, a lot steadier on my feet than I had been earlier in the evening.

I had my doubts that Dottie would be able to make it upright.

I hadn't seen Carlos for hours so I figured I needed to make my own way home. In the nearest powder room, I found a telephone and paged Wesley, punching in Dottie Moss's unlisted number. It was after 2:30 a.m. and I wasn't sure how long ago the midnight show of *Gasp!* had let out.

Three minutes later the phone rang. I lunged at it, jumpy as its shrill ring jangled the clock-ticking silence.

"Wes?"

"Mad?"

"I need a ride home," I told him. "Where are you?"

"Driving the teenagers back to the duplex," Wes said. "They're dozing in the back seat."

"Sweet," I said, remembering the fun we'd had. Where had that pleasant evening gone?

"I'll swing by. No problemo," Wes offered. "I'm on Sunset. I should be there in five minutes."

"Great," I said. This was working out perfectly. I needed to talk to Wes right away.

"Donald's movie was cool," Wes informed me.

"Really? Good for him!"

"Not bad, for action-adventure. Pretty ironic, actually."

This was extremely high praise coming from Wesley Westcott.

"I got quite a story out of Ms. Moss," I said, lowering my voice in case the lady was close by.

"Can't wait to hear it," Wes said, and then there was some break-up interference on the line.

"My cell phone . . . drop . . . later."

He must have been driving through a bad patch of cellular stress. Before I could respond we were no longer connected.

I hung up the phone and dialed another number. A sleepy voice answered on the seventh or eighth ring. The man told me that he would go wake up Brother Xavier Jones. I regretted calling. I wasn't used to friends who lived in dormitories.

"Xavier. It's so late. Sorry." This was awkward. "Uh, it's Madeline."

"Maddie? What time is it?"

"After two," I said, guilty.

"Is something wrong?"

"I know this sounds paranoid, but I feel you may be in danger."

"Me?"

"Is it possible for you to sleep somewhere else tonight? Somewhere that no one would think to look for you? I'm worried."

"You're so crazy," he said warmly and I suddenly remembered that's what he used to say. "You don't need to worry about me."

"I can't help it." I heard the crunch of tires pulling onto the faux cobblestones out front. Wes must have arrived.

"What worries me is the sad news about Monsignor Picca," Xavier said, sighing.

"Picca . . ." I had to think hard to try to place the name, so many hours and stories had drifted by since my visit with the old gentleman of St. Bede's the Venerable.

"Yes," Xavier said. And as the sound of sleep dropped away and his voice grew clearer, he said, "But, of course, you haven't heard yet. They found him this evening. His cat was yowling. When they opened his office door they discovered him lying on the floor. I'm sorry to break this bad news to you, Maddie. But the monsignor is dead."

Chapter 13

"The monsignor you met this morning?"

"I'm totally, totally creeped," I said to Wesley, talking low so as not to wake the sleeping passengers in the back of the van.

Wes was driving fast, zooming eastward on Sunset past the dark campus of UCLA.

"What happened?"

"They're not exactly sure. He collapsed and then his heart failed. Xavier said the old man died in his office."

"The office you met him in this morning?"

"Don't you think I get it? Two religious men are dead and they died right after they spent time with me."

"Aw, honey," Wes said. "This stinks."

Wes thought about it all for a few minutes. I trust Wes's logical brain. I waited.

"Here's the part that doesn't add up," he said finally. "Frank is a young Jesuit from the barrio. Brand new to his order. Now what does he have in common with an old parish priest from the suburbs? One's close to twenty and the other's closer to eighty."

"I'm worried about Xavier. Maybe it's all about him."

"You think the first time they got the wrong victim? Like some gangbanger was really after Xavier, but got confused."

"Well, no. No gangbanger fits in my scenario. No gangbanger I ever heard of would kill a guy this way, would they? I mean, they don't stop in for a *visit*, they just like to *drive-by*."

"Brother Frank's death doesn't have that gang-slaying *je ne se quoi*," Wesley agreed. "But the man who confessed . . ."

"I know!" I said, exasperated to the point of laughter. "But we can't get distracted by the facts."

Just then, our quiet consultation was abruptly shattered by a ripping loud snore emanating from the seats behind us. I shot a look over my shoulder and saw Donald curled up on the back seat. Sound asleep, he looked about fourteen years old, with his head peacefully resting in Holly's lap. It was the second grinding snore that made me look up. Holly, sitting straight with her head thrown back, was generating a lot of noise.

"I've been thinking, Mad, maybe this has some connection to the pope's breakfast," Wes said, slowly.

"That's a thought," I agreed.

"You should have called the police this afternoon, like I told you when those creeps grabbed you."

"If I'd gotten their license number," I said, "but I was too . . ." I shook my head. It was too late to regret everything after the fact. I'd been shaking. I'd been shocked. I was disappointed in myself.

"I know. I know," Wes said. "But you've got to talk to them now."

The police. We weren't their biggest fans. And to be honest, in the past they hadn't been all that impressed with me either. They had no interest in my collection of instincts and anecdotes and gut feelings. They frowned on gossip. They had little faith in the logic of gestalt. I found them pathetically left-brained and hideously rule-driven. But perhaps I was still angry over some disagreements we'd had in the past.

"Look," I said, "what really happened? A guy yelled at me. No big."

Wes gave me that look.

"But if it makes you feel better," I continued, "I'll tell

the cops all about it. Believe me, they'll yawn."

Wes had driven Sunset all the way across town and was now making the familiar left under the Hollywood Freeway overpass, that would take us up Cahuenga and into my section of Whitley Heights.

As he turned onto my cul-de-sac and pulled up in front of my house I was jogged awake by something that seemed oddly out of the ordinary.

Parked in front of my garage was Arlo's white Saab convertible. When Arlo was working on a script he rarely dropped by. What was he doing here?

As a caterer, I was used to late parties and on many occasions I found myself shifting to an up-all-night, asleep-all-day cycle. But Arlo was more of a regular bedtime wimp.

"Look who's here," I remarked.

"And he's not the only one," Wes said. He gestured for me to look out the van window. Sitting on the steps that lead up the hill to my house was Lieutenant Chuck Honnett of the LAPD.

"I told you I'd be reporting to the police," I said, virtuously. Since I apparently had no choice. "And the time would be?" I asked.

"According to the digital on our trusty Town & Country," Wes informed me, "it is three-twelve."

"It's lucky I'm a night person."

"See ya later," Wes said, "and tell all your admirers that a lady needs her beauty sleep." He kissed me on the forehead before I grabbed my shoulder bag and hopped down out of the van.

"Hey, sister," Honnett said, drawling like he was leaning on a rail in Texas instead of sitting on a curb in Hollywood. He gave me that regulation cop stare, his clear blue eyes squinting at me as I approached. I doubted much about my wild hair or my lack of lipstick or the cling of my knit dress escaped him, but I had passed the point in the evening where I gave a damn.

After a long moment his face softened a touch. "Your

boyfriend upstairs suggested I wait for you out here. Friendly guy, huh?''

Lieutenant Chuck Honnett and I had met a few months earlier and I still wasn't quite sure what I thought of him. It was complicated. He's a detective, a policeman, which I do not like at all. I am uncomfortable around authority. I was born that way.

But Honnett's got something, I had to admit. There's the physical thing. A look. He's tall and lean and rough-faced. He's got good thick hair with some gray showing in the brown. He's got a gravelly voice and a mocking kind of humor. He's smart. He could take care of himself in trouble. And perhaps, most appealing, the man has no problem handling my sarcasm.

I stood there in front of him, stretching my arms behind my head after the long drive. He watched. I knew he liked what he saw but he'd never give it up.

There are plenty of other things that make a relationship with Honnett complicated. One being I'm still involved with Arlo. And while Arlo and I may not be a perfect match, we've been hooked up for a long time. I hate to think about things like this. So mostly I don't.

Honnett moved over on the step, making room.

Half the time I don't really know if I'm attracted to Honnett or if I'd just like to piss off Arlo. A while back, Chuck and I tried to go out. We didn't get through dinner before his beeper went off and he had to take charge of some crime scene. We never got around to trying to finish a meal together after that.

''Haven't seen you in a while,'' I said, sitting next to him on the steps.

''Yeah, well, you know. Been busy.''

''Sure,'' I said, laughing at how clichéd everything sounds after 3 a.m.

''I'm working on a case,'' he said.

''I figured.''

''Want to talk about it?''

''I've been wondering when someone was going to ask

me about Brother Frank's death. It sure took you long enough. After all, I was the one who found the Ace Award that probably killed him."

"Come again?"

"In Dottie Moss's dressing room trailer. I told the fools not to move the poor man's body, but no one would listen to me."

Nobody ever listens. This was actually a leitmotif that ran though my life. I sighed.

"Very interesting. But I'm not working on any case that features a Brother Frank. So all of your squirrelly Ace Awards and bodies that have been moved are not my problem. For which I am thankful. My fellow's name is Picca. Remember him?"

"So is it true? The monsignor was killed?"

"Slow down. No one said 'killed.' The priest had a heart condition. For all we know it was natural causes. But you know how it is. Folks were upset. Some questions were raised at his parish. A witness came forward to say she overheard shouting coming from the monsignor's office before he died, but no one could tell me who was doing the shouting. So right now we are checking it out."

"At three in the morning." These police types liked to keep their cards close to their chest. It was like taking a crowbar to a clam.

I started again. "Look, that's what I'm trying to tell you. Another man was killed and there was *shouting* in that case, too." This certainly would capture Honnett's attention.

"Madeline, why is it you seem to find yourself involved with so many dead men?"

"Nothing is penetrating, is it? You simply don't have any interest in what I know." I hate this part. I always hate this part. I don't want to go on about women's lib and which gender is ignored, mocked, and shut out of the conversation. Let's just say that the chip that was forming on my shoulder had jumped to such proportions that even the lieutenant noticed.

Honnett took out his little notebook. "I'm writing it down, okay?"

"Okay," I said, trying to stay calm.

"But you're not telling me much, are you?" He glanced back at his notebook. "Monsignor Benecio Picca, age eighty-seven. We looked at the monsignor's daily calendar and guess whose name we found?"

"I went to see him this morning for a friend," I said. "But that's not important."

"You don't think so?" Honnett asked, sounding sorely put out. "Then what exactly do you think is important? What is this whole thing about, in your opinion?"

"I think this whole thing is about the pope."

Chuck Honnett stopped writing and looked up at me, reassessing. "Have you been drinking?"

"Not recently."

"The *pope*, you say." Honnett couldn't help himself. He let out a little laugh and then caught it. I amuse the hell out of him.

I gave him a sidelong stare just to let him know I got it. "The pope," I repeated, patiently, like I'm the grownup waiting for the youngster to settle down. I liked that. "You know he's coming to Los Angeles, right?"

"Sure."

"Wes and I are working on the pope's welcome party—the big one at the Otis Mayfield Pavilion."

"Yeah. I've read about it. Before mass at Dodger Stadium."

"Right. Today some maniac grabbed me in the monsignor's parking lot and told me to drop out of doing the event."

"Hold on," he interrupted. "There was a maniac involved here somewhere? Why didn't you mention him before?"

"I, well . . ." I suddenly realized why I don't like to be questioned. I hate feeling on the defensive, like a child who's got to answer for everything. "Sorry."

We had passed a small hurdle and we both knew it. In

a gentler tone, Honnett suggested, "Tell me about this maniac."

"Some very angry guy. He was upset about the pope thing. He said back out of the event or I'd be sorry. His buddy held on to me so I could hear better."

"Did you report it?" Honnett asked, sounding like the cop he was. He was taking notes, which removed a bit of the romantic overtones I'd been imagining.

"No. Sorry."

Honnett eyed me, like he'd wanted to start a lecture.

I turned my palms upwards and shrugged, "I should have. Wes told me to."

Honnett let it go. "So who the hell was this guy—a competitor?"

"Maybe some kind of fanatic."

"A religious catering fanatic," Honnett repeated, and stared at me.

Since we had found ourselves communicating in a civilized fashion, for once, Honnett stopped short of hooting. I could feel him hold one back. Instead, he showed off his sensitive side and said, "Right. Well, let's leave that theory to one side, for a minute. Who else have you been rubbing the wrong way?"

"You?" I suggested.

Chuck Honnett had the kind of male chemistry that mingled well with late-night rendezvous under halogen lampposts.

"Well, much as I like to sit and chat with you about the weird things you've got going on, we haven't really touched on the subject at hand."

"What subject?"

"Picca," he said softly, patiently.

I told him everything I could think of, the whole convoluted mess; how kind Monsignor Picca had seemed, the killing on the Warner Bros. lot, the odd connection between the two deaths and my old fiancé. I dropped my head into my hands and continued, knowing I was not making any sense. ''See, it seems to have something to do with me or Xavier, but I can't figure out what.''

I knew Honnett wanted to touch me. Put his arm around me. I could feel it. The air seemed thick with possibilities and matted with confusion and early-morning stillness and hormones.

''Madeline . . .'' Honnett started to say, his breath close to my hair.

A door opened somewhere.

''Honnett.'' I looked into his eyes, waiting. If there was going to be a move, it was important that he make it.

''That you down there, Mad?''

The last voice was Arlo's. He stood at the top of the landing, a thin young man in an oversize THE TRUTH IS OUT THERE T-shirt and white boxers.

Chapter 14

It was close to four in the morning and Arlo felt like talking. I had to take a shower. Arlo joined me in the bathroom and took up a post sitting on the toilet with the lid down.

"So am I being paranoid?" Arlo shouted.

The hot water rushed over my head, sprinkling down my tired shoulders and back.

"Honey, with you that's a given," I called out under the spray.

"So there's nothing going on with you and Mr. LAPD Blue?"

"Well, I'm getting on his nerves. Does that count?"

"Don't kid. That's not too far from love," Arlo pouted.

"Honey, we have enough problems. I don't think we need to imagine any extra ones, okay." I turned off the hot water and let the spray run cold.

"Yeah. Okay," Arlo agreed. "But what's with you and Wes lately?"

"What?" I turned off the cold water, shivering slightly.

"Like what do you guys do together until all hours of the night?"

I pulled back the shower curtain and stared at Arlo. "What?" Was Arlo spooking on me? Was he seriously suggesting that Wesley and I . . .

"Okay. Okay. That's crazy. I know Wesley's . . ."

"Arlo!" This was beneath all of us. "He's my best friend for God's sake."

I stepped out of the clawfoot tub and onto a white rug, reaching for a fresh towel. Arlo handed one to me. Standing there naked, I didn't feel Arlo's eyes on me with half the intensity I'd felt Lieutenant Honnett's. And he'd been staring at me fully clothed. I wondered if that was a reflection of the feelings of the beholders or the beheld.

What was with this night?

"And Brother Xavier," Arlo picked at another fraying thread in our relationship.

I wrapped the towel very tightly around my dripping body and looked for my wide-tooth comb.

"What about Xavier?" I believed we might have arrived at the real issue at last.

"Back in San Francisco. What happened? Did you guys sleep together or what?"

"Look, Arlo," I said, stopping my tugging on the comb to look at him. "This was years and years ago. Long before there was an Arlo and Maddie."

"Long before the guy decided to *lay off chicks*?" he asked.

"Honey, this is way past your bedtime. What's really bugging you?"

"I care about you, Mad," Arlo said. "I care about you, damn it." Even under extreme emotional duress, Arlo never even veered near the "L" word. "And then I meet your old boyfriend. Is he a jerk? Is he a loser? No! He's too good to be true. He's great. I mean, I think I have a crush on him myself," Arlo said, turning back into the old Arlo and going for the laugh.

"And your point would be . . . ?"

"So why would you be going with an asshole like me? I mean, I work in goddamned television." Kidding, but serious, he yelled at me, "You're slumming!"

It was almost sweet. Arlo, the hot young sitcom millionaire, with his fucking Emmy and his need for space. Arlo, the funniest guy at any party. Arlo, the king of noncommitment. Arlo was having self-doubts.

"You know, you're right," I agreed, trying to get him

back to the Arlo who was so self-absorbed he'd rather spit than analyze a relationship. "You're gutter trash."

"Okay, so I'm having a problem here. How do you think I should feel? You were going to marry a guy who was perfect."

I took Arlo's hand and dragged him back into the bedroom where I could find some leggings and a T-shirt. "Xavier Jones was so perfect, Arlo, he left me."

"But I mean," continued the king of angst, "he was the better man. I may be shallow but even I can see that." Arlo looked at me. "I'm waiting for you to jump to my defense, here."

I laughed.

"No, I mean it, Mad. Xavier got to me. And nobody gets to me." Arlo was joking, but as usual, it held a core of truth.

"I think he probably made the right choice," I said. "It was best for him, and best for his family, and best for your sitcom, and best for all of humanity, for all I know."

"Because he's so good," Arlo agreed.

"Yes. He's very, very good," I said, pinning up my hair.

"Don't you even hate him a little bit for dumping you?" Arlo asked, with a twinkle.

I climbed into bed and held the quilt open for Arlo.

"Oh, yes. I believe I do."

Arlo turned out the light and joined me in bed. Having come to the understanding that he was for me and Xavier was for all of mankind, he rolled on his side, more or less content. And while I believe he was reassured that I could never fall for a cop and I would always hate the priest and my best friend was out of the question, I found I could not go to sleep.

I raised up on one elbow and said, "Hey."

Arlo kept his eyes closed and, chuckling, said, "Too bad I'm already sleeping."

Taking advantage of a sleeping man sounded like fun. I lay on top of him, put my hand inside his shorts and said, "Arlo, wake up."

In the complete darkness of my bedroom, Arlo squinted at my bedside clock. The lit numerals read 4:24. He said, "All right! Morning already!" in a voice that sounded more alert than I'd heard him sound all night.

Chapter 15

With the spins and twists of the last twenty hours I felt the loom of unknown demons flying close. Questions begged answers. I could barely close my eyes let alone fall asleep. In the dark, the faceless anxiety of death and love and my own messed-up needs poked my conscious mind like a sharp stick. It required a tremendous effort just to fend them off unexamined. What to do.

Mindless albeit satisfying sex was not thrill enough to blot it all out. And now, the suffocating regularity of Arlo's rhythmic breathing made me want to bolt. Overhot and claustrophobic in the warm bed, I crawled out and headed downstairs.

In the kitchen, I turned on the bright working lights and set the kettle on the range. As I waited to make tea, I noticed the stack of recipes gathered from Xavier's research. He had been on my mind and I was curious about some of the documents. Slowly, I flipped through the notes Xavier had made. I stopped to look at a page taken from the Custom Book of the American Assistancy of the Society of Jesus. It appeared to be an official book of procedures for the operation of Jesuit residences. Reading it, I began to realize what life had been like for Xavier these past years.

> *The daily hour for rising is 5:00 a.m . . . The caller opens the door of each room, but without looking in, says* "Benedicamus Domino," *and waits until he*

hears the response "Deo gratias." *A quarter of an hour later, he visits the rooms again.*

The custom may be kept which exists in some provinces, whereby the community is permitted to rise one-half hour later on the weekly vacation day.

One who for any reason has not risen at the assigned time without having previously obtained permission, should report the matter to the minister or to the superior.

I looked at the wall clock and noticed the time. In five minutes a caller would be coming to wake up Xavier.

I rubbed my temples with both hands. What a life he had chosen. How different it would have been had we married. He might have slept through all the five o'clocks he chose, without another soul's permission. I sighed. It might have been our bed out of which I was crawling now.

I flipped though the Jesuit Custom Book and began to suspect how little I had really known the heart of the man I had loved.

Among the old recipes were several which Xavier and I had been planning to try out for the cookbook project. I paged through, mentally checking them against the ingredients I had on hand. In times of stress there was nothing that soothed me like baking did. I read through a nice traditional brioche recipe that had been sent to Xavier from the Jesuit community at Rue de Grenelle in France. A tall round loaf of brioche—dense, egg-rich, and crusty. It would be perfect with strong coffee. Yes, this was just what I needed.

Making bread in your own hands is a humble and sensuous experience, but no one does it anymore. It's popular these days to bypass all the work and simply use an electric breadmaker. People are afraid of the work involved in baking, the time commitment, the risk of failure after such an investment.

For me, the work is where I find peace.

I paid attention to what I was doing and checked the

brioche recipe. Quickly, I pulled together all the ingredients that were needed, measuring them out into a variety of clear glass bowls. It's the way I begin all new recipes. This allows me to concentrate on the techniques and timing instead of searching for measuring cups at a critical point.

Each time I bake bread, I am reminded that by the combination of simple ingredients one can produce a thing of beauty, delight, and nourishment. The first step is always the same: start the yeast.

I used the fresh kind, fawn-colored and crumbly, which I mixed with warm water in a small creamware bowl. Yeast is a living plant that has needs like any of us. It needs warmth, moisture, food, dare I say love? I enjoyed a nice tragic sigh. Perhaps I was turning a tad melancholy?

Fresh yeast can be a pain. It needs to stay well wrapped in the refrigerator and will only last around three weeks. I tell my friends to use the active dry variety, which is quite good.

Touching the yeast gently, pushing it with the tips of my fingers, I always feel like I am coaxing the cells awake. In the small bowl, the yeast began to fizz and release its pleasant sour odor and I moved the bowl aside to rest for five minutes in a nice warm spot.

Without any sleep, my mind was wont to do as it would, and so without bidding pingponged back to Xavier and the day we baked bread together. It had been the first day we met after our long separation. Things had gone well at first, small talk, catching up, jokes, but then we grew quiet.

To avoid the obvious subjects neither of us wanted to mention, we decided to bake. I said baking bread reminded me of our days back in cooking school. Xavier said that's funny, because it reminded him of his religion.

As we worked side by side, he told me a little about his training. At the novitiate he was taught about St. Ignatius. This founding father of the Society of Jesus believed that the authentic search for God must pass through one's ordinary life. He prescribed for Jesuits a daily spiritual exercise called the Examen of Conscience.

Xavier had never spoken with me about his religious practice before. I listened closely, as perhaps any former girlfriend listens to a man describe the rival he chose to spend his life with. I was trying to imagine how his Jesuit life could be better than the one he left behind. What had persuaded him to abandon me? I was always on alert for the overlooked clue that would unlock that mystery. Hesitantly, I asked him to tell me more.

Xavier said he found that he was happiest when he performed the Examen of Conscience while he did simple chores, like baking bread from scratch.

First, he would think of all the good things that had come into his life and thank God for them. He would examine his recent actions, and thoughts, and desires. He would ask himself questions. Had he spent any time doing something generous for another? Had he prayed for another's needs? Had he been kind? Had he remembered that God is lovingly watching over us all?

Who wouldn't be drawn to Xavier's innocent desire to serve God? How petty I was to think only of myself, my old wounds. How selfish.

This was becoming painful to remember. But in the middle of the night, alone, I couldn't stop these thoughts.

I shook my head. With the sky still black outside the multipaned windows in my kitchen, I pulled myself out of my ego death spiral and got my mind on the work before me. The process was calming. I creamed the butter and added sugar, salt, eggs, and an extra egg yolk in my favorite blue and white pottery bowl. Following the old Jesuit brioche recipe closely, I mixed in warm milk along with the yeast, which was foaming to life.

While I beat the dough I added the flour slowly. As I worked, I tentatively took a shot at finding my own spiritual side. I began to perform an Examen of Conscience. I thought about all that I had to be thankful for: my friends, my health, my energy, and enthusiasm. I asked myself, had I been kind? Had I spent enough time doing something for another?

Ten minutes of beating thick dough by hand and I began to feel the burn, but I must admit this is my kind of exercise. Between the physical exhaustion and the spiritual cleansing, some of the tension that had been building all night began to pass. I dusted my old marble countertop with flour. The dough had begun pulling away from the sides of the blue and white bowl and now I carefully turned it out onto the floured marble in order to knead it properly.

With my thoughts now gently focused, I really needed to stop moping about what might have been and get on with the work that had to be. We had the pope and guests to feed. There were questions about Brother Frank's death. And I was not going to sit by and let the odd coincidences between that death and Monsignor Picca's go. If the police weren't connecting the two, maybe I could come up with something new that would open their eyes.

Before dawn, I figured to have a pretty good shot at getting through on AOL. My notebook PC was already plugged into the phone line and it sat where I'd left it, on a wooden kitchen chair. I scooched the chair closer to me, flipped open the notebook, and turned it on, waiting as it began its startup routine.

The trick would be punching the proper commands into my computer at the same time I was working the dough. My hands were out of commission. And then I struck upon a plan to leave one small finger out of the kneading. This one clean finger was all I needed to operate in the twenty-first century, while I devoted the other nine to practicing an art that went back to a time before Christ.

Kneading by hand is both meditation and physical exertion. I inhaled deeply, loving the smell of the yeast while squishing my hands, minus one finger, through the dense slippery mound. The world may be pushing me in incomprehensible directions, towards lessons I'd sooner not learn, but right now in this hour just before dawn, all I knew was the weight and bulk growing smooth and elastic in the warmth of my hands. I guess this was the only peace I really knew.

The computer beeped as my network connection came through. I was pleased to hear the little guy tell me, "You've got mail." But for the moment it would have to wait. I pleaded with the machine to let me stay connected to AOL until I could get back to it in a minute, as I swirled a touch of oil into the big bowl. Then, I turned my brioche dough in the bowl quickly to coat it on all sides.

It was now time to let it rise. I covered the bowl with plastic and moved it to stay warm next to my oven where all it needed was to be left alone for an hour. Baking is fair. It demands hard work and then rewards you with a break.

I wiped my hands and then ten-fingered my way through to my e-mail.

That was odd. Who was epressman? I clicked on the message and my screen became filled with an electronic letter from Edward Pressman, of St. Bede's the Venerable Catholic Church.

And as I read the e-mail, a chill traveled down my spine.

It was a polite note from the church secretary inviting me to meet Monsignor Picca at the home of his sister at ten o'clock this morning.

Is there anything eerier than receiving e-mail from a dead man?

Chapter 16

I looked up at the information at the top of the e-mail to check the time it had been sent. "1514." That meant 3:14 in the afternoon, East Coast time, which translated to 12:14 here. It must have been sent before the old man became ill and died.

A noise registered just beneath my conscious perception. I held my breath and listened. Was it something outside? I looked at the clock. 5:35. I listened hard, but could hear nothing. I remained in that heightened state, every sensation sharpened, until the clock moved to 5:36, and then, slowly I relaxed.

When we met, Monsignor Picca had told me that the documents from his time in Rome were kept in boxes in his sister's garage. Perhaps he had found something and wanted to show it to me.

I studied the e-mail. It gave his sister's name and address.

When Xavier and I began our investigation into Brother Ugo's note of confession, I believe we may have unknowingly kicked open a long closed door. It seemed impossible, but somehow our search in Los Angeles had upset the calm. Whom had we provoked?

What was that? A loud metallic sound, a scrape from down the hall, and, oh my God! I heard the front door open. Shocked, adrenaline rushing, I jumped up off my stool and dove for the wall. My hand flew to the light switch. Instantly, the kitchen was pitch black.

My heart was beating too loud. I eased the drawer open and reached for my eight-inch chef's knife, familiar in my grip as an old friend's hand.

A faint light flipped on down the hall, and then, footsteps.

Barefoot, I creeped silently toward the pantry. Clutching my knife, I slipped into the closet and closed myself inside. I heard the squeak of hinges as the pantry door shut behind me and my blood froze. Fingers clutching, I tried to stop the door from moving, stop the sound.

The main overhead lights were instantly blazing in the kitchen. Someone was there and they didn't care who knew about it. I tried to see out the crack in the door and felt, suddenly, foolish. What if Wes was stopping by? What if . . .

I caught a glimpse of a dark figure, and then he moved out of range.

My stomach flopped. Arlo was upstairs, asleep. Arlo could sleep through a train wreck. There was no chance he'd be awakened by any sounds from downstairs.

I had to do something fast. How long would it take before the pantry door was ripped open and I was exposed?

My house has been equipped with an old-fashioned dumbwaiter. It's a miniature elevator that goes from the kitchen pantry up to the converted dining room above. Food and dishes go up, dirty trays and leftovers come down. As quietly as I could, I pulled open the hatch, stepped up onto the counter and climbed into an opening that was only about thirty inches square. From the inside I slid the hatch shut.

Almost immediately, the door to the pantry swung open from the other side. Shoved into the dumbwaiter, its hatch shut tight, I waited and listened. My whole body vibrated with tension as I tried to slow my breathing down, desperate not to move a muscle. I clutched the chef's knife between my knees and its point was close to my chin. Squashed as I was in that awkward position, I couldn't tell who was there and if they suspected I was inches away, behind that hatch above the counter.

Moments went by. Then darkness returned to the small pantry. The outer door must have been shut. Whoever was after me had moved on.

My muscles couldn't take being so cramped for much longer. Slowly, silently, I inched open the hatch to the dumbwaiter to catch some air. There was no movement and no further noise. In the safety of darkness, I began to move. But before I came out, I noticed the door between the pantry and the well-lit kitchen stood slightly ajar. The figure of a man wearing black could be seen moving around my kitchen, silhouetted against the white cabinets and tiles.

I couldn't risk scrambling down. I dared not stay where I was. I did the only thing I could think of. I hit the wall switch that sent the dumbwaiter up to the next floor and ducked my head and arm quickly back inside.

Problem was, the dumbwaiter moved horrendously slowly.

Second and more critical problem—the dumbwaiter's motor was horrendously loud.

Immediately, I could hear movement coming from the kitchen.

The dumbwaiter had not been built to carry a weight over seventy pounds, and I didn't make the limit. As the machinery groaned to lift me I could feel it slowing down.

Below, in the pantry, the door must have been opened again as a shaft of light from that direction brightened.

"Hey!" a man's voice called out, startled, as whomever it was managed to piece together what was going on and realized I was making my escape.

The dumbwaiter had made it up about five feet on its fourteen-foot climb, but then it just gave out. The smell of burned-out motor parts came down at me, and in my enclosed space I gagged.

"Hey!" I heard again, although by this time my fright had started to play tricks on my ears. This time, the voice shouting at me sounded like a woman's. Could that be?

Could I have mistaken the body I saw dressed in black? Was a large, bulky woman after me? I was trapped between floors in a stifling wooden coffin, a knife between my knees, and stuck.

"Hey! Maddie!" the voice shouted at me, alarmed and louder this time. "MADDIE! ARE YOU IN THERE?"

I could barely breathe in the tight space. I couldn't lean an inch without stabbing myself. I was feeling faint from the heat and the fear. My brilliant escape pod had failed. And now, I was hallucinating that Holly was calling up to me.

"FOR GOD'S SAKE! ARE YOU OKAY? SHOULD I CALL THE PARAMEDICS?" Holly screamed.

"Holly?" I asked, but after holding my breath for so long, I could only let out a squeak.

"DON'T MOVE," she called up to me.

As if I could.

The air was probably getting to me fine, but curled up in that tiny space, I started imagining that it was running out. I was faint, but luckily there was nowhere for me to fall. Except onto the point of the chef's knife.

"Holly, hurry," I called.

Two hours later, I sat in my kitchen sipping a cup of tea. The fire truck had left. The paramedics had departed.

Sometimes when you least expect it, useful new information may come your way, virtually slapping your face with facts. There is no easy way to get out of a dumbwaiter that has become stuck with you inside it between floors. They are not equipped with safety devices and escape mechanisms because no fool is ever supposed to get into one. Note to self: replace burnt out and destroyed dumbwaiter motor with one that can lift my weight. P.S. Add a backup motor.

When Holly had arrived, my house had been totally dark except for the lights blazing from the kitchen windows. The front door had been left wide open and so she walked right in. She expected to find me up early baking, which she would have done had I not decided to grab a big knife and climb into a tiny box and go for a ride.

Police patrolmen, fingerprint experts, frightened neighbors had come and gone. Arlo even woke up and joined the party. While the parade of humanity used my kitchen as its right-of-way, I sipped tea and finished baking my brioche. At that point, what else could I do? Wesley insists that I like to distance myself from emotional upset. If that's true, then this morning's events had sent me, emotionally speaking, to Nome.

While being questioned by a young officer, I greased my two-quart copper brioche pan. It was a gift and had come from the kitchens at Windsor castle, a royal comfort for those times when you're talking to the police about home invasion.

As I spoke on the phone to Wesley, catching him up on my night, one humiliation at a time, I punched down the dough, turned it out on the marble, and kneaded it for a couple of minutes, punching at it with perhaps more vigor than was actually required.

When Holly took charge and shooed everyone out of my way so I could have a little peace, I chose to spend my peaceful minute cutting off a section of dough that measured about one-fifth of the whole, which I set aside. Then I rolled the remainder into a ball and placed it in Queen Elizabeth's greased copper brioche pan.

My favorite part came next, and I didn't even mind that my neighbor's husband and Arlo were arguing over whether they should try to take apart the dumbwaiter's motor on my kitchen tile. I let them work it out as I took a sharp pair of kitchen shears and cut an X in the top of the dough. Then I shaped the reserved piece of dough into a teardrop and placed the pointed end into the X.

While I worked, Holly told me the entire story of *her* night. Naturally, she and Donald woke up as soon as Wesley drove them home and couldn't go back to sleep. As Holly described the rest of their evening, during which they did more or less what Arlo and I had been doing, I covered the brioche dough with a blue tea towel to let it rise. For the full thirty minutes that Holly went on, graphically detailing just how spectacular her Donald was, I allowed the dough to sit. In the time it took to give Donald's prowess its full due, the dough had doubled in bulk.

By eight, when Xavier called and discovered to his shock what had occurred in the nighttime, I'd already beaten together an egg yolk and a tablespoon of milk. I was just brushing the prepared dough with egg-glaze as I told Xavier about my suspicions, that we may have gotten too close to a secret.

I told him, just as I'd told Arlo and everyone else, that I was mad as hell and humiliated beyond speaking. Of course, I was determined to get to the bottom of it all. But, yes, I agreed to be extra careful. I'd turn on my alarm, never go out alone, and sleep over at Wesley's until things were resolved. I'm not a fool, I repeated to Xavier before we hung up, and then I slipped the brioche into a 375-degree oven.

Thirty-five minutes later, I pulled out the beautifully golden, heavenly scented, perfectly done puffed crown of a brioche. By the time I'd transferred it onto a wire rack to cool, Arlo came back just to see if I needed anything. Then, Wesley dropped in to check on me and while he was at it, look at the dumbwaiter motor. And then, Xavier walked through the door to implore me to avoid any more investigating, at least until after the pope had departed from our fair city.

Holly had brewed some dynamite Guatemalan coffee and set out a fresh pot of tea, as this large, mostly uninvited group sat down to sample my baked goods.

It was not without irony, then, that at that very moment the doorbell should ring. I opened the door to see Lieutenant Honnett standing on my doormat. He walked right on in, pulled a chair up to the long pine farm table joining Arlo, Wes, and Xavier, and said, thanks, ma'am, to Holly as she poured him a cup of coffee.

The brioche was sliced and served with some cinnamon-spiced orange marmalade I'd made a few days before. Cream was poured into tea. Cantaloupes were sliced and served with fresh raspberries and yogurt. As everyone was politely passing the honey and complimenting the bread, Honnett made a quiet announcement.

"We had a few officers check the area and one of them found this stuffed in a neighbor's trash can." He pulled out a large plastic evidence bag that contained a legal-size burgundy leather folder with the initials M.O.B. in gold. "This yours?"

"Oh my God." I stared at my leather folder. I'd left it on the kitchen counter yesterday, after I came home from visiting Monsignor Picca.

"The initials . . ."

"Madeline Olivia Bean," I answered, stunned by the evidence that the break-in had been for real after all.

"The folder was empty when we found it. You remember what you had in it?"

"Yes. Directions to St. Bede's."

"That all?" Honnett asked, alert.

"No."

Wesley looked at Holly. Holly looked at Arlo. Arlo looked at Xavier, while Honnett just kept watching me.

"It held a copy of Brother Ugo's confession."

Chapter 17

With all that, Honnett was not convinced we had any real leads. According to him, the burglar could have been after anything, and grabbed the nearest item when he heard Holly coming. There was no conclusive evidence that Monsignor Picca's death wasn't natural, and they already had the killer of Brother Frank in custody. He did intend, however, to track down any disgruntled caterers who may have had a connection to the pope's visit.

I suggested he might check Monsignor Picca's office, to see if the copy of Brother Ugo's confession note I'd left with him was still in his office, and Honnett gave me a look like I should know he'd have this covered.

And then, Lieutenant Chuck Honnett reminded us that there could be a much simpler explanation to the trouble I had had.

"Men break into houses when they're after something," he noted. "Sometimes they're looking for stuff they can sell off to make a few bucks. Sometimes a jerk sees a beautiful woman in the window, alone, in the middle of the night, lit up like that with no one around. It happens," he said.

Basically, he was implying that I was "beautiful" and that gave me a nice jolt. As for the weight of his argument, I was unimpressed.

"I know Miss Bean is convinced that the fellow we've arrested for the murder of Brother Frank del Valle is the wrong man,'' Honnett said, ''which is her privilege. In spite of the fact that he *confessed.* Even so, I looked into it further . . .''

''You did?''

''. . . and it turns out this creep, Anthony Ramona, had both opportunity and motive to back up his confession.''

''No way,'' I said, sure as ever that I had to be right.

''Ramona was on the Warner Bros. lot Thursday night. Did you know that? He was there filling a seat in the audience.''

Arlo looked up, startled. ''Sitting in the audience at 'Woman's Work'? Someone let a gang killer on the lot? That's impossible.''

''Apparently not,'' Honnett said.

Producing situation comedies is a lively industry, but like any manufacturing process, cranking out a high volume of laughs isn't easy. The recipe is delicate. The timing in comedy is tricky. Audiences are crucial. Sitcoms need real people reacting to the jokes to help the performers get the beats right.

With nearly fifty-five comedy series in production, attracting enough people who are willing to sit all night from six to eleven is tough. Tourists are interested, but they're around in the summer when most sitcoms shut down. So, the studios rely on audience wranglers to round up live bodies to sit though all those long tapings.

Even though the seats are free, the people of L.A. have better things to do on a school night. Audience brokers end up paying fundraising groups to entice enough people to sit through each episode of all the crap that comes out of the studios' mills. Even hit shows like Arlo's end up buying audiences.

''You mean we paid a gang of crackheads to watch our show?'' Arlo said, nonplussed. ''No wonder we were getting such easy laughs.''

''Wait. We were in that audience,'' Holly said, indicating Xavier and me.

''Naturally,'' Honnett said, stirring his coffee. ''But VIPs get seated way down in front. They bus in the rest of the audience from wherever they can. That night they had a group in from South Central who were raising funds for their church baseball team. And a couple of gangbangers with brothers on the team apparently got on the bus."

"So why did Ramona kill Brother Frank?" Xavier asked, in a low voice.

"According to the confession, Ramona knew Frank and his cousins from life on the street. There had been bad blood. Ramona says he spotted Frank in the audience, waited until he could get him alone, and that's it."

I had to admit the pieces could be made to fit. If Anthony Ramona had been at the studio and saw Brother Frank . . . I drifted off, trying to rearrange the puzzle with this new odd-shaped piece.

Soon everyone had places to go and people to meet. I promised every man and woman I knew that I would pack a bag and get out of the house. Xavier was planning to move residences as well, since Honnett was in the mood to play things safe. If there was a chance that Xavier's life had been the one they were after, he needed to keep a lower profile.

Arlo had to go to the studio and Honnett gave Xavier a lift.

The pope was expected to arrive this evening, and with our big event only one day away, Wesley was in overdrive. He was going to a meeting with all the volunteers. I told him I'd pass and meet up with him later. We agreed to lunch at his place, since I had to bring some things over for my enforced stay. Holly agreed to baby-sit me until she could safely turn me over to Wes. I mean, really.

It was time to get back to our gig. We weren't actually going to be working the stoves for the reception for the pontiff, so this event had one less element than we were used to. After the frenzy of previous years, this little job seemed to almost run itself. Of course there were a million details to confirm, but unlike most events I'd worked, everyone involved wanted to make sure things ran as smoothly as possible.

Perhaps it was the sheer awesome power of the pope, but everywhere a code or a permit or a problem could have gotten stuck, it didn't. Wesley said it was Xavier who was so unbelievably prepared. Xavier said it was God's path, so why shouldn't it be smooth?

Holly and I were astonished at the number of celebrities who were vying to be invited, even though the official invitations had gone out already. My message machine was loaded with big names I'd catered parties for in the past, who just needed this one little favor. Holly was hoping I'd pull strings and find a place for her personal favorite, Robin Williams, just so he could do five minutes of pontifical schtick. Holly enjoyed pushing my buttons.

I ran upstairs to change. Off came the leggings and on went a pair of black jeans and a white tee. I pulled a clean denim shirt out of a cellophane bag, buttoned it up, and grabbed my purse. Holly had traipsed around after me, taking down instructions on her notepad. As I put some finishing touches on my makeup she looked up.

"Where are you going?" she asked, suddenly realizing I was getting ready to depart.

"I want to visit Monsignor Picca's sister. He was going to show me something he had stored at her house."

"But didn't he just die?" Holly asked.

"I know, but Hol, if we don't come up with some clue as to who this Brother Ugo guy is soon, I may wind up living with Wesley for the rest of my life."

"Well, I'm coming with you."

I looked at her, dressed head to toe in a floor-length purple sweaterdress.

"Fine. You can make your phone calls from the car and I'll drive."

"Yes?" the woman said, as she opened the arched front door and peeked outside.

Holly and I stood on the shaded veranda of an elegant

old Mediterranean-style house, on a deep-lawned expanse of property, studded with Californial live oaks. My faithful black Grand Wagoneer stood parked on the sweeping circular driveway. There were several other cars parked there as well.

On this residential street, La Canada–Flintridge was a lush suburban oasis from the urban crawl that is most of L.A. Up and down Indianola Way, large well-kept homes sat on impressive lots, each exuding the quiet comfort afforded to the residences of doctors and investment analysts. The UPS truck, brown and squat, was making stops along the street, as the sound of gardeners and sprinklers kept up with the background music of the birds.

"Mrs. Castiglione?" I asked. Her address and full name were on the e-mail from the St. Bede's assistant.

"Yes," she said, smiling at me. Her white hair, which had been done in a salon, swept up in an impressive chignon. Although certainly in her late seventies, at least, she stood with straight posture, wearing a dark suit.

Stan, the gray-striped cat from St. Bede's, appeared at the entrance.

"May I introduce myself?" I began. "My name is Madeline Bean, and this is Holly Atkins."

Stan walked up to me and rubbed against my ankle.

"It looks like Stan has found a friend. Would you two girls like to come in?"

"Thank you."

As she opened the door to admit us, we could see the entry beyond the front door. We stepped into a cool, dark room. The grandfather clock that stood against the wall chimed the quarter hour as we passed.

The tiny, perfectly coifed lady tottered for a moment as she showed us into the spacious living room where forest green was the color. Large, old-fashioned sofas covered in green damask faced each other in front of the stone fireplace. Dark green and red were used in the slightly threadbare oriental carpet underfoot. The room looked as if it had seldom been used and a slight musty odor clung to the upholstery.

As we sat, Mrs. Castiglione looked us over, but not unkindly.

"Madeline *Bean.* I know your name, of course. *Madeline Bean,*" she said again, and stared off, her petite head at a tilt.

"Yes, ma'am, I'm the . . ."

"I'll get it. I'll get it. Just give me a moment. Madeline Bean . . ." She spoke with a slight Italian accent, but the most notable quality to her voice was the dramatic emphasis she placed on the occasional odd word.

She paused in thought, and Holly nudged me. Stan circled my chair and sat near my feet.

"Oh! Are you the Madeline Bean who married *Antonio Banderas?* He's a *wonderful* looking boy."

"That's Melanie Griffith," Holly put in, dishing with Mrs. Castiglione. "She's the blonde."

"Yes. *Right!*" the old lady said. And then she stared at me more carefully. "Well, *you* don't have blonde hair. You're a *red.*" She looked at Holly for confirmation.

"Reddish-blonde," Holly suggested.

"Is *that* it? Perhaps I need my specs," Mrs. Castiglione muttered.

Just then, a tiny middle-aged lady came to the doorway. She was dressed in black and carrying a casserole dish.

"Do you need help, Mama?" she called, not quite sure who the new guests might be.

"This is my daughter, Maria," the old woman said.

"I'm not sure my mother is up to having visitors. Her brother just passed away and the family . . ."

"I like these girls," Mrs. Castiglione said. "It's so much better when my mind is busy, Maria dear."

Maria wanted to say something, but instead she turned and left.

"Mrs. Castiglione," I tried to get back on track. "I met with your brother yesterday. I'm so sorry to hear . . ."

"We're really awfully sorry," Holly added.

Mrs. Castiglione put a hand on Holly's purple sweater-covered knee and confided, "It is not such a shock, you know. Benny was eighty-seven years old. But I am going to miss him. He had a *good* life, a life of service to God. Yes, he lived a life which was blessed. He was always a star to me, from the days we lived in Italy and after when we came to Los Angeles."

"We are sorry to bother you at this sad time, but we are most urgently concerned about information your brother intended to give us today."

"Then we must see to it," Mrs. Castiglione said, nodding her head, her grand hairdo sprayed so heavily that not a hair bobbed out of place. "The ladies from the guild will be coming soon. They are a help. The parish is planning the service. And my daughter told me there may be *a possibility* that His Holiness will come." There may have been a tear caught in Mrs. Castigione's eyelash, but her small face was bright.

"Since my husband was taken almost twenty years ago, and my *grandchildren* are all grown *up*, this house seems quiet, don't you think?"

"It's a great old house," Holly said, looking up at the wooden beams that spanned the twelve-foot ceiling.

"Perhaps you young *ladies* would care for a tour?" she asked us, trying to get to her feet.

"We don't want to bother you."

"Nonsense. It will give me something to do."

"Thank you," I said standing quickly and helping to steady the woman who almost tripped over the monsignor's cat.

"Splendid," she said. "Where would you like to start?"

I shared a look with Holly. "How 'bout the garage?"

Chapter 18

I pulled and Holly pushed, and soon the brown crate marked 1933 was jerked free from the shelf. The three-car garage held not a vehicle, but its walls were lined floor-to-ceiling with open shelving units, which contained several hundred packing crates. At the back wall, the crates were ordered by year and had the seal of the Vatican. We started there.

Mrs. Castiglione returned to the house almost as soon as we'd entered the garage, in need, she said, of some coffee. We helped ourselves, as our hostess bid us, to look around. Although less than steady, Mrs. Castiglione did remember speaking with her brother's secretary the day before. She remembered clearly that the boxes were to be made available for a research project. We thanked her and got to work.

The crates were of an old design, with lids and leather straps that fit into buckles. They were quite beautiful in themselves. I imagined them sitting in a storeroom at the Vatican and felt the thrill of being close to history.

Inside the crate, files and notebooks were neatly stacked. Ledger books, which contained daily journals, were filed at the back. The dark blue covers opened upwards where two strong metal brads held each page, punched at the top for that purpose. The long legal-size sheets fastened within contained handwriting in blue fountain pen ink. In places the blue ink was quite light, in others it blobbed.

Up until this moment, I'd kept fatigue at bay by sheer

will chased by a shot of adrenaline. But now, with the truth written somewhere nearby, I lost it. As my eyes tried to focus on the tight script, they blurred. The harder I tried to pull them into focus, the more my eyes stung. I was toast.

I put my hand over my eyes and tried to relax them, rubbing the sockets gently.

"How much sleep did you get last night?" Holly asked, yawning herself.

"Holly," I said, sitting down on the cool cement floor, "I'm getting old."

"I hear you," she said.

With my eyes somewhat rested, I tried to read the fine penmanship again. The writing was elegant, with perfectly formed letters that slanted to the left in compressed pointy parallels. Beyond that I had little to observe. The words were swimming.

"Holly," I said, defeated. "Read this to me."

Holly took the ledger and turned it towards herself.

"Houston, I think we have a problem," Holly announced.

I looked again and sighed. The pages were written in Italian. What the hell had I been thinking? Without someone to translate, I was lost. And by the number of crates, even a fluent translator could be stuck for years trying to make it through all the notebooks and files and ledger journals.

Holly yawned again and sat down on the floor beside me. "What now?" The cat silently jumped onto her purple lap.

"Mrs. Castiglione?" I suggested, with little conviction. "She can read Italian."

Holly looked at me and shook her head. "Dead end."

I put the ledgers back in the crate, adjusted the straps, and fastened the buckle.

"Let's take it with us," I suggested, for lack of a better idea. "Maybe someone Xavier knows will have an idea of how to get through this stuff."

Holly scooted the cat off her lap and got to her feet. She

took a handle on one side of the crate. I took the other.

When we stopped into the main house, Mrs. Castiglione's voice could be heard singsonging with its odd emphasis down the hall in the direction of the kitchen. Holly and I carried our prize there and put it down on the dark tile floor.

The monsignor's elderly sister was sitting on a settee at the back of the kitchen along a bank of French doors. Next to her were another senior citizen and her daughter, Maria.

''Are you girls *finished* already?'' asked Mrs. Castiglione. ''My, that was fast.''

''We ran into a little glitch,'' Holly said.

''Oh, dear. And we've *just* had the exterminators,'' Mrs. Castiglione said, and turned to Maria. ''Could you call those pest people? The very nice gentlemen. You know the ones. *Dewey*. That's the name. I can always remember a name. Let's have Dewey come again.''

''That's not the trouble, Mom,'' Maria said, smiling up at Mrs. Castiglione.

''Nothing like that,'' I added. ''We didn't realize just how many documents we'd have to look through.''

''What kind of project are you working on?'' the second elderly lady asked. She had more wrinkles than a prune, but her hair was an interesting shade of jet black.

''Research,'' Mrs. Castiglione answered her. ''Benny's *memoirs*, I should imagine.''

''We really don't want to disturb you any further,'' I told her. ''Do you think we might borrow this one crate of files so that we can go over the papers in greater depth?''

''Be my guest, dear,'' Mrs. Castiglione said, her head bobbing ever so slightly to the left.

''We should get a receipt, I imagine,'' Maria suggested.

''Splendid,'' Mrs. Castiglione agreed. She pulled out a slip of paper and found a pen and began to write.

''I'm surprised you'd take *this* one,'' she said, handing me the pen to sign for it.

''Why? Is there a better year?''

''I'm *sure* I wouldn't know,'' Mrs. Castiglione sighed.

''Never looked through the boxes myself. I just naturally thought you would be more *comfortable* reading Benny's journals in English.''

The room really did rock. As an adopted Californian, I immediately looked up at the chandelier hanging over the kitchen table, the better to judge the magnitude. It swung in a slow arc about one inch off plumb. For the little quakes, we're a bunch of amateur seismologists, trying to outguess each other as to how strong the jolt actually is before the experts at Cal Tech give the official number. On the Richter scale, this one had felt like maybe a 2.3, 2.4 tops.

''I think perhaps, Maria, I've had quite enough coffee for the morning,'' Mrs. Castiglione said resolutely, setting down her cup.

We don't fuss too much over the small temblors. As soon as we figure it's over and nothing fell on us, we simply go on. Holly and I were already over it, but Maria looked unsettled, Mrs. C was confused, and I was convinced the elderly lady with the jet-black hair never even felt it. As for Stan, he was nowhere to be seen.

''Excuse me, Mrs. Castiglione, what English journals?''

''My dear brother, may God rest his soul, had a nice boy out not too long ago to help put the journals into English. Now *what* was the dear child's name? Maria, you remember that nice young man who came to us from a cathedral in Liverpool and lived at the house for those two years. He was called Raymond Something. Yes, I've got it. Raymond Moon. Isn't that right, Maria?''

''I think the man was here when I was away at college, Mother. I never knew the fellow.''

''Can that be true? It couldn't have been too long ago. Now I remember. He loved to listen to the Beatles. So loud. But a nice man just the same. How long ago did the Beatles sing?'' she asked Holly, who was Mrs. C's entertainment reference guide.

''Sixties,'' Holly said.

''*Yes,* it must have been in the sixties. Anyway, we've

got his manuscripts in English. Such a *shame* you can't use them.''

I was so overtired, I had actually begun drifting. Conversations with Mrs. Castiglione took their own precious time, but with a little help from Maria we were soon out of the house and the back of my Grand Wagoneer held six cardboard boxes with the entire contents of Monsignor Picca's personal journals from 1922 until 1964.

In English. Thank the Lord.

Chapter 19

I crashed in Wesley's guestroom. I surrendered to sleep as my brain found the darkness it craved, and Saturday afternoon disappeared.

Five hours were all I dared steal, and my head ached as I climbed out of the king-size bed and splashed water on my face. The business of running a major event requires organization. I sat down at Wesley's dining room table and began to work. We were in the final countdown, just a few more hours until the city of Los Angeles welcomed the leader of the Roman Catholic Church over maple-chicken brochettes. And since they were *our* maple-chicken brochettes, the team recently dubbed Mad Bean Events was in high gear to make sure it all came off right.

From 6 until 8 p.m., I returned calls and e-mails that seemed critical. While I was sleeping, a message had been left by Chuck Honnett. The police had gone back over the monsignor's office and come up empty. No copy of Brother Ugo's Latin confession had been found in his office or at the rectory. He suggested that Wes and I and Xavier come down to the station so we could put together our best memory of what the thing had said, after the pope event, of course. With all three copies of that old document now missing, I wondered what secret it might have contained that all of us missed.

I looked at my watch. Wesley was out at the venue, overseeing the load-in. The floor looked good, Wes reported in his understated way by cell phone. The custom-ordered slipcovers for the chairs weren't there. The food had been delivered without major mishap. All in all, a promising report.

Holly had grabbed a few hours of sleep and was now at my side, going over lists and making reconfirmation calls to florists, candy-makers, rental houses, linen suppliers, and the ladies from St. Mary's who were sewing the slipcovers. Virtually every item had been donated to the city, and many were donated by good Catholic businesses and families. Xavier told me there was one faithful gentleman who donated one hundred thousand dollars to the city to cover the additional cost of hiring extra security and traffic cops.

This party was causing deep anxiety at many levels. From the cubicle of the lowliest grunt at city hall to the chambers outside the most venerated office in Rome, men and women were working furiously. Secretaries were charged with procuring unobtainable tickets, speechwriters were up all night polishing speeches for insecure politicians, and network news directors were ordered to produce the unbookable interview of the year, with the pontiff himself.

What we were doing, frankly, was the fun part. We developed the creative concept, designed the menu and décor, and fashioned everything else from invites to party favors to custom white chocolates. Wes and I selected every item. We talked Tiffany's into creating three thousand tiny commemorative gold crucifixes which then had to be FedExed to Rome for advance papal blessing and returned to us within our two-week deadline. Wes and I strongly believe in the right party favors.

We color-coordinated everything, from the lights under the ballroom floor to the centerpieces of bright red tulips to the postage stamps with white doves on the invitations. We also took care of the nitty-gritty. We got approvals from the Vatican, pulled city permits, and submitted every detail for okay from the FBI, LAPD, and Archdiocese of L.A. In addition, we fielded requests from journalists, agreed to interviews, coordinated the volunteers, trained the staff, placed all orders, managed the money, and prayed that it all would work like a dream.

Each member of Mad Bean Events fills a specific function. Wesley is our line manager, out in the trenches. Holly coordinates all vendors. There is nothing she can't procure on a moment's notice. I book contracts, handle PR, make final design decisions, and plan all preproduction. As the party nears, I am available to handle the unexpected. But some events are blessedly free of major last-minute crises, and sometimes I find myself without much to do in the hours right before show time.

While Holly kept to her endless list of calls, I felt I could steal a few minutes to look at Monsignor Picca's journals, which began with a summary of his childhood and continued through 1964, translated into English by the visiting Beatles fan.

I love history. Benecio Picca was born in La Storta, Italy, just outside of Rome, in November of 1912. As a boy of ten, he witnessed the pageantry at St. Peter's Basilica as Cardinal Achille Ratti was elevated to the church's highest office and became Pope Pius XI. In 1929, when Picca was just seventeen, he entered the seminary and began his studies for the priesthood. It was the same year that Pius XI worked the political miracle that saw Vatican City established as an independent state.

Young Picca was a rising star in his class. Even at twenty, he showed a gift for writing and documenting church history. It was March 19, 1933, on the Feast of St. Joseph, when the twenty-one-year-old was ordained to the priesthood, with his future bright. Looking back, how could he ever have imagined the path he would find ahead. I sighed, wondering what my journals would look like when I'm eighty-seven.

Picca recorded his personal story with the same objectivity that he used to detail the political climate in Rome. In the year he was ordained, 1933, he reported what to me seemed like a staggering event. He calmly noted that Pius

XI signed an agreement that would provide protection for the Roman Catholic Church in Germany during the political upheaval that was threatening Europe. In essence, the church agreed to cooperate with the Nazis.

I stopped reading. If true, this information was explosive. Recently, there were many stories floating around regarding the church and its apparent passivity with the Nazis. But the date was significant. It was too early for the world to predict the coming madness. Back in 1933, the Nazis were a bunch of thugs, gaining a frightening amount of political power. Rome must have felt vulnerable to their heavy breathing. With the Vatican's independence only a few years old, the church was on the defensive.

I wondered if any of this history was known.

I wanted to read further, but I stopped myself. I didn't have the luxury of time. I had been hoping to find some mention of Brother Ugo and the affair that Monsignor Picca remembered. If Picca, as a young priest, was given an assignment to investigate the death of the Jesuit brother baker, I'd seen no mention of it. I flipped ahead quickly through the next several years.

I was stunned, therefore, when I saw some further notations regarding how Rome was planning to deal with the growing horror of Hitler. Too caught up in the vivid story, I had to read on.

According to Picca's journal, by 1938, relations between the Vatican and Nazi Germany were strained. Under mounting concern, Pope Pius XI called a secret meeting with his staff. Picca, as secretary to one of the cardinals present, was there taking notes.

The pope was no longer willing to remain altogether passive. While his advisers worried about what might become of the millions of Catholics living in Europe should Hitler make them his special target, Pius XI persisted. He was still critically aware of the enormous threat to Rome, but the pontiff did not believe the church could remain silent.

Perhaps to maintain their tenuous neutrality, the Vatican would not attack Hitler nor mention the Nazi movement by name. Instead, the pope commissioned a select group of priests to draft an ''encyclical'' that would denounce the evils of anti-Semitism.

Again, I was stunned. There had been bad feelings for almost sixty years because the Vatican had remained silent during the Holocaust. I wondered what had happened?

I called Wesley at the Otis Mayfield and got through to him as he was testing the lights placed under the banquet floor.

''I've found something in the monsignor's papers.''

''Do you know what happened to Brother Ugo?'' Wes asked with interest.

''Not yet. But I'm reading a lot about the Nazis and I need to know, what exactly is an 'encyclical'?''

''An encyclical?'' Wes barely paused before beginning his spiel. ''When the Catholic church wants to come out with their position on something major, they prepare an official document and publish it. It's like a very heavy speech from the head man. Popes issue encyclicals, but not very often. It's the most influential form of communication between popes and the universal church. You know. It sends the word down from Rome to all the churches throughout the world on the party line. Why?''

Simply put, Wes knew everything.

''I've been reading Picca's old journals. He says Pope Pius XI ordered an encyclical condemning the Nazis.''

''Impossible,'' Wes said. ''The pope never did anything like that. Wow, are you kidding? It would have been a monster deal. An encyclical would have spelled out for all Catholics that they must fight the Nazis. I doubt the Nazi party could have survived the defections. If such a document was ever published it might have ended the Nazi domination of Europe. Believe me, it never happened.''

''That's odd, isn't it? Because Picca was there when the pope discussed it. He was actually at the meeting taking notes for a cardinal.''

''Maddie, these are very controversial ideas. The news is full of stories of how the Vatican handled this very subject. The state of Israel has been insisting for years that the church rectify its past silence. The point being, my dear, that now even Rome has agreed that they didn't do very much at the time. I believe Rome even half-apologized.''

''Yes. That's what's so intriguing. From these private journals, I'm getting the impression that Picca was in on some secret plans. Don't you wonder what happened?''

''This is a much hotter topic that we should be discussing right now,'' Wes warned me. ''The pope has landed in Los Angeles, for Pete's sake. His Holiness has trod upon our miserable soil. He's going lead a mass tomorrow for sixty thousand. I know we're supposed to entertain the man, but I do not recall our contract specifying that, in addition, we inflame the Jewish community.''

''But Wesley,'' I said, using my most persuasive tone of voice. ''Use your brain. These papers support the idea that the Pius XI was *against* the Nazis. This is a positive thing, controversy-wise.''

''Yes, well . . .'' Wes thought it over. ''Then riddle me this. Why, when the weight of ecumenical pressure came down on the Vatican a couple of years ago, did Rome apologize for keeping mum while the Nazis ripped across Europe?''

''I'll keep reading,'' I said.

''Mad, honey, maybe you should come over here and look things over.''

Distraction stopped working on me when I was six.

''I hear you, Wesley. This is not a light subject. Don't worry about me.''

''Any bad guys breaking in over there?'' Wes asked, just to mother hen me.

''One or two. But Holly is beating them all off with her Rolodex. Bye.''

I went back to Father Picca's journals. I was up to 1938 and had expected to find some mention of Ugo the baker by this time.

I should have skipped ahead, but something about the mystery of the secret encyclical drew me back into the young Father Picca's clear narrative. At that time, Picca was the assistant to Cardinal Eugene Tisserant, who was the prefect of the Vatican library. That was the year, I learned, in which the Italian government began imposing racial legislation on Jews. I became overwhelmed with sadness. My mother's family was Jewish. I couldn't imagine that period of darkness. I knew distant relatives of hers lived in Europe during that time. But she had always been vague about who and where and what had been their fate.

I reread the part where Picca had transcribed the pope's instructions for the drawing up of the dangerous document. Pius XI denounced anti-Semitism as "a deplorable movement, a movement in which we, as Christians, must have no part." He had apparently been moved to say such things in public, for which he and the church had come under increasing pressure from the Nazis. Still, he meant to persist.

Cardinal Tisserant had Father Picca contact an obscure Jesuit from France. He was the Reverend John LaFarge. This unassuming man, Picca wrote, was Harvard-educated and had committed his life to fighting segregation. In his humble way, LaFarge wrote and spoke out often, displaying exemplary concern for the rights of all men. It appears his calling was leading him to Rome.

LaFarge was personally selected by Pius XI to draft the secret encyclical denouncing anti-Semitism. Pius XI instructed LaFarge, a most obscure and unknown Jesuit, to say "what you would say if you yourself were pope."

The pope's own words. I was fascinated. The journals were recorded in date order, and many of the entries concerned the daily routines at the Vatican. I skipped ahead, trying to pick up the thread of the encyclical. What had become of it? I skimmed along, looking for another entry about LaFarge, turning the pages quickly until a familiar name jumped from the page and stopped me cold. Finally, I found what I had originally been looking for: the name of Brother Ugo Spadero.

The entry was posted in 1939. It was datelined from the

pope's summer residence in the Alban Hills. There were only a few brief sentences, telling much the same story Monsignor Picca had recalled. Brother Ugo Spadero's death seemed sudden. He took violently sick in the night. Rumors circulated. He had been morose in the days before his death, some said inconsolable. The death was considered suspicious, the key piece of evidence being that no one had ever before seen the gentle brother baker depressed. Slim. Even Perry Mason would not have been able to make a case.

A little later, a notation mentioned that Picca was asked to drop the inquiries into the death of Brother Ugo Spadero by the office of Pope Pius XII.

There was no more to go on than before.

Occasionally, in the margins of the typed journal, I would notice words, which had been scribbled in pencil. I began to recognize Monsignor Picca's handwriting in those scribbles as he notated items that he found worthy of further research. I tried to read the scribble at the top of the page that dealt with the investigation surrounding the question of Brother Ugo Spadero's death.

It was short. It said, simply, "Call with Q's" and next to it, "Doesn't want to talk about it," and then underneath was a telephone number. With a Valley area code.

Naturally, I dialed it.

Chapter 20

After only one ring, the phone was answered by a man.

"Hello," I began. "I'm sorry to disturb you this evening. I'm the event planner in charge of the pope's official reception tomorrow. My name is Madeline Bean."

"Yes?"

"I was doing some work and I came across your telephone number. I wonder if I might ask you some questions."

"Of course," the man said, quietly. He spoke with a slight Italian accent and the more words I heard him speak, the more I was convinced he was not young.

"Perhaps it would be convenient for you to come to my house," the unknown man suggested.

"Your address?" I asked, nonchalantly. I follow the rule of never looking a gift horse in the mouth, or, for that matter, any of the animal's other private parts.

"Didn't they give it to you? Oh, my," he said.

He sounded like he had been expecting me to call. Now, how on earth . . . ? I jotted down the address.

Encino. The suburb was pure San Fernando Valley: lawns, strip malls, and those personality-deficient single-family homes that spread across both sides of Ventura Boulevard like diaper rash. It was one of those middle-class, flat ranch-style neighborhoods that sprung up like a tract of mushrooms after the war. While real estate prices had shoved the area upscale during the eighties, the homes were a hodgepodge of remodeling jobs, displaying widely varying degrees of taste.

I took my bodyguard, Holly, along. She rode shotgun in my old Jeep Grand Wagoneer, not taking a breath between confirmation calls on the cell phone that was now growing out of her ear. With her notebook PC and extra batteries, she was a triumph in mobile workaholism. Gotta love her.

The house we were looking for was standard-issue Encino. It managed to present about four thousand square feet of lateral living space in the blandest architectural style possible. The exterior was covered in the ubiquitous stucco, this time painted a sad shade of washed-out green. Color trends being what they were, the tint of the stucco alone proclaimed that no one had prettied the place up in forty years.

These were the fixers that real estate bloodhounds sniff around for on Sundays. They've got "potential" if for no other reason than they are so butt ugly. If you simply replace the aluminum windows with wood sash, put in French doors in place of the old aluminum sliders, repaint the outside white with taupe trim, slap the front door with a coat of high-gloss black, rip the green shag wall-to-wall off the hardwood underneath, and whitewash the interior, you can turn around and sell it for $75,000 more than you paid for it.

It was dark out and nearing 9 p.m. I parked at the curb and left Holly to work in the car. As I stepped outside, I noticed the deep front yard. Globular bushes, shaved into strange perfectly round shapes, dotted a tangle of overgrown ivy. This yard had apparently not been updated since the fifties.

The doorbell was answered quickly. I stared at the man at the door, startled to find I recognized him.

"Would you care to come in?" he asked with a shy smile.

"Thank you," I said to the little old man. He was the self-same one I'd observed on the morning I'd visited the mayor of Los Angeles. He had been sitting in the waiting room with the flamboyant young woman. His name was . . .

"You must be the one who called," he said, leading me though the dark house until we reached a family room at the back. "Madeline Bean, was it?"

What the hell was his name? I knew I had it deep in there, somewhere. The mayor called him by name. It was . . .

"Would you like a cookie?" he asked me as we got settled on the brown Naugahyde, he on the sofa, I on the matching love seat. He offered me a box of Thin Mints. The Girl Scouts in this neighborhood had a rep. Man, they could hustle.

"Is this about Security, then?" asked the man. His name was on the tip of my tongue. It was like watching *Jeopardy!* when you know you should know.

"For the Pope?" I asked, startled, wondering how this elderly gentlemen fit into the picture.

"Of course," he said, kindly. "That's why you wanted to see me, isn't it? Is there a need for more money? I can get my checkbook."

Victor. His name was Victor. But how could I call a man old enough to be my grandpa by his first name. "I'm sorry to confuse you," I said, "but my visit has nothing to do with security."

"Oh. I only thought . . ." he petered out. In the stillness of his pause, he chose a Thin Mint. Then he explained.

People do that. If you can just stay quiet enough, I find that people will most graciously rush into the void and explain everything. I just have the devil of a time keeping my mouth shut long enough for it to work.

"I suppose you know my secret," he said. He still had a bit of cookie in his mouth, so he continued to chew.

"Your secret?" This is the way caterers work. We wait until the client gets all their ideas out. We don't judge or jump in too fast. If they really love the idea of having an Apollo 13 party for their son, and adore the notion of building a replica of the capsule in their backyard so that a dozen eight-year-olds can be locked inside, we listen. There are other times to come back at them with our concerns about feeding macaroni and cheese to a bunch of kids through a tube, and to offer a saner alternate suggestion. Although, even then, we rarely allow ourselves the luxury of screaming at them, "Are you crazy?"

"Well, I hoped to keep it a secret," Victor Somebody explained. "About my contribution."

"You . . . paid for the extra security." Somehow I pulled it together. This must be the generous man I'd heard about who was helping support the pope's visit. The morning I'd eavesdropped, his great granddaughter was making a fuss about the money he'd donated. Small world.

"But I don't like too many people to know," he confided, small and gnomelike, swallowed up by the giant sofa he sat on.

"You can count on me," I assured him.

"Thank you, Miss Bean."

"Please call me Madeline," I said.

"A nice old-fashioned name, like my great-granddaughter. Her name is Beatrice. She is an artist, of sorts. Or so she tells me. She never lets me come to see her."

I remembered the serious buzz-cut and the nose ring. I was sure I knew to which great-granddaughter he was referring.

"So what is the problem?" asked Victor. "Does His Holiness require something that I can provide?"

"I'm here to ask some questions about Monsignor Benecio Picca," I said, quickly. "You do know him?"

"Why, yes. Of course. We go back a very long way," he said pleasantly. "Do you know Father Picca, too?"

I suspected he had not yet heard the sad news and realized I would have to tell him.

When I finished explaining, he sat still and didn't speak. After a time, his nose became redder and a tear escaped from each eye. Victor pulled a snow-white linen handkerchief from his shirt pocket, the old-fashioned kind, and rubbed his cheeks. It cannot be easy to be close to ninety and hear that all your friends are dying off, one by one.

"So," he finally said.

"The monsignor was doing research and he let me look at his journals," I said.

Victor carefully folded his handkerchief and tucked it back into his pocket.

I told him that I was concerned about an obscure baker who died in the late thirties. He nodded as I talked and waited until I was through.

"Oh, my, Rome is a magnificent city," he said. "Have you been there?"

"Why, yes. When I was studying cooking," I said.

"The food. Yes, it is without equal, in my humble opinion," he said, and found the spirit to smile, faintly. Food will comfort us all.

"You lived in Rome?" I asked.

"Yes, yes. I was born there. I lived there for many years. That is where I first met Benny. We were boys together. I wanted to go into the government. He went into the church, but we remained friends. It was always good, in Rome, to have friends inside of the Vatican, yes?"

I understood how that goes. Sort of like here, it's nice to have friends who work for Universal.

"So you read my old friend's journal," Victor said. "He and I would meet, to work on various research projects. It was just a hobby, you see? We had other friends from the old days, but many of them have passed." He crossed himself. "When Benny Picca and I moved to Los Angeles, after the war, we became even closer. Expatriates, both of us."

"Did you ever hear of this Jesuit baker I'm investigating, Brother Ugo Spadero? Maybe when you were living in Italy? He worked in the kitchens of the pope's summer villa in the late thirties. We think he may have been involved in some trouble."

"There were a lot of troubles, to be sure, but I do not recall his name."

Another dead-end. This was really the last time I'd go

chasing after such a flimsy trail. I didn't know what I was expecting to find, anyway. The old man was looking at me, waiting for a response.

"What do you mean, there was trouble?" I asked.

"Ah, well. With the Nazis, of course. Do you know, the Holy See had a very chancy time just surviving those animals."

With less energy than he'd had when he met me at the door, he dipped again into the Thin Mints. I figured the local scouts had him pegged as an addict. His address is probably circled in red and fought over in a troop turf war of fierce proportions. I imagined the bruised carcasses of uniformed Brownies littering the battle zone of Encino. And then I realized what happens when I don't get enough sleep.

"I have been reading about the Nazis in the monsignor's journals," I said. "And I have been wondering about something he reported that seems almost impossible, about a secret document."

"Ha!" Victor laughed. "Yes, we were two old peas in a pod. We both had our obsessions, you see? Secrets, that's what we loved. Two old hunters of secrets. The monsignor was always searching for evidence about the missing encyclical, as you must know."

"Was there really such a document?" I asked.

"Oh, my, I should say there was," Victor answered, leaning back with his fifth or sixth cookie. I noticed he had not taken a sip from the mug of tea that was placed on the side table.

"This was Benny's pet project. He was there, you see, at the secret meetings in the Vatican. He heard the pope's orders."

"What happened?" I asked. I hadn't eaten in hours and eyed the box of cookies. There were only a few left.

"You know about LaFarge?" he asked, his sharp eyes darting to meet mine.

"Yes. I just read about him. The French Jesuit who believed in equality for all people," I said.

"An unknown," Victor scoffed, "which suited His Eminence especially well. The encyclical was a bombshell. And there were many inside the Vatican who found the idea of such a public statement a little too close to an act of suicide for our church."

I was content to help this old guy finish off his cookies and listen to the tale of long ago. I love puzzles and, hearing about the secret encyclical from his old friend, Victor, made me feel a little closer to that man whose journals I'd been reading.

"Ah," said Victor, shaking his head, "the encyclical was madness."

"But it was the right thing to do," I said. "Wasn't it?"

"There are often many right things, and then how does one choose? Eh?"

"With one's heart?" I suggested, and in my sleep-deprived state began to look at the issues that had tormented me regarding Xavier's decision in a different light.

"You are a nice young lady," Victor said, smiling, "but you know very little of politics. Power and survival, they are very important to men. But where was I? Oh, yes.

"I was speaking about the men who were charged with the task of writing the pope's position paper regarding the Jews. LaFarge, along with three other Jesuits, worked on the draft of this possibly revolutionary encyclical all through the summer of 1938. They worked throughout the oppressive heat of Paris. They called their draft *Humani Generis Unitas*, 'The Unity of the Human Race.' "

"Did they ever finish it?" I asked.

"Oh, yes. Late in 1938, LaFarge went to Rome to deliver it to the pope himself. And that is all we know."

"But what happened?" I offered the box with the last Thin Mint to Victor. He took it and smiled.

"There are many theories. Our friend, Monsignor Picca, believed Pius XI meant to deliver the speech revealing the encyclical to the world, but was hampered by poor health. He was not well. A few weeks later, on February ninth, nineteen thiry-nine, Pius XI died. And then, mysteriously, the paper just vanished and has never been heard of again. This is why Benny continued his studies. He truly believed word of the encyclical, even at this late date, would correct a long-standing misconception of the Holy See's responsibility during the war. Some day, he felt, the document would surface."

"It disappeared?" I wondered if this could in any way be connected to Brother Ugo. His death was near enough to these times to require further investigation.

"It was an old man's romantic quest," Victor said, shaking his head sadly. "And my dear old friend will no longer pursue this, or any other quest on earth."

"It's late," I said, rising.

"Stay a minute longer, Miss Bean," Victor said. "Let an old man tell you about his own passionate quest."

I sat back down, aware I had left Holly too long in the car and there was work pressing for me as well. But when a ninety-year-old man has just lost one of his oldest friends, it seemed the right thing to do to sit with him a few minutes more.

"Benny Picca was searching for clues to the location of a piece of paper," Victor said, encouraged. "But I am looking for a lost room."

"I'd love to hear about it," I said with as much sincerity as I could manage.

"Ah, the Amber Room is magnificent, Miss Bean. At least it was. It once graced the palace of Catherine the Great. Now, it is one of the biggest mysteries of World War Two."

I smiled in what I hoped seemed an encouraging manner and stole a peek at my watch. It was 10:30 p.m. Ah, well.

"Imagine an enormous ballroom where every square inch is covered in dazzling precious stones. One hundred and twenty-nine mosaic panels made up the jeweled chamber. In all, it took six tons of amber to create these panels. The room was priceless. It was a gift to Tsar Peter the Great in seventeen sixteen from the King of Prussia. The amber panels were installed at the tsar's summer palace in the town of Tsarskoe Selo, which is now the town of Pushkin.''

''Pushkin,'' I said. ''The Soviets had a way with names. It certainly loses some of its oomph.''

''To be sure,'' Victor said, chuckling. ''But this is a small town approximately fifteen miles south of St. Petersburg. Anyway, the Amber Room held treasures so magnificent it was considered by the Russians to be the eighth wonder of the world. Incorporated into the room were four prized eighteenth-century Florentine mosaics made of marble and onyx. And there were mirrors and gilded carved wood to enhance the amber's effect.''

''Beautiful,'' I mumbled.

''My dear, the room was brilliant. The entire room was a gigantic piece of jewelry. It was said to have a very high ceiling and measure one thousand square feet. Imagine when the western beams of sunlight entered the room and lit up the panels. It was like the room was shining from the inside!''

''You must have traveled to Russia to see it,'' I said, politely.

''But of course not,'' Victor said, shocked. ''The entire room was stolen by the Nazis. At the start of World War Two, Hitler ordered his troops to capture the Amber Room and 'return' it to Prussia, which was then part of Germany. As the Nazis advanced, the Soviets were desperate. In an attempt to save their treasure, they disassembled the room and packed the one hundred and twenty-nine large amber panels to ship them to safety. But the Nazis captured the amber.''

''Oh!'' I enjoy an adventure story.

''But of course they never took it to Prussia. They sent the jewels to the German village of Koenigsberg, where in nineteen forty-two, it was installed in an old castle.''

''Wait a minute, you say the Nazis stole the amber panels and set the entire room up in their own castle?''

''Yes. Back in Germany.''

''What happened in nineteen forty-five? Did the Russians get their Amber Room back after the Allies won the war?''

I was now pretty hooked on this treasure story. I saw it as a Disney movie, with perhaps a heroic Russian soldier searching for the stolen room and meeting a beautiful German girl, who'd been kept prisoner in the castle. Disney had not had an animated blonde in a while . . .

"This is a good question, young lady. Of course, at war's end, the Soviets went after their prize. Troops advanced on Koenigsberg and the only escape route for the Germans was by sea. The panels were taken to the basement of the castle and again packed for shipment. And that, my dear, was the last reported sighting of the Amber Room."

"How could six tons of carved amber panels disappear?" I asked, wondering if my Disney film treatment was doomed. The mice in Burbank require happy endings.

"Who knows? Over the years, countless treasure seekers have searched for the amber. They've torn up caves and mines, dived in lakes, and ripped apart wartime ruins and Nazi strongholds, but never found a clue to the disappearance of the amber panels. Some suspect that just before the fall of Koenigsberg, the treasure was put aboard a German submarine or ship that was torpedoed as it tried to escape. Others speculate that the amber was hidden beneath Koenigsberg or in one of many secret bunkers and subterranean towns built by the Nazis."

"I'm surprised that half of East Germany has not been dug up by now," I said.

"A good joke," Victor said, smiling broadly. "It is not such a farfetched idea, that. But still no one can find any trace."

"What do you think happened to it?" I asked.

"Me? I think the world will never know," and the old codger winked at me. "But it has been my little hobby to study this room. My granddaughter and now my great-granddaughter have helped me to make a miniature replica of the room, a model, you understand? Would you care to see it?"

"Not right now, sir," I said, standing. My condolence call was ending.

"Another time, perhaps," said Victor, getting to his feet. The old boy had more pep than one would suspect. It's the wiry ones who maintain their strength.

"Oh, by the way," I said as he showed me to the door amid a scatter of cookie crumbs, "when exactly did Pope Pius XI die?"

I believe the pale old man may have bleached a half shade. "You are not Catholic, are you my dear?" he asked, his voice stiff.

Now what had I done? Stupid me, poking and prying, right after the pain of hearing about his dear old friend's death. What I was saying was probably sacrilege to this man. "I'm sorry. Just forget about it," I said, stammering, and left the house fast.

I got to the Wagoneer, where Holly was sitting with the windows rolled up, chewing gum and bopping her head. As I opened the driver side door, the jumping rock of R.E.M. burst from the enclosed space. Holly could entertain herself on a deserted island, as long as it had electricity.

"What's the haps?" she asked, turning the volume to a more or less reasonable level.

"Nothing. Dead-end. Nada," I said, turning the ignition.

"Too bad," said Holly. "Hey, remember you told me you were doing all this research-type stuff on the Nazis and Rome?"

"Yeah?"

"I just got off the cell with Donald and he's got a friend you should meet over at Spaceland."

Right. Just what I wanted to do. Hit a hot club in Silverlake and take in a few bands.

"Thanks, Hol. But maybe we should just go home. It's been a long day and tomorrow morning is the . . ."

"I know, I know," she said. "The Popemeister. But I told Donald we'd pick him up at Spaceland," she said, in what was approaching a wheedle. "And that's where he's seeing his friend, you know, the girl who gave him those stories for his movie. The one about the people who escaped from the Nazis with fake papers. Come on. It'll be fun."

"Okay, Hol," I said, "but we're not drinking and we're definitely not staying, got it?" I suddenly heard myself sounding exactly like somebody's mother.

"I know. I know. It's a school night." Obviously, Holly heard it, too. It made me shiver.

If I had enough energy to sit through a sad old man's fairy story I was damned if I couldn't rock with my friends. I pulled the clip that was holding my hair up and shook my head. I could take off the denim shirt and just wear the camisole under my leather jacket. I punched up the volume on the R.E.M. CD just as lead singer Michael Stipe began to wail the last plaintive verse of "Losing My Religion."

"Hey!" Holly said, checking me out with a grin. "I do believe we've been visited by Mad-woman Bean, the wild party animal who just astral-projected herself into the body of my very responsible friend."

"So who are we going to hear?" I asked, as I squirmed out of my shirt at the red light before we merged onto the Ventura Freeway.

"It's this amazing lesbian punk group. Wicked B and the Dairy Foundation. You're gonna dig them. Their lead singer, B Zoda, rocks."

Who, after all, needs sleep when you have a chance to hear the punk-rock stylings of a great lesbian like Wicked B?

Chapter 21

Spaceland was the largest and most established of the hot music clubs in Silverlake. Some of its earliest stars, like Beck and the Dust Brothers, had become huge in the music business, and Spaceland had become even hotter. There were some who raved that Silverlake was becoming the next Seattle, with this crop of L.A. power pop musicians ready to replace the aging grunge scene. But, naturally, such out-and-out hype made the cool-cat Silverlake musicians go ballistic.

Groups with names like The Neptunas, and Hello, I'm a Truck, and Expectorant were the newest draw. The club scene was hopping seven nights a week and wherever late-night L.A. went, Holly had already been there and scoped out the best table.

At the door, there was the usual business of showing I.D. and getting hand stamped, and then we were inside, feeling the pump of adrenaline from the noise and the bodies and the gleams flashing off the mirror disco ball. The dark lively space was filled with small tables and crowded with scenesters. There was a retro sixties flavor to the attire, with flower power a recurrent theme.

Donald Lake was already there, sitting at a good table, surrounded by four women. Holly spotted him and, grabbing me by my shoulder bag, wove her way through the tightly spaced tables until we were near the front of the house. On stage, a roadie was setting up a guitar stand with a white Fender Stratocaster, completely covered in tiny iridescent stickers. There was a miniature Barbie doll hanging from its tuning pegs.

"This is too cool," Holly said. "Remember I saw The Julies at Poptopia and told you about them?" I nodded, and unbuttoned my leather jacket. I figured we could at least stay until I'd gotten to hear this group. I ordered a Diet Coke and found a chair.

Donald was happy to see Holly. She scooted him over so she could share his chair as Donald introduced me to the group of women at the table. It was Wicked B and her crew.

I just stared. Amazing! For the second time in one evening I was shocked to find myself looking at a face I'd seen before. What's more, I'd seen this face in the same waiting room outside the mayor's office where I'd first set eyes on old Victor.

"Hi," I said to B, cupping my hand to be heard over the piped-in music while The Julies were setting up. "I just came from talking to your great-grandfather."

"No shit!" said B, happily. This was the Beatrice of the old-fashioned name and artistic temperament that Victor had been talking about earlier this evening. How small a world can one city with ten million inhabitants be?

"You saw Grandpa Vic?" she asked. Now if B was a lesbian, as Holly had stated, she was definitely of the "lipstick" persuasion. She wore a tight silver mini-skirt and shiny Lurex tights. Her halter top revealed a stunning chest behind all the sequins. The rest of the Dairy Foundation, as her group was named, had the more utilitarian look of jeans and white button-down collar shirts. What contrast. B was still wearing her hair in a multihued buzzcut and the nose ring was in place, but looking at her up close, she seemed softer. Maybe it was the tattoo that said "mommy" on her bicep.

"How do you know B's family?" Donald asked, smiling in amazement.

"Long story," I said. My Diet Coke was delivered and

The Julies lead singer, Julie, came on stage ready to rock the house.

Donald put a hand up to the side of his mouth. "B's great-grandfather is the guy I was telling you about, the guy who worked with the rescue group called *Stille Hilfe* during World War Two," Donald continued, over the opening to "Surfer Duane," a song that got the crowd in the club shouting and applauding.

"What guy?" I asked Donald.

"You know. When I was doing research for my masters, B told me about her great-grandfather and his experiences in Europe during World War Two. He was the guy who smuggled Jews out through Rome. He managed to get them travel documents through the Vatican, somehow."

"Because the Vatican is an independent country?" asked one of the serious-looking Dairy Foundation, a young woman with glasses and a pretty smile.

"Right," Donald answered.

"Of course," I said, turning over these new facts in my mind. Old Victor had contacts in high places within the Vatican. Maybe that's why he thought Pius XI's encyclical would make too many waves. It might have jeopardized the work Victor was doing behind the scenes to secure escape for some fortunate Jews. He didn't see the big picture. If the church had come out against the anti-Semitic policies of Hitler, they may have saved a few million lives. Still, Victor had clearly been a hero.

"Why haven't we heard about this?" I asked B. "Look at *Schindler's List*. Everyone knows about Schindler. Someone should write about Victor Zoda."

"That's what I thought," yelled Donald over the music. "The man probably saved a hundred lives. You know, originally, *Gasp!* was about Victor. But then the studio changed the concept and we found ourselves in outer space."

The Julies were finishing up a tune with wry humor, sung loud. The audience was into it.

I began to see how all this added up. Victor liked to keep his philanthropy work very quiet. He didn't want public acknowledgement for the money he donated to the church. He might not have enjoyed the limelight from a movie about his work during the war.

B pulled her chair closer to mine. "So why did you see my great gramps?"

"A whole different thing," I said.

"Yeah," Holly piped in, "Madeline and I are working on the big breakfast party for the pope tomorrow morning."

"Really?" B asked, as Julie started singing "Road Kill."

"Oooh!" Holly interrupted, "You've gotta listen to this song. It's way dark."

We all listened. I must say, without trying hard I was starting to relax and have fun.

"You know that big party you guys are doing?" B said after a while. "The pope's party? I'm going to be there. Grandpa Vic invited me. I drive him around a lot."

"That's nice of you," Donald said.

"Well. He bought me the Miata, so . . ." Wicked B was making fun of her wicked self, which I like.

The Julies were on a roll and they swung into another tune. Julie, herself, has a great voice and a wild art-rock way with lyrics. Her look is pure sex kitten fun. She was wearing baby doll pajamas in shocking pink with red fuzzy slippers, her thick hair pulled up in an "I Dream of Jeannie" ponytail.

I turned back to B. "I was looking into research that Monsignor Picca was doing," I said, leaning over so she could hear me.

"Hey, I know him," B shouted over the applause. We all clapped and smiled as Julie looked at our table. B stood up and whistled, like a truck driver. When she dropped back into her seat she explained, "Julie's so fine. Her new CD is coming out soon."

"You knew Monsignor Picca?" I asked, curious.

"Sure, I drove Grandpa Vic out to see him in La Canada all the time. We went there yesterday, matter of fact."

The band on stage was getting frantic and the crowd was

with them all the way. Julie was belting out "Are We Even Here?" and Wicked B and her entire Dairy Foundation were bopping their heads to the beat.

Holly said to Donald, "This psychedelic metal insanity just creeps into your brain!"

They were having an intellectual discussion, so I reached out and touched B's arm to get her attention.

"Did you say you saw the Monsignor *yesterday*?" I shouted over the music, alarmed.

"Uh huh," she mouthed, giving me half her attention, but quickly turning back to the musicians on stage.

"B!" I yelled. "What time were you and Victor Zoda there?"

She turned back to me and thought. "Afternoon. Maybe three. I don't go out early." She shrugged her delicate shoulders, which made the sequins on her halter glitter. "That's why this pope thing tomorrow is such a bitch. Waking up tomorrow morning is gonna kill me. I think the women and I may just stay up all night. Right Sheryl?" she asked the one nearest her.

"That's what Julie does," Holly informed us. "She stays up all night."

As B and Holly got into a discussion on how to deal with the schedule of the real world when you really want to rock all night long, I considered what I'd just found out. If B had taken Victor to St. Bede's yesterday afternoon, they may have been the last people to see the old priest before he died.

Now, in all the time I'd just spent out in Encino, listening to ancient history, why had Victor said nothing about the last time he saw his old pal Monsignor Benny?

Chapter 22

Waking up groggy from too little sleep, I jerked to consciousness, startled with apprehension. I'd been dreaming of ants escaping across a thin twig above a rain-puddled patio. I poked the cloud cover that was fogging over my unconscious to remember the end of the dream. The ants were marching, now that I thought about it, to Encino.

It was 4 a.m. and time to scramble. In the darkness of Wesley's guestroom, I felt lonely and out of place. I had missed Wes again. He had just left the duplex before I got in at midnight. We'd meet up at the Otis Mayfield Pavilion at five.

While showering, I reviewed the schedule for the party ahead. The guests would begin to arrive at seven, while waiters passed trays of juice. Coffee stations, along with platters of fresh bakery goods, would flank the lobby of the Otis Mayfield Pavilion. We would then open the doors to the auditorium at eight o'clock.

If all went according to plan, the mayor and his entourage would arrive shortly after that and then, finally, the pope himself would make an appearance at eight-thirty.

Xavier had already informed me that the pope would not be eating from our menu. His food was meticulously fussed over by a special team of Vatican chefs who traveled with him. Nevertheless, he would certainly see my food, even in passing, and so I was going over early to make sure that everything looked right and to give Wesley moral support.

I wiped the steam from the guest bathroom's mirror with the corner of my towel, and sighed. Too much hair is just a pain. I sat down and began the careful process of French braiding it up off my face. Whenever I do this I'm reminded that my hair has really gotten long. It normally shrinks up in tight ringlets, but now, wrestled into a plait, the subdued curls reached well past my shoulders.

Chefs, especially the young ones that Wes and I hang around with in California, work in a uniform, of sorts, mixing elements of the traditional with the hip. Most of us still honor the classic chef's white tunic, but we like to update the look by wearing it with clogs and a baseball cap.

Even though we had assembled a great staff of chefs to work the pope's breakfast, I always like to be prepared to cook. I slipped into a fresh tunic, with its double row of white buttons and "Madeline Bean" stitched in black above my heart, zipped into a pair of white jeans, pulled on white cotton anklets, and stepped into my trademark red clogs.

Clogs are it. They can save your back. This, of course, means everything to a crowd who spends night after night, hour after hour, standing on hard floors. There's a wonderful little shop near the Beverly Center that supplies Swedish clogs for all the best chefs in Los Angeles, and the owner special orders my favorite model in red. She has this amazing talent to fit anyone and know exactly what style one should buy. How could I argue?

For today's event, I selected a charcoal-colored baseball cap from Notre Dame and put it on, pulling my braid through the small opening in the back. I had a lucky superstition about matching the hat to the occasion, and although Holly had bought me a special cap that said "I ♡ Pope," it was not me.

My hanging suitcase held my good clothes and I planned to change before the mayor arrived. I grabbed it and stepped into Wesley's dining room, where I'd left my purse and my toolbox.

Professional chefs can be weird about cooking utensils.

We get fond of a vegetable brush. Or, we discover a whisk or a peppermill that fits our hand perfectly. Over the years, we build up a personal *batterie de cuisine.* Those of us who travel put our indispensable spatulas and our discontinued instruments and our revered knives into a toolbox. Mine was the big kind you can buy at Sears.

I poured hot tea into a thermos cup, clicked on the top, and loaded my Wagoneer. From Wesley's duplex in Hancock Park, I was able to make it downtown to the Otis Mayfield Pavilion in fifteen minutes. There's something to be said for driving before 5 a.m. I parked in the loading dock and showed the officer stationed there my pass. Security would be tight all day, and I was glad.

The kitchen complex at the pavilion was in the basement and I headed there, toting toolbox, purse, and suitcase. It was quite a walk through the complex maze of halls. In the bowels of the Mayfield I passed several cooks I knew from past events. Everyone had that special zing: excitement mixed with espresso. We were stoked.

I entered one of the main tunnels that led to the cooking rooms. The Otis Mayfield was equipped with three hulking commercial kitchens, with enough oven capacity between them to cater a dinner for three thousand. In one of the mammoth stainless steel and white rooms stood Wesley, tall and handsome and alert, amidst the bustle and noise of over fifty cooks doing their thing.

Miniature lemon croissants were popping out of the ovens, moist and chewy and the size of a baby's hand. These pastries were destined for the silver trays, which would line the outer foyer of the Mayfield auditorium. Bite-sized was our opening theme. These goodies were the perfect size to nibble while standing around and schmoozing. Since most of our guests would be politicos and others who had friends in high places, we figured no one would want his mouth too full to make a false promise or his hand too sticky to shake on it.

Many of the morning's most complicated dishes would have to be prepared immediately before they were served, so this was a time of baking, prepping our special ingredients and creating fresh sauces.

"Madeline, you're here." Wes came over as soon as he spotted me. He was wearing jeans and a black T-shirt with a half-apron wrapped around his thin waist. And of course his Dodgers cap and a pair of black Converse sneakers.

I set down my stuff in a clean corner. "Hey, what's with that?" I asked, surprised, nodding to his footgear.

"I've put in twenty miles since I got here," Wes said. "I stuck your sneaks in my bag. I'm just waiting for you to beg for them."

"It's looking good," I said, checking out the action. "What's going on?" I was happy to see the level of activity, which was a controlled burst of industrious hard work, rather than a frenzied explosion. I can walk into a kitchen and know in an instant when all hell is breaking loose.

"We're happening," Wes said, smiling at me. "We're ready."

"The waffles?" I asked.

"Batter's up."

I love this guy despite the puns. But, of course, I still had to punch him.

It had been controversial to attempt to cook fresh waffles and omelets for a sit-down party of two thousand diners. We'd come up with a neat little plan. Wes designed these clever little placecards with a detachable sheet on which one could mark their own selection. Tiny golden pens, with an inscription to commemorate the pope's historic visit, were provided at each place. These would disappear quickly. I only worried that they would remain on the tables long enough to do their job.

In a few hours, each guest will mark the exact custom omelet or waffle combination he or she desires and our waiters will bring the orders back to the kitchen. Station captains were organizing the whole operation, so that each table of ten would be served their main courses at the same time.

It was ambitious to do it this way, to custom cook two

thousand individual dishes at the very last minute, but we only get one chance in life, and frankly, Wes and I are crazy. Each of our chefs had an assistant and they'd rehearsed their moves. Half of our chefs would be working Belgian wafflemakers capable of producing ten waffles each, which gave us the capacity to produce 250 fresh waffles every three minutes. The remaining twenty-five chefs were each working an array of omelet pans and should be cranking out an equal number of custom egg dishes at the same rate. We planned to serve these entrees to our guests, still hot, within a window of just twelve minutes. You may recall the gentleman who twirled plates on Ed Sullivan.

Wes and I would normally bet on such an ambitious plan, but we were both feeling a little too superstitious this time. Let's just say that we asked Xavier to pray for us.

"Walk with me," I suggested to Wes, as I was anxious to see how the main Mayfield auditorium had been transformed.

"Here's our problem," Wes said, as he fell into step alongside me. "We can cook the damn dishes, we can plate them and dress them . . ."

"Uh-huh." This was the technical part where you tried and tried to whittle down the time it took to cook food and then add the necessary sauces and garnishes and accoutrements that would make the presentation a knockout.

"But then we're faced with this damned hustle from the kitchen back to the theater," Wes said.

"It's a haul," I said, noting that we'd been walking a full minute and hadn't yet reached the main entrance.

"And a half," Wes concurred. Then he added, with a twinkle, "I offered a prize to the waiter who could make it the fastest."

"Yesterday?" Wes likes to motivate our crew.

"Yep. They had to carry four bowls of soup on a tray . . ."

"Soup!" I said, laughing. "Did you clock them?"

"Of course. Would you believe Adam Voron made it in

thirty-five seconds, with most of the soup still in the bowls?''

''Did you consider Roller Blades?'' I asked, and then we were at the double doors to the auditorium. A guard with a walkie-talkie approached and checked out my badge. All the staff had been issued laminated picture I.D.s that we wore from chains, like dogtags.

After we were cleared, Wes opened one of the heavy doors and said, ''After you.''

Inside was a wonderland of white and gold, accented in red. I stood still, amazed.

The small ramp that normally takes you down to the floor of the auditorium was covered in frosted Plexiglas sheeting, which extended across the tops of the fifteen hundred seats found in the orchestra section. I took a step on the slightly pebbled surface and was reassured to feel it was bolted tight to the scaffolding underneath. This astonishing temporary floor was suspended over thousands of twinkle lights, creating a fairylike underglow, which illuminated the enormous space from below.

And the tables! Two hundred ten-top rounds had been dressed in pure white, their cloths reaching the floor. Overlaying each were squares of gold netting. Each table was circled by ten metal garden chairs, which had been slipcovered in flimsy white gauze with the pope's seal embroidered in gold. And draped from the back of each chair was a garland of fresh flowers.

Hundreds of votive candles would flicker in clear glass globes, which had been set on a circular mirror centerpiece on each table. The effect was breathtaking.

''My God, Wes,'' I said, stunned. ''I want to get married here.''

''Well,'' Wes said, sensibly, ''we do have the pope hanging around somewhere. It could be done.''

Then, all of a sudden, the eight million twinkle lights underfoot were instantly extinguished. The auditorium went completely dark.

''What the . . . ?'' Both Wes and I spoke out as one.

Alone in the cavernous theater, where no light save the faintest dull glow of emergency exit signs could now just barely be seen, brought quite a rush of fear. Not being able to see Wesley, who might have been only a foot away, didn't help.

Blindly, I reached into my purse and searched. I always feel around inside this old leather bag while driving, so I was familiar with the shape of my compact and the feel of my pen. In an instant I found what I was looking for and another instant later the match sprang to life.

"Sensible girl," Wes said, and moved quickly to the nearest table. He brought a couple of the votives in their holders, which I lit rapidly. Just one match and we had light. There must be something of the scout in all of us.

"What happened?" I asked, alarmed.

"Circuit?" Wes said, puzzled.

The radio on Wesley's belt spit out a loud burst of static as we moved toward the door and then a voice mumbled a loud squawk of words. As I reached for the handle on the auditorium door, all of a sudden, the lights came back on.

"Yes," Wes was saying back into the radio. He turned to me and looked worried. "The power was out in the kitchen, too. I'd better get back there."

"Me, too," I said. Out in the foyer, the grand chandeliers were glowing, but there was no sign of the security guard who had been on duty when we arrived.

Wes and I raced back to the underground kitchens, grabbing the safety railing on the landing, taking steps on the fly. True, we didn't have four bowls of soup on a tray, but I believe we bested Adam Voron's fastest time by ten seconds.

As we rounded the last corner before the kitchens, I huffed a bit, my calves aching, and whimpered, "Wes, I need my tennis shoes."

No signs of security outside the kitchen. I was beginning to get concerned.

Inside, there had obviously been a problem. The smell of faintly burned food is not one we're accustomed to, but that unmistakably bitter odor filled the large space, while the drone of high-powered ventilators whirred from the shafts overhead.

''We were on a timer,'' Del Wipp said, as soon as Wes and I entered the room.

''The thing's electric. It was screwed up when the power shut down,'' Marcy Kaplan added, joining us as we surveyed the damage.

''But couldn't you just . . .'' Wes was frustrated, but what could anyone have done? Spread out on every surface were muffin tins filled with blackened blueberry muffinettes.

''The place was totally black, man,'' Del Wipp said. ''It was cool.''

''We couldn't try to open the ovens in the dark,'' Marcy said. ''It was pitch black. I couldn't see my hand in front of my face.''

''We got scared the smoke alarms were about to blow!'' a blonde girl said. I checked her name badge, Deborah Besset. A crowd was gathering around us as we got the gist of the scene down here.

''I got mine out,'' Rolando Cruz said. He stood at his worktable, beaming, and the crowd parted to see his trays of eight dozen perfectly cooked muffinettes. ''What's a matter you guys, eh?'' he asked, laughing.

''He's real smart,'' Deborah complained to Marcy. ''Imagine sticking your arms into a four-hundred-degree oven, blind.''

''Nothin' to it, chica,'' Rolando said, loudly.

''Dump the burnt muffins,'' Wes said, reminding everyone to concentrate on the solutions and stop all the complaining.

A security officer entered the kitchen and headed over to Wes, who was busy giving instructions for fixing the muffin mess.

''I'm Madeline Bean,'' I stepped into the officer's path. ''Wesley is my partner and he's going to be busy for awhile. Can you tell me what happened here?''

"I'll wait for Mr. Westcott," he said, annoyed and not trying very hard to hide it.

At not quite five foot five, I was just some girl in red clogs and a baseball cap to him. I usually have to yell or something to get men like these to listen to me. It was a fight I'd rather not get into, but I was more than prepared.

Wes was supervising as 960 black miniature muffins hit the trash and dozens of muffin pans were scrubbed and regreased.

"Look," I said, injecting that edge of annoying menace in my voice that got men's attention, that tone that felt like a poke in the chest. "Tell me what happened or get me your supervisor. Now."

"Calm down, lady."

Just then, an LAPD captain entered the kitchen and called out, "Who's in charge here?"

Newly prepared batter was being paddled in gigantic mixers and Wes was passing out flashlights to each chef's assistant as everyone in the room kind of stopped what they were doing for a moment and said, "She is."

"You got problems?" the captain asked me. "I'm Todd, Douglas Todd. I hear you had a power outage."

"Right," I said. "This cop you've assigned to me abandoned the kitchen during the blackout."

"I thought I should go for help or something."

The captain looked me up and down, no doubt taking in the clogs and cap.

"Sorry about that Ms. Bean." He either read the embroidery or the badge, but at least he was polite. "This guy's not one of ours. He's private."

Great. I wasted all my heat on a rent-a-cop.

The man looked contrite. I looked satisfied. Captain Todd looked unhappy. He spoke into his radio, calling for backup.

"Don't leave here until your replacement arrives," Captain Todd instructed the man. "I'm sending you out to guard the shuttle parking lot."

The room grew quieter as the cooks concentrated on getting the new batches of blueberry muffins into the ovens.

"What happened here?" I asked Todd. "Was it just a circuit overload?"

"Not exactly. The guard outside the power plant was off in the john when the lights went out. The system is programmed to switch to the backup generator in that event."

"So we're on generator?"

"Right. But in a few minutes the facility engineer will restart the juice and we'll be back on full power."

"So what happened?"

"We don't know yet. It could have been a computer malfunction. Or someone may have sabotaged the current. We'll investigate and see what we come up with."

"So we're not worried, right?" I asked the captain, hoping to lighten his mood.

"You bet your ass we are," he said, laughing.

In the background I was aware of the buzzing of the timer, which meant our new batches of mini-muffins were ready. The next second, all the lights blinked out once again. Amidst cries of "Oh no!" and "Not again!" the room was plunged into blackest night. But almost at once, ten, then twenty-five, then forty flashlights blazed.

"Help out here, people," Wes said, fully in command, as our chefs, now experienced in the art of baking in bunker conditions, saved every last tray of blueberry muffinettes in the flickering illumination of about four dozen crisscrossing beams of battery-powered light.

Chapter 23

Downtown L.A. is a deserted canyon of high-rises at 7 a.m. on a Sunday morning. Except when the pope's in town. Crowd control here, perfected for such events as the Oscars, was as professional as it comes. Two giant bleachers were filled with pope admirers. There would have been more, I figured, but nearly sixty thousand faithful were putting on their Sunday best and heading for Dodger Stadium about now, in preparation for the papal mass that would begin at ten.

The giant square that comprised the auditorium complex was surrounded by satellite uplink trucks and portable video control booths. The television news buzzards had circled this event, signaling they'd found their prey. On north Grand Avenue near the main entrance to the Otis Mayfield, valet parkers were attending to the vehicles of invited guests. After relinquishing their cars, the elite moved across a long red carpet through white tents where security had been set up to check invitations and distribute badges. I was told many of these security officers had been involved with the 1984 Olympics.

Wes looked at the scene and said, "I know we usually have bouncers for our parties, but we may have gone a little overboard this time."

"I'm afraid if Arnold Schwarzenegger is watching the '*Today*' show, he's going to insist we bring the FBI to his next party, too," I said. Actually, I wasn't joking.

Guests proudly wore their laminated badges, plastic cards hanging from metal neckchains, over their Pradas and Armanis, and walked past the Otis Mayfield fountain and up the steps to the main doors. Wes and I watched as they greeted one another, friends of the city or the mayor or the archdiocese of Los Angeles.

A long dark car pulled up and L.A.'s Cardinal O'Grady stepped out. I could see that Brother Xavier Jones was there to greet him. The press corps came alive and surged forward. The crowd in the stands screamed.

"You'd think Tom Hanks had just arrived," I said to Wes, noticing the frenzy of microphones that were being waved by the crush of reporters.

"That is Tom Hanks," Wes acknowledged.

I looked closer. It was true. Cardinal O'Grady and his distinguished party were ushered by Xavier into the foyer of the Otis Mayfield with a minimum of fanfare as Mr. Hanks and his wife were mobbed by the television media. I had wondered why *Entertainment Tonight* had sent a truck.

Inside the foyer, our waiters were dipping through the gathering crowd, offering an assortment of pastel-colored fruit smoothies in crystal shot glasses from their trays. They were dressed, male and female alike, in black slacks and crisp white shirts, with security name badges as required.

There had been some discussion about the pope's feelings regarding women wearing pants. It was not allowed, we'd been informed, in the Vatican. Xavier succinctly reminded the overly nervous pope handlers that this was L.A., the city was the host of this event, and he advised the conservative Romans they might follow the sage down-home advice, "When in Rome . . ." I'd always admired Xavier's chutzpah and sly wit.

I felt a sense of relief wash over me. It dawned on me, as it always does at the start of a great party, that somehow we all finally made it here in one piece. I was proud of the job we'd done.

Allen, a big beefcake of a guy and one of our most trustworthy employees, was carrying a tray.

"What do you have here?" I asked him.

"Banana-strawberry, kiwi-lime-pineapple, and tangerine fizz," Allen said. "Everyone likes the shot glass idea," he commented, "especially the men. They take a quick shot of fruit juice and then get rid of the glass. It's a big hit."

"That was Mad's idea," Wes said. I blushed.

"But we've got some real weirdos in the crowd," Allen said.

"Trouble?" I asked. Like everyone else, I was on edge about the frightening potential of this morning's event. We had stepped upon the world stage and I was aware that it was just such a platform that could draw the extremely disturbed to make a sometimes explosive debut.

"That lady in the purple," Allen said, aiming his chin to his right.

I noticed a tall woman wearing an eggplant-colored raw silk suit and holding a large black patent leather shoulder bag.

"She looks okay to me," Wes said. "Except who would wear eggplant?"

"It's in the purse," Allen said.

"What? A gun?" I asked.

"A Pekinese," Allen said.

Just then, a female server moved toward eggplant woman and started to dip her tray down to offer a tiny smoothie or miniature pastry. What looked like a messy brown wig bounced up out of the tote bag and scarfed several muffins. The waitress was so startled, she fell back and just barely got control of her tray.

"Allen, please go straight to the juice bar and put out the alert."

Wesley and I walked through the crowd and felt the power in that room. Our guests were very excited to be here, and I knew that it had more to do with the guest of honor than our catering. Still, until the pontiff arrived, our décor and food would have to hold their attention.

Holly arrived at our sides. I stared at her. She was six feet of extremely thin woman dressed in a long flowing black gown with a severe white collar.

"Holly!" Wes said, speechless.

"You look like . . ." I couldn't get the words out.

"What?" she asked, happy with our reaction. "A nun? That's what I was going for."

"You got there," Wes said, with awe in his voice.

"Do you think the hat's too much?" she asked.

"Definitely," I said, eyeing the thing. It looked like a big black bat.

She whipped it off and fluffed her stick-straight platinum-blonde hair. "Hey, you guys seen my Donald?"

"Not yours nor any other," Wes replied, and Holly drifted off, checking out the crowd as she went.

At all our events, Holly is the emergency utility sub. If any of the staff cancels at the last minute, whether it be a waiter or a chef, Holly is superwoman. But none of our people were about to miss playing their part in history. So, without any no shows, we thought she and Donald might enjoy the honor of being guests at an event that was the hardest ticket to get on the planet.

I looked at Wesley, always perfectly groomed and attired. This morning he'd changed into a charcoal suit of meticulous cut, a white shirt, and gray and white tie. A good suit on such a tall man is a classic look. But I had little time to think about clothes, and was quickly back to other more crucial concerns.

"So the electricity hasn't been a further problem, after all," I commented to Wesley.

"Not after that second time, no." The second blackout was due to the facility engineer for the Otis Mayfield Pavilion switching off the auxiliary generator and switching us back to full main power. It might have been nice if we'd received some warning, but we'd managed remarkably well by flashlight for five minutes.

"I'm worried about those guys who attacked you the

other day,'' Wes said, not for the first time. ''What if they were serious. Maybe they have some connection to the power cutoff.''

''I know, Wes. That's what I told that Captain Todd this morning. You were there,'' I said. ''The cops were checking on the names of any disgruntled contractors, but they'd been over this whole thing before. You remember, I told Honnett about the guys who'd grabbed me a couple of days ago.''

''I'm glad you did,'' Wes said, still fussing over me.

''But I have another thing that's been worrying me even more.''

All morning, something wasn't right. I had an uneasy feeling that wouldn't go away. Something was going bzzzz in the back of my head. And unless I paid attention and got the damn message, pretty soon we'd all be smelling smoke.

I told Wes about my odd encounter with old Victor Zoda in Encino and with his great-granddaughter, Wicked B, at Spaceland.

Wes listened to my story without interrupting and then asked, ''So the fact is, this old guy was a war hero?''

''Something like that. He saved the lives of hundreds of Jews, helping them to escape from the Nazis and then secretly smuggling them out of Europe as part of an underground organization, a charity group known as *Stille Hilfe*.''

Wesley spun and looked at me. ''*Stille Hilfe*?'' he said, suddenly deadly serious.

''I think that's what B said, yes. Why?''

''Madeline, *Stille Hilfe* is German.'' Wes, the encyclopedia.

''I know that.''

''It means 'Quiet Aid' and it was definitely not about helping save the Jews.'' Wes sounded very upset.

''You're scaring me,'' I said, suddenly chilled. ''What is it, then?''

"Madeline, the so-called charity called *Stille Hilfe* still exists. In Germany and some say in other countries as well. Its members are what remain of the family and friends of high-ranking Nazi officers and to this day, they continue to help these fugitive criminals. Even now, when some old Nazi concentration camp guard is caught and prosecuted for war crimes, it's *Stille Hilfe* that provides all the money to defend him."

"Oh my God."

"The group is run by the daughter of Heinrich Himmler."

"Adolf Hitler's leading henchman," I said, shocked. My head ached and I began to feel dizzy.

"Right. Himmler's daughter, a woman named Gudrun Burwitz, has helped support some of the Third Reich's most stunning piece-of-shit officers, like Klaus Barbie. The only thing I ever heard about the group helping people escape from Europe was the rumor that *Stille Hilfe* may have secretly helped dozens of top Nazi assholes escape at the end of the war."

"Wesley . . ." I said, stunned. "What does this all have to do with Victor Zoda? He's not German . . ."

My cell phone rang and I answered it, moving slightly so I'd hear better. The arriving guests had gathered into a huge group by now.

"Honnett here," Detective Chuck Honnett said in my ear.

"Honnett. We need to talk." I said.

"That's why I called. I've got something I want to show you. Can you find the KTLA news truck? It's parked at the curb on Grand."

KTLA is the local station, which broadcasts on Channel 5 in Los Angeles. I watch their morning show and I'm familiar with their on-air news talent. They, along with everyone else in the world, were covering every move the pope makes on his brief visit to L.A. Since this was their home turf, KTLA got an exceptionally good location from which to broadcast.

Stepping outside, I crossed the plaza past the fountain, and jumped up the two steps to the portable control booth truck. Before I knocked on the aluminum door, I smoothed my new skirt.

Arlo bought me the designer suit, the color of molten bronze, for my birthday because he knew I had a problem spending big money on clothes. He said the color was perfect with my hair. The rich, tight metallic skirt fell at a circumspect length, a few inches above the knee, while the short, fitted black and bronze check jacket skimmed my body. I was wearing all the real gold jewelry I owned and I'd taken time with my makeup. Somehow the enormity of getting to be in the presence of His Holiness had knocked most of the irreverence right out of me.

Since no one answered, I pulled the door open and walked into the truck. A bank of miniature screens flickered from the console across the darkened room. The director of the morning news sat in a roller chair at the panel, wearing headphones and calling shots. Staring at the wall filled with moving images, he was flanked by technical engineers and assistants. Masking tape beneath each of the small monitors had been marked in black marker "Cam 1 ED," "Cam 2 BOB," etc. I noticed they had ten camera positions, and this was just the local news. A lot of freelance camera crews were making overtime this morning.

Chuck Honnett was sitting in the second room, talking on a phone. When he saw me he motioned for me to join him. There were several KTLA production assistants and writers in that room, working on their next spots. I sat down as Honnett got off the phone.

"Thanks for coming," he said, looking me over. And then he couldn't resist a dig, "Real dressed up today, aren't you?"

"The pope is not a jeans-type guy," I said, shrugging. "But, wait. I need to tell you something."

I proceeded to fill him in about elderly Victor Zoda, about his visit to Monsignor Picca on the afternoon the old priest died, and Zoda's possible secret connection to the

Nazi relocation charity known as *Stille Hilfe*.

Honnett swore as he dialed up the security post at the main entrance. Before he got through he warned me, "None of this is evidence of a crime, Madeline." But I knew I'd gotten through to him.

"Well, that's lucky," he told me when he got off. "Zoda hasn't arrived yet. If and when he does, they've got instructions to hold him. Under no circumstances will he be allowed to enter the pavilion until we have a chance to question him. Satisfied?"

"Well, actually, yes."

It was not at all like Honnett to take my ideas so seriously. I liked it. "And another thing . . ." I started.

Honnett interrupted, "In a minute, okay. First I need to tell you, you might have been right . . ."

". . . no, this is really important, I . . ." and then I stopped. "What did you say?"

Not to belabor the point, but when a man who hasn't listened to me time and time again finally says those magic words—not "I love you," but "You were right"—I'm afraid he goes straight to the top of the list.

"Our suspect in the del Valle homicide," Honnett explained. "Anthony Ramona was let go this morning."

"No shit!" I was sure I'd been right, of course. But there was the little matter that I had absolutely no proof. "I know you respect me, Honnett, but you didn't let Ramona go just 'cause I had a hunch, right?"

That got a slight smile out of the bastard. He said, "Ramona's girlfriend had a birthday party out in San Fernando the night our Jesuit brother was killed. So he calls his legal aid attorney at two this morning and says the girlfriend's got a videotape of the birthday party complete with Ramona dancing the macarena."

Honnett called out to a guy named Randy in the booth, and soon the video operator began to roll tape on the monitor in our little alcove. I watched as Ramona and friends drank beer and generally had a great time. There was a date and time stamp on the bottom left of the frame. Thursday night at 9:30 p.m. There was no way Ramona could have simultaneously been at Warner Bros. in Burbank killing a Jesuit.

"Are you sure this wasn't doctored?" I asked, knowing of course it would have been checked.

"We're sure. So isn't this just what you were trying to tell me, Madeline? That you didn't buy it for a minute that a gangbanger did the job on Brother Frank?"

"Yes. It was impossible. But what I don't understand is why that idiot Ramona went and confessed to something he couldn't have done."

"You'll like this," Honnett said in a weary voice. "I hate it, so I know you'll like it. It seems Ramona's sister was nervous. She was afraid that if someone wasn't arrested for the murder of this Roman Catholic brother, the pope might cancel his trip to L.A. She had tickets for the mass."

I looked at him, almost ready to laugh. "She didn't want to lose her seats?"

"She told him it was a blessing in the eyes of the church. He'd go sit in county lockup for a few days, something I might add he'd had plenty of experience with, and then once the pope was out of town, he could recant his confession. She came up with this brilliant idea because she had been on that fundraising trip to Warner Bros. and she figured he could just lie and say he'd been there, too."

I could almost see their cockeyed logic. "They both were counting on the fact that the LAPD were pretty eager to arrest someone, and a Latino gangmember would make you guys salivate."

"Well, whatever," Honnett grumbled. "We look for nut jobs to give false confessions, not hard cases like Ramona. Anyway, it turns out that life inside our county jail was more of a trauma than Ramona expected. A gang member usually gets left alone in lockup, but when the guy is the confessed murderer of a priest, the regular rules don't apply. He was roughed up pretty bad. As soon as he heard that the pope's plane had landed, he demanded his release."

"So that leaves you without a suspect in the murder of Brother Frank."

"For the moment," Honnett agreed.

"There a Miss Bean here?" called out a P.A. who had just answered the booth phone.

"That's me." I picked up the extension on the desk in front of me.

"Miss Bean?" a male voice inquired. "This is Richard Burke. I hope I'm not bothering you at a busy time."

The mayor. The mayor was calling me and hoping he wasn't being a bother.

"No, sir," I said. I hate it when I say "sir." It just slipped out.

"I'm in my car just heading over to the Mayfield, now," the mayor said. "I should be there any time, but I wanted to take a minute to let you know what a bang-up job you're doing. You saved the city's butt. We'd gotten a bad start, I'm afraid, with the wrong folks trying to take on this big an event. Well, I wanted to let you know I'm proud of you, Miss Bean."

"Thank you."

"There's been nothing but praise for how well you've planned this event. From the archdiocese, from the city, from the music center, from security. I'd like to show our appreciation. Is there anything I can get for you? Anything you'd like?"

"A free lifetime parking pass for the beach lot in Santa Monica?" I asked, back to my old self.

"Ah, if it were only possible," the mayor said, chuckling, "but, alas, this isn't Chicago."

In awe, I hung up and said, as nonchalantly as I could manage, "The mayor."

"Congratulations," Honnett said.

On the multiple screens on the wall, we could see guests arriving on the red carpet in front of the fountains as well as several views of the Otis Mayfield. One monitor displayed the slowly panning overhead view from the blimp, showing the entire auditorium complex below with the streets clogged with traffic.

On one screen, we could see the news reporter talking to the later-arriving dignitaries. On another screen, one marked Camera 6, Bill the cameraman was taking random shots of people coming out of the security tent. This camera shot was not being broadcast live, but was probably being saved to tape for a later program where an editor would select shots to compile a montage of arrivals and party-goers.

A group of three nuns in black habits walked out of the security tent and headed for the main doors of the Mayfield. A guard there opened the door for them to enter. Right behind them was a face I would never forget. It was the dark-haired, out-of-shape, red-faced bastard who had accosted me in the parking lot of St. Bede's Church.

''Honnett,'' I said. My voice must have been pretty charged, because I grabbed the attention of everyone working in that small room.

The director even paused between saying ''Ready Camera Four . . .'' and the next command to his assistant, which should have been ''Take Four.''

Instead, all of KTLA's viewers were momentarily stuck on the shot coming from Camera 1, the closeup of the anchorman back in KTLA's studio, while I blurted out to the whole control truck, ''That's the man who attacked me at the church!''

The director urgently spoke into his headset, ''Okay Bill, get focus on the guy in the navy blazer. Ready Six, take Six!''

Broadcast live all over the city was a closeup of the man who had tried to scare me off from working on this event. I was too excited to stay seated.

''Are you sure?'' Honnett asked, while simultaneously giving directions into his radio.

''Positive,'' I said.

I could hear the anchorman's voice talking over the live video shot of my attacker, who was now walking across the open plaza toward the entrance of the Mayfield. The announcer was saying that they had received word that this man may be wanted by the police. I'd just heard the assistant director speaking almost the same exact words into his headset the moment before. These boys were fast.

Into the picture stepped a half dozen plainclothesmen, who circled my nemesis. All of this was going out live to the city.

"Get his badge," the director whispered into the headset to his cameraman.

The shot on our monitor zoomed and quickly pulled into focus. The badge read Michael Stone.

"The name mean anything to you?" Honnett asked from the door of the truck, about to charge out.

"Nothing," I said. "But it's him."

Honnett left the booth and the voiceover of the announcer kept repeating the very little that was known about the situation they had been lucky enough to have fall into their laps.

"Apparently," the man's voice announced, "this man, Michael Stone, is being detained by security forces including the LAPD, the FBI, and we understand, even members of the pope's own Swiss guard. It's interesting to note that the Swiss guard, when traveling with the pope, forego their customary uniforms the world has grown to love with the bright red and yellow stripes . . ."

"Ready Camera Two . . . take Two" the director instructed.

By now more cameramen had gotten into position. Camera 2 had a different angle, showing the phalanx of security operatives surrounding Stone and moving him out of sight into the white tent.

As Camera 2 pulled in to follow their retreating backs, the director was readying the next shot. "Okay, ready Camera One . . . Take One". He snapped his fingers, giving the exact cue for the live cut to the technical director, who was pushing the buttons on the console. As the shot changed on the director's monitor, which displayed the show as it was being broadcast to the folks at home, I watched as the mayor's limousine pulled up and the field reporter began to inform the people at home that Mayor Burke had arrived.

My radio squawked and I answered. Wesley was wondering where the heck I was. He told me Arlo had been there a while and was looking for me. He said Holly still couldn't locate Donald and she was getting antsy. And, he'd just heard from Xavier that the pope was going to be delayed. I looked at my watch. It was already nearly eight o'clock. We agreed to meet up in the main theater/ballroom, where the doors would be opened to the throng in five minutes.

As I stepped to the door of the truck I noticed on the broadcast monitor that Mayor Burke and his entourage did not go through the main security checkpoint, but proceeded directly to the pavilion. The mayor was just outside, only a few steps away from where this KTLA truck was parked, and if I opened the door I would probably see him. I was about to do just that when out of the corner of my eye, something caused me to stop and do a double take. The director had cut to another camera angle.

Victor Zoda, smiling and waving to the crowds in the temporary grandstands, was walking into the main entrance of the Otis Mayfield Pavilion. He had not been detained, as Detective Chuck Honnett had assured me. He had bypassed the security checkpoint because he was in the mayor's party.

In a panic, I pulled open the door. The bright Sunday morning light dazzled me as I stepped out of the dark control booth truck. Shielding my eyes, I tried to get my bearings in the real world and then I spotted the tail end of the mayor's entourage across the large open square as they slipped inside the Mayfield. I became aware of voices around me, as news producers followed me out of the truck with questions. Who was that man, Michael Stone, anyway? Why was he being held?

It was not Michael Stone that I was worried about. I began running. I had to find Honnett. Victor Zoda had not been stopped by security. And now, Victor Zoda was inside the most rigorously guarded building in Los Angeles.

Chapter 24

I ran as quickly as I could, whipping across the plaza, past the fountain, and up the steps of the Mayfield Pavilion. My black shoes had tall chunky heels and a thick ankle strap, so at least I didn't run out of them. At the door to the Mayfield, there was a line of guests waiting to be admitted. I pushed to the front, excusing myself as I elbowed aside the wife of the city's chief of police.

"You have a security band radio," I said to the guard at the door. "Call Detective Chuck Honnett!" The guard was asking me to slow down and repeat that name. Hell! I waved my badge in his face and entered the noisy foyer of the Mayfield. Just as I stepped inside, I saw two thousand expectant guests begin gathering outside the doors of the auditorium. As I moved among them, looking for Zoda, looking for Honnett, looking for someone, anyone, the inner doors opened and the crush of the well-dressed and well-connected attendees surged towards the reconfigured theater.

The sounds of oohs and ahs rippled back toward me as each wave of guests entered the space, amazed by the splendor, startled to find themselves stepping upon a suspended floor with an ethereal glow. Damn it! I love this part of the event. And instead of standing with Wesley, feeling duly proud, I was desperate to get to Honnett so he could round up Zoda.

The guests had been assigned tables according to a carefully worked out seating chart. The design of that chart had taken the full attention for two weeks of a committee of fourteen from the mayor's office, ten from the county supervisor's office, and Cardinal O'Grady's four top aides.

I scanned the crowd, but there were too many suits, too much movement. As the guests were finding their tables and chatting with friends, I kept my eye out for Zoda. I immediately looked at the mayor's table. No one was there yet.

I felt a sudden increase in heat, a frisson of electric current as someone approached from behind and touched my elbow. I jumped from the warmth of that contact and spun to see Chuck Honnett, tall and at ease, as always.

"Simmer down," Honnett said, kindly. "It's me."

Like that wasn't the whole problem.

"My God, I'm so happy you found me," I said, taking a deep breath, my first in too long a time.

"Don't worry. We got Zoda. The security boys just called. They're holding Zoda in the tent outside."

"Thank goodness," I said, relieved. The kaleidoscope of the room seemed to focus back to its usual appearance. I could now actually make out faces of people I recognized. Many of the county supervisors were present, and I was surprised to see a familiar ponytail over the collar of a tailored suit coat. I didn't see the man's face, but I thought it must have been Carlos Schwartz. Fancy that. I even spotted the mayor in the crowd. Zoda was no longer with his group.

"We picked up that fellow, Michael Stone," Honnett said, as we continued to watch the people find their places and pick up their menus. "I think he's the guy, all right. His sister-in-law is miserable, so he's been taking it upon himself to harass you."

I looked at him utterly confused.

"She and her guild at St. Bartholomew's were originally in charge of organizing this party. They do quite a good job, I hear, raising money for their school. But when this job got too political, the mayor stopped making nice with the church and hired you.''

''I knew the city hadn't been satisfied with the previous caterer. I just had no idea I'd replaced a group of well-meaning church ladies.''

''Well, Stone isn't so well-meaning. He just wanted to throw a scare into you, he said. But we'll get his prints, and if they match the ones we found near the power plant downstairs, we can write him up.''

As groups and clusters of guests began to settle into their seats around us, I noticed the woman in the eggplant-colored suit. She had found her table, located near the center of the massive room, and was setting her large tote bag on the empty seat beside her. On the other side of the tote bag sat a tall nun.

I thought I'd better warn the sister to keep her plate as far away as possible from that tote bag. And then I relaxed. Looking closely, I realized it was Holly. And Holly could fend for herself.

The reaction to our menu was gratifying. As waiters circulated, collecting the engraved order forms from each table, I could hear comments from those sitting closest to me.

''I love asparagus,'' I heard one woman say to her companion.

I smiled and Honnett looked over at me, interested.

''What's that?'' he asked.

''We're trying some unusual combinations. This is a pretty conservative crowd, so there was a question if all the items would fly. That woman mentioned my favorite, the asparagus frittata with avocado and bacon in warm lemon vinaigrette.''

Honnett gave me a full look into his clear blue eyes and said, smiling slowly, ''You make me hungry.''

I laughed.

Allen, my favorite waiter, came up to me with a Diet Coke, which I will happily drink any time of the day.

''Madeline, we got a pair of Demento sisters at Table

Nineteen. You gotta check them out. They're sitting right next to Arlo,'' Allen said, amused.

I looked back over to the table in the center of the room. Two plump thirtysomething women were huddled together, talking to a waitress. Near them, Arlo was seated, looking forlorn. Next to Arlo was Sister Holly, then a tote bag full of doggie and finally eggplant woman. What a table. I could see Arlo craning his neck around and knew he was bugged I hadn't said hello.

'' 'Scuse me,'' I said to Honnett, and turned to Allen and whispered, ''bring the lieutenant here some of the asparagus frittata.''

I drifted my way among the round tables, with their candles all aglow, brushing against the backs of chairs covered in gold embroidered gauze, smelling the lovely scent of the two thousand flower garlands in the room.

As I worked my way to Table Nineteen, I overheard a conversation that had been in progress for some time.

''I can't eat this!'' one of the women was saying, plaintively, to the waitress as I approached.

''It's not on our list,'' said the other woman. ''Haven't you got anything we can eat?''

''I'm sure we can prepare something,'' the waitress said. By her cheerfulness, I could tell she was on a tight schedule and had spent too much time with these ladies.

''We can eat broccoli,'' one woman said to the other, after digging through her bag and coming up with a wrinkled sheet of paper.

''But only with celery,'' the other said, looking at the list.

''We don't have broccoli,'' the waitress replied.

Arlo looked up and saw me there. ''This has been going on for ten minutes,'' he whispered. ''If they don't shut up and eat something I'm going to shoot myself.''

''Cope, Arlo,'' I said.

''Mad!'' Holly was seated next to Arlo. ''Have you seen Donald? I'm really worried about him.''

"Did you come here together this morning?" I asked her, concerned.

"Yep. And he went to the men's room and that's the last I saw of him."

"He'll turn up," I said. "I'll mention it to Honnett, okay? They'll find him for you."

"Thanks, Mad. You're a doll."

"So, 'doll,' " Arlo said, putting his arm around me. With Arlo seated at the table and me standing, that meant his hand was resting on my, well, behind. He seemed content. I kept looking over my shoulder to see if the table of nuns next to us was praying for my soul.

"This won't do," said the plump woman to her friend across the table.

The waitress had just brought her a dish of melon.

"We can't eat fruit until after two o'clock. You're going to have to take this away."

"Right now," the second woman agreed.

The first woman took a large zip-top bag out of her purse. It was filled with raw celery. The other woman helped herself to a stalk and sprayed it with some kind of diet dressing in what looked like a Windex bottle.

"I need to go find Xavier," I told Arlo. "The pope is delayed and I better find out when he's expected."

"Hang on a sec, I need to talk to you," Arlo said.

"Can't it wait?" I asked, distracted with the demands of running a party that's begun to get challenging.

"I need to talk to you alone."

I looked at Arlo and inwardly sighed. "C'mon," I told him, and led him, weaving between tables, across the glowing floor, and out through a side exit into a service hallway.

"Okay," I said. "I don't have much time, here, but you got me. What?"

"You sure you can talk now?" Arlo asked. The weasel.

"Arlo."

"Okay. Look. I think we should stop seeing each other for a while."

"What was that?" I asked, not sure for a moment where

the punch that knocked the wind out of me came from.

"You need space. I need space. It's for the best, right?"

"Space? Space!" I was dizzy. "Arlo, people needed space in the seventies. We were kids in the seventies. What are you talking about?"

"You never wanted a commitment, so I never pushed you. You always wanted to have your independence. And that was fine. But now, I think it's time to grow up."

The irony. Arlo lecturing me about growing up. I could almost laugh if my head wasn't suddenly aching so hard.

"Arlo," I said in a slow, calm voice. "Arlo, the pope will be here in a few minutes. I am in charge here. I'd love to talk to you about 'space' any other time. But for the moment, you must excuse me."

"See what I mean? You can't even have a simple conversation about our relationship without running away."

"Okay, I get your point. But this is not a good . . ."

Down the service aisle, far away, still out of sight, we could hear a strange, deep rumbling. The noise grew louder and louder.

Arlo looked at me quizzically. "What is it?" he asked, trying to make sense of the sound of galloping that was coming towards us.

"Stampede!" I yelled at Arlo, and pulled him ahead, as fast as I could drag him.

I pushed open the door into the main hall and hurried Arlo away from the opening. Five seconds later a rush of waiters carrying trays piled with breakfast entrees descended upon us. They swarmed out of the doorways into the hall and made a rapid move towards their tables. Each silver-domed dish was set down at once in front of each guest. There was a smattering of applause as the guests were riveted by the unexpected service.

Meanwhile, Arlo sat back down at Table Nineteen and began talking to Holly. I wondered if he was casually mentioning that he had just broken up a relationship that had been the longest one either of us had ever sustained.

I moved out to the foyer, which was now a vast empty

area patrolled by dozens of cops. Wesley spotted me and came over.

"We can't seem to find Brother Xavier."

"Isn't he on a radio?" I asked. Security had their own network of Motorolas, and so had we.

"Yes. But he's not answering. And we just heard that the pope should be here any minute."

"Great," I said, checking my watch. It was eight-thirty. He'd made it after all. "Holly's worried. Has anyone seen Donald?"

"No," Wes said, subdued.

"Wesley, what aren't you telling me?"

"Nothing," Wes said, in a voice that wasn't all that convincing.

I was about to grill him further when Honnett joined us. Almost at once, Wes had an "emergency" and had to go fix it.

"He's not too fond of me, is he?" Honnett asked.

"Can you blame him?" I asked.

"Guess not. Things seem to be going well. We caught some bad guys, which always gets my blood going. And the mayor and the chief of police look pretty happy. That's saying something. And your party food here looked swell."

I remembered that I'd had Allen bring Honnett a meal. "Did you like the frittata?" I asked.

"Oh, it looked real good. But I can't eat anything while I'm on duty."

"Really? I thought that rule had to do with alcohol."

"Any and all distractions."

"Oh."

Honnett looked me over and sighed. "You want to know what your trouble is?"

I must say that is about my least favorite question in the universe. It means someone is about to analyze your life and find you at fault.

"Okay, Honnett, why don't you go ahead and tell me. My boyfriend, Arlo, just decided to end our relationship after three and a half years, so I expect this is my morning for insight. Let 'er rip.''

He leaned against the railing and looked down at me.

''When did you start splintering men into need groups?''

''Pardon me?''

''Or have you always done that? You know you figure out what you need and then you find yourself a guy to take care of it.''

''I do not.''

''No? You need a soul mate, you run to Wesley. For jokes, you've got Arlo. You need money, and some Hollywood producer like Bruno Huntley comes to mind.''

''Are you saying I would use a man to get money?'' I was shocked.

''Of course not. You work for your money. But you always have some guy on the line who can hire your company. I'm just talking about 'needs' mentality, here.''

''Oh, really,'' I said, totally insulted. ''And what do I do for sex?''

''For sex, I guess Arlo's been the starter. But I'd say lately you've been auditioning me for the role,'' Honnett said.

''My God!'' I said, blaspheming just moments before the Holy Father was scheduled to arrive. ''You must be crazy. Where did you ever get such a load of shit?''

''Hear me out,'' Honnett said.

''I will not! The arrogance,'' I said, shaking my head. ''How did my life get filled up with so many severely flawed men?''

''Don't you know?'' Honnett asked, in a soft drawl. ''You seek us out.''

''What!''

''We may be jerks. I don't doubt we are. But at least you can count on us. Hell, we're the least likely men in the world to run off and become a priest.''

I sputtered. What was happening today?

'' 'Big Father' is here,'' said a plainclothesman who I

believe was from the FBI. Even an eight-year-old would figure out he was talking about the pope.

Honnett said, "Catch you later," and walked over to the glass doors to join the other security men.

I turned to go and find Xavier. I knew he would want to be here when the pope arrived. But instead, I bumped into Holly going down a service hall to where the restrooms were located.

"Hi, Holly," I called to her.

She stopped and turned around, waiting for me.

"There's a men's room down this hall," Holly said. "I thought I just better go check it out."

"I'll go with you," I said.

We walked down the long service hall and found ourselves outside an area that was used as a storage room. Across from the storage room was a men's room that was for the use of the Otis Mayfield Pavilion employees.

The entire area looked deserted, since the party was going strong on the other side of the building.

Holly stood outside the men's room and looked at me. "Well, here goes."

She pulled on the handle and nothing happened. She jiggled it. Nothing. She pulled harder.

"Madeline, this door is locked," Holly said, surprised.

"Let me try," I offered. I grabbed onto the handle and gave the door a hard yank. It didn't budge. I thought it was strange. They never lock restrooms.

"Together," I suggested, and Holly and I both gripped the door. "One, two . . . three!"

The stuck door gave way and I waved to Holly. "After you."

Laughing we walked into the men's room together. I dropped my shoulder bag on the floor, holding the door ajar, so we couldn't get locked in. And then, I noticed something odd. When we first opened the door, I'd thought I'd heard some noise coming from inside, but as soon as we entered, it went silent.

"Donald, honey?" Holly called out. Neither of us was

anxious to walk all the way into a men's room, in case a strange man was making use of the facilities.

There was a long pause. Then we heard Donald's voice, "Uh, Holly?" he said, and he walked out of the furthermost stall, the extra-large one that is meant for handicapped use, zipping his fly.

"Sweetie?" Holly said, confused. "Were you just taking the longest whiz on the planet?"

"I, uh . . ." Donald saw me standing back by the entrance to the men's room. "Oh, hi there, Maddie. That door was stuck. I called for help, but then, well . . ."

"Whatcha doing in here all alone all by yourself for so long, you naughty boy?" Holly asked, getting ideas. She began to pull Donald along, moving back toward that furthest stall he'd just emerged from, the one with all the room and the door that could be latched.

I ran over to stop her.

"Wait, Hol. I mean, the pope will be here any second. Is this really the right time to . . ."

We were standing outside the toilet stall at the end of the row. The door stood slightly open, the way Donald had left it. But all of a sudden a movement from inside that end stall caught my eye. It had apparently caught Holly's eye as well. She was closer to the stall than I was. Her view was better. Holly screamed. Then she pushed open the door.

Standing there, buck naked, was the lovely Dottie Moss.

Chapter 25

Holly, her pale skin even paler, ran out of the men's room without a word. Donald, red-faced and stammering, hit his fist on the tile wall and then took off after her.

"Hi, Dottie," I said.

"Well, don't that beat all!" Dottie said, displaying her perfect body without a trace of shame.

I turned to leave the men's room and retrieved my shoulder bag from the floor where it had been holding the door ajar. Could I allow the inevitable? I contemplated the ruckus of having the press discover a guest locked into a faulty john and the headlines if that guest was our own beloved Dottie Moss. Even if she managed to get back into her clothes by then, it wasn't good P.R. Wedging my foot into the doorway, I pulled a spare pad of Post-its from my purse, positioned it between door and frame, and then carefully removed my foot. The yellow pad kept the door just far enough ajar to prevent it from sticking shut again.

Holly and Donald were long gone and the service hallway was deserted. I called on my radio and Wesley answered. The pope had finally arrived, he told me. The mayor and other city officials were delaying their remarks until the pontiff made it to the banquet, but His Holiness was not quite there.

"So is Xavier with the pope?" I asked.

"Nobody's seen Brother Xavier," Wes said. "Perhaps he's with the missing Donald."

"No. Donald's been found," I said. "So you can call those dogs off."

"Good," Wes said over the radio.

"I'm going to look around for Xavier," I said. "Radio me if you see him first."

"Roger that," Wes said.

I did a complete round of the Otis Mayfield complex, from the loading dock, where I saw my Wagoneer proudly occupying its supremely good parking spot, to the steps outside the Mayfield, and back again. By the time I'd retraced my steps, I found myself pulling on random doors, looking into broom closets and empty custodial offices. Every time I saw a security guard or police officer, I told them about Brother Xavier and my search. No one remembered seeing him. When I made it full circle and was back down the original service corridor, I once again noticed the storage room door that was opposite the employee restrooms. Many doors like this one had been locked. But as I tried it, the handle turned.

Startled, I pulled on the door and walked into the darkened room.

"Xavier," I called.

There was no response.

I looked around and saw a roomful of storage boxes, piled into stacks on pallets. One wall featured loading dock bays with motorized garage-style doors. I calculated where I was in the Mayfield complex and figured this storage garage must allow forklifts to move equipment and goods into the facility. High factory-style windows allowed some faint morning light to filter into the space, but the overhead lights were off, and the dimness in the shadows of the mountains of cartons made it difficult to see clearly.

"Hello," I called out. The skin on the back of my neck became chilled.

I pulled out my radio and called for Wesley to pick up. In a few moments he did.

"Where are you?" he asked.

"Some storage area downstairs near the employee restrooms,'' I said. ''I wonder if you could get some security guys to meet me down here.''

''Something wrong?'' Wes asked, his voice sharp.

''Not really. I'm just feeling spooky.''

''Well we've got a little situation going on up here,'' Wes said calmly. ''They seem to have lost the pope . . .''

I looked at the black handheld Motorola with its aggressive rubberized antenna.

''. . . so the security team is pretty much up to their ass in . . .''

''Wes, how can someone lose the pope?''

''That, my dear, is the question of the day up here. Luckily, no one inside the banquet hall has heard this bit of strange news. I think they are just going to inform the mayor, now.''

''Have I missed anything else?''

''We had a wonderful compliment on your spiced raisin waffles from Julia Child.''

I was missing everything.

''Call me when they find the pontiff,'' I said, and then signed off.

I had become used to the dim stillness of the room, so I nearly fainted when a voice from very close behind me said, ''Madeline?''

I spun. Moving quickly down the row, I found him. Behind the second nearest pallet of boxes, lying prone on a full-sized crate.

''Xavier! What happened? Are you all right?''

''Madeline,'' he said again, his voice thick like he was just waking up.

''Did you fall?'' I was at his side, looking at him, giving him my arm to help him sit up atop the low crate. When I'd pulled him up I noticed his left arm was caught in something. I looked close. He was handcuffed to the metal handle on the crate.

''Oh my God.''

''I'm okay,'' Xavier said, feeling gently along the back of his head.

"Who did this to you?"

"I'm not sure. I was told to come here. Some change in the pope's plans. What happened after I got here, I just don't remember. I think I may have been ambushed by some old man. Does that make sense?"

"Victor Zoda," I said, swearing to myself and then feeling guilty about it in front of Xav. "Don't worry," I told him. "The police already have him. This is somehow connected to Zoda's past in Rome." I filled him in quickly.

"But what time is it? Has the pope arrived?" Xav asked, concerned that he was not at his post.

"I'm told he's here." Why get Xav all worked up about the pontiff's present whereabouts when there wasn't a thing he could do about it handcuffed to a crate.

I tried getting Wes on the radio.

"Madeline," Xavier said, looking at me with a jumble of emotions, revealing more of his feelings than he'd let show since he'd come back to town. He reached his free right hand out and put it on mine, lowering the radio from my ear.

Just then the radio chirped to life. Wesley listened to my story and he said he'd tell the cops.

"While we wait here," Xavier said, speaking carefully, "maybe we can talk."

I perched myself on a large carton next to his crate, trying to maintain some dignity in my finest clothes. The metallic skirt, being rather tight, crept up.

"So," I said. "Here we are."

"You look beautiful, Maddie," Xavier said with a sigh.

"So do you. I guess there's no chance we could start dating again, huh?" I asked, mostly just to keep it light.

"Jesuits don't date."

"I didn't really think so."

"But we can have friends of the opposite sex," Xav said, seriously.

I watched his eyes as they inadvertently swept over my hips and legs and then quickly looked away.

I didn't have the strength, anymore, to avoid the truth. I

don't know. Maybe it was the morning I'd been having. I tried the direct approach.

"I know you're a Jesuit now, Xavier, but can you actually stop yourself from being attracted to a woman?"

"No," he confessed, looking directly at me.

Tears sprang up, just like that, and rested inside my lower lids.

"Maddie, nothing happens to us at the time of entering the seminary that eliminates normal human needs."

"What about normal human desires?" I asked, noticing the clench of his strong jaw, the softness of his wide mouth.

"As celibate people," he said carefully, "we choose to channel these feelings and express our love for others in a wide range of means other than in . . . well, physical expressions."

"Ah," I said.

Xavier felt gently along the back of his head, moving his fingers through his thick blond hair, where I imagined he'd discovered quite a lump.

Propped up against the stiff carton, I shifted my weight, which seemed to bring a bit of comfort to my back but also hiked my skirt a few inches higher. I tugged it back down. When I looked up, Xavier was staring at me.

"Maddie, I loved you. You cannot doubt that, can you?"

"Oh, of course not." A single tear escaped, but I tried to ignore it.

"How can I explain? I knew I had a calling. I felt the pull of it. My family was always religious, you knew that."

"But I told you I would convert to Catholicism," I said, rushing in. "I thought that was what you wanted."

"My sister, Teresa, talked to me, Maddie."

Teresa? I suddenly felt I was finally going to hear the truth. His twin sister, Teresa, lived back with his family in Philadelphia. At least she did when Xavier and I had been engaged.

"What about Teresa?" I asked, perhaps a little too harshly. "Did she tell you I would ruin your life? Does she hate me so much?" I began to suspect that his jealous twin had somehow gotten to Xavier all those years ago, turned him against me so she could bring him back east, back to the family.

"Maddie, Teresa is dead, may God rest her soul."

That stopped me cold. How anyone who hadn't been raised a Catholic could so swiftly be overtaken with guilt, I couldn't say, but I started blathering, "Oh, Xavier. Oh I'm so sorry. Why didn't you ever tell me?" I moved from my perch and came to sit next to him on the large crate.

"Teresa had wanted to become a nun. But her health was never good. When she found out she was not strong enough to make it into a convent, she called me. We talked about our dreams as kids. We had each of us felt that our relationship with God gave us strength, gave our lives special meaning. I was reminded, Madeline, of who I have always wanted to be. When I realized Teresa might not live, I was struck by what I had to do. Can you understand? I loved you, but I couldn't promise that I would always be happy with the life we had planned. Talking with my sister, I felt strong enough to make the commitment I needed to make. To join the Society of Jesus. To enter the novitiate. To take vows of poverty and chastity and obedience."

"I see," I said. "And what does your order suggest a future priest should do with the girl you've fallen in love with?"

I was sitting so close to Xav that our shoulders were almost rubbing. When he turned to look at me we were close enough to kiss. He didn't pull away.

"The basic responsibility is to preserve our commitment to our life in Christ," Xav said, reaching for my hand.

"And what happens to the poor girl who loves you?"

"Sometimes that means developing the relationship with the woman, but within the bounds of one's commitments to celibacy."

"I see," I said, barely audible, but close to his ear. "But you disappeared."

"Other times," Xav continued, avoiding my eyes, "if the stress of the temptation seems too great, it may be necessary to drop the person out of one's life all together.''

I winced in pain.

''Maddie, what can I do to make you feel better?''

I looked at his blue eyes. Sitting so close, I could smell the clean soap smell of his face and neck.

''Hold me,'' I said.

Xavier paused. Then he lifted his chained arm as high as it would go and circled it around me. It's what I wanted, but it only made the hurting worse. I melted into him, tears falling now.

''How can I feel good about my decision, Maddie, when it causes you so much pain? Can't you see what I did was for the best? I have an opportunity to serve God. I feel blessed to live this life. And I believe you are living a better life as well.''

''That's just not true,'' I said fiercely. ''Don't twist this. It may have been the best decision for you, Xavier, but leave me out of it.''

''Really? That's not how it looks. You wanted to follow me, Maddie. You wanted to help me be a great chef. But what kind of life would it have been for you?''

''Oh, Xavier,'' I said, thoroughly frustrated. ''You're a genius in the kitchen. You were so talented.''

''No, Maddie. You were always the gifted one. Don't you see? You could always do anything with food and people. If we'd gone on together, you might have taken a back seat as you helped me move ahead. Maybe this was really the way things were meant to be. Perhaps God meant for you to face this challenge and become your own person. Look where you are today. Look how strong you are.''

I rested my head on his chest and thought about the years.

''I don't think God was planning anything for me,'' I said.

''You know how frustrated you get with me when I tell you that sometimes I can't always understand God's plan?''

I nodded against his shirt.

''But, Maddie, sometimes I suspect you can. You can

understand things other people can't. That understanding, that may just be your calling. That's why it always made you crazy when you couldn't figure everything out at once. That's why you get so burnt up when you do figure things out and no one will pay attention.''

I sat straight up, about to tell him how wrong he was about me. Tell him he had no idea who I was. Tell him that God was not pulling my strings. But, suddenly, I couldn't. Instead, I felt this odd sensation that perhaps, after all, there might be one individual on earth who truly did understand me.

I heard the door open to the storage room. Our rescuers here at last. I hoped it was someone with a key to Xavier's handcuffs. I was about to call out when a voice spoke up from beyond the stacks of boxes.

''Young man? Are you awake? I'm afraid I must finish some unpleasant business.''

It was the voice of Victor Zoda.

Chapter 26

I nearly fell off the crate. I just managed to recover my balance enough to roll into a crouch and hide behind a pile of empty cardboard boxes stacked nearby. The noise I made caught Zoda's attention as he rounded the corner. I didn't think he saw me.

"What was that noise?" Zoda demanded from Xavier. With a frightening amount of energy for such an old man, he pulled at the handcuffs, making certain they were secure.

"Some boxes fell over," Xav said. "I was hoping the noise might get someone's attention."

"You have my attention, young man," Zoda said, sternly, "so stop that noisemaking at once."

"Who are you?" Xavier asked. "What is this all about? I'm a Jesuit . . ."

"A priest, yes I know," Zoda said, rubbing his bald head with one hand in a nervous gesture. "But you should have left me alone. There is nothing worse than a nosy priest."

"You're making a mistake," Xavier tried to explain. "I don't even know who you are."

"Victor Zoda? You expect me to believe you have never heard of me, sir? You've been stalking me, dogging my steps. I am an old man. I will not permit it."

"Mr. Zoda, I am a Jesuit Brother. Surely you must understand that I've dedicated my life to helping people in trouble. Maybe if you told me what your . . ."

"Enough talking," Zoda said, when he had finally satisfied himself that the handcuffs were intact.

"Why did you attack me? If you're planning to harm the Holy Father, I must warn you . . ."

At that Zoda began laughing, as loud and as hearty a laugh as one would expect to come from a man half his age.

"Please, dear God, you can't mean to injure His Holiness," Xavier said, nearly distraught.

"You don't know the joke," Victor was saying, as he moved around into a clear spot. "If you only knew the lengths to which I have . . ."

I jumped off the highest pallet, straight onto Victor's back. In an instant I had crushed the old man, landing spread-eagled atop him, his now crumpled body breaking my fall.

"Madeline!" Xavier shouted.

Before I could speak, the man beneath me began to squirm, lashing out with hands and feet. Twisting violently, Zoda almost overturned me with the strength of one agitated kick. Quickly, I drew up on one knee and then pounded the force of my body onto him again, slamming down hard on the man's mid-back. While I had him on his stomach, I clutched about wildly, trying to seize one of his flailing arms.

He was yelling incoherently, stronger than an old man should be, resistant as a steel spring, heaving, trying to buck me off. One more desperate lunge and, at last, I grabbed hold of his swinging right arm and pinned it down. Then I yanked it with all my power up behind his shoulder blade until I believed it was close to breaking.

"Stop!" he screamed.

"Maddie, you're hurting him," Xavier said, shocked.

"Please, can we worry about that later!"

With his arm pinned back high, Zoda stopped wriggling so much. Only on his stomach, I knew, could a man be restrained.

Zoda sputtered. "What insanity . . . ! Have you gone mad? What do you want from me?"

In the elegant surprise of my attack, he had barely gotten a look at me. And in that moment, I felt exultant. I had truly done it. For once, I had taken action. No more swearing after the tailgate of trucks. No more slinking off in fear into my own dumbwaiter. With the extreme abuse I'd taken that morning, I didn't need a shrink to tell me what I was doing with all my pent-up anger and frustration. This was probably as emotionally healthy as I was going to get all year.

"Mr. Zoda. Victor," I said. "Don't you remember me? I visited you only last night."

"What do you want?" he hissed.

"Why didn't you tell me the full story last night, Mr. Zoda? You enjoyed talking so much about the old days, why leave out the part where you smuggled Nazi war criminal scum into South America?"

"What do you know?" he asked, as he once again came alive beneath me, jerking almost out of my grasp. I pulled his right arm even tighter and he yelped loudly.

"Tell us about the Nazis," I yelled, breathing heavily, angrier than I can ever remember being.

"It's nothing. You know nothing," he said, now lying still, but with his muscles tightly flexed. "I am Victor Zoda, a respected man in my community. Do you realize how much money I have donated to my church, Miss Bean? I have given over twenty-five million dollars! Do you think of me as a criminal? Well, I can assure you no one else in this building does."

"They don't know you like we do, Victor," I said. "Tell Brother Xavier about *Stille Hilfe*."

The man seemed to wilt beneath me. I felt the energy ebb away from his resistance. But I couldn't let down my guard, not until someone came to take charge.

This position, me astride Victor Zoda forcing his right arm up behind his back, was problematic. It meant I couldn't reach my radio, which had smashed to the floor and skittered away down the aisle, when I'd made my jump. I still had my bag over my shoulder, but I couldn't loosen my hold on Zoda to feel around for my cell phone. And Xavier, handcuffed five feet away, was of no use.

"*Stille Hilfe*," I prompted.

"Who told you about that?" he asked. "Did the same person ever tell you how many Jews Victor Zoda saved? It's true. I saved more lives than any priest in this building," he said.

"What's he talking about?" Xavier asked me.

"In the late thirties, I had a job in the Mussolini government. Not a grand job, you would probably tell me. How could I not be disappointed when my promotions did not come through? With my qualifications, it was preposterous! Politics. But I learned quickly. I made it my business to become friendly with the powerful people I met."

"You mean with Nazis, don't you?"

"Don't be so quick to judge. During the war, I also had special friends inside the Vatican. Boyhood friends, men I'd grown up with. Some of these priests knew of families, Jews who needed special help, but what could the priests do? Their hands were tied. It was *I* who saved these wretched men, *I* who took the risk, *I* who gave them back their lives. My access to government schedules and the falsified travel papers procured through my Vatican sources permitted many, many Jews to get out of Europe alive, one step ahead of the Gestapo."

"For how much money?" I asked him, coldly.

"Money was the key, Miss Bean. Nothing happened without money. Yes, the Jews paid. They paid dearly, as who would not if it was their own children's necks they wished to save? Are you suggesting I should not have collected their payment? Are you so naïve to expect men to risk their lives without hope of profit?"

"And while you were getting rich off your 'humanitarian' scheme, you somehow kept this black market activity from the notice of your Nazi friends."

"Of course. I was clever. I told you."

"Then tell us about *Stille Hilfe*," I said, grimly.

"When the war began to go badly for the Third Reich,

there were many Nazi officers who were anxious to escape Europe with their lives. These were men I had become friendly with, in the line of my work, men of great wealth."

"Stolen wealth, you mean. The money and jewels and artwork of the continent, stolen by murdering thugs."

"Stolen or not, these objects were worth unspeakable amounts of money. Some items were indeed priceless. This is what they offered me to get them to South America before they were captured by the Allies and put on trial for their crimes. And think, the underground path out of Europe had already been established and I controlled the gate."

"So you used your contacts within the Vatican?"

"The Vatican was an independent state. As such they were permitted to issue their own travel visas for the use of clerics," Zoda said. "This is how my Jews escaped. Do you enjoy the irony? My Jews traveled in cassocks with false papers which showed them to be priests traveling to a mission in South America."

"So while some helpful priest arranged for documents to allow Jewish families to escape those monsters, you lined your pockets with those families' life savings. And if that wasn't despicable enough, you used the same unwitting priest's kindness to rescue the Nazi monsters when their money looked better."

I was sick to think I was that close to such a villain. Such callous, commerce-minded evil.

"Maddie, don't," Xavier said.

I looked down and realized I was close to breaking Zoda's arm.

"Please, I told you what you wanted to hear. These stories are old. The men we speak of are dead. Of what importance are these ancient matters today? Let me up and . . ."

"Let you up?" I screamed. "You ambushed an innocent Jesuit brother and murdered him. Why did you kill Brother Frank del Valle? What madness was that?"

"It was a mistake," Zoda said, giving in to his own tears. "I never meant . . ."

"Madeline, is this true?" Xavier asked.

"He was after you, Xavier," I said, watching Xav's face lose its color as he took in the news. Then I turned back to the old man who lay quietly on the ground, and demanded, "Weren't you?"

Zoda said nothing.

"Was it Picca who acquired the travel documents for you back in Rome?" I asked.

"Through him. He was not important enough yet. But he knew men who were."

"So Monsignor Picca thought you were a hero," I said, disgusted with how easily Zoda had fooled everyone all these years. He was a respected man in the community. It was shocking.

"Benny knew the good I had done. Although he had sworn to keep silent about our clandestine arrangements to help the Jews escape from Rome, he knew," Zoda said, actually sounding proud of himself.

"We were from the old country together," Zoda continued, "and we had interests in common. Naturally, I saw him often. Then, one day last week, I noticed a diocesan newsletter on his desk. A notice was posted by a Brother Xavier asking for information about a certain Jesuit brother named Ugo. Of course, Benny remembered Brother Ugo from the old days. He told me he planned to respond to the notice.

"That evening, I called the parish where this Brother Xavier was staying. I was informed he was attending a performance at a television studio. I was able to call a friend and get permission to enter the lot. Once I was there, I sent a note, but when the Jesuit brother I was looking for came to meet me, I saw he was not alone. There was a woman with him. So I stayed away and watched. What else could I do? Of course at that time, I thought I was watching Xavier Jones."

"You meant to find *me*?" Xavier asked, shocked.

"And kill you, Xavier," I said.

"No! I meant to talk with the brother. Why would I kill

anyone? I simply wanted to tell him to leave this ancient issue involving Brother Ugo alone.

"I kept my eye on that trailer he entered. Soon, through the back window, I could see the brother standing all alone. I moved nearer and heard the sound of the shower running, so I took the chance I could have my quiet word with Brother Xavier and be out again before the lady emerged from her bath.

"But when I spoke to the Jesuit in that trailer, he denied everything. Don't you see? I thought he already knew my secrets and was about to reveal them. I couldn't allow that! Not now. Not with the pope coming to see us. I was pushed beyond reason. He denied looking into the matter of Brother Ugo. He even denied that he was Xavier Jones."

I grimaced. Poor Brother Frank. He'd gotten caught up in something he couldn't begin to understand. He tried talking sense to a madman.

"I didn't mean to kill him. But he was holding a statue. A heavy statue. I thought he meant to attack me with it. So I wrestled it away from him. I don't know what happened next. Perhaps he thought I was a thief. He became very agitated that I was in the trailer. When he tried to take the statue back, I swung. The next thing I knew, the man had fallen back onto the bed. I threw down the statue and ran."

"And no one saw you?" I asked, amazed. "No one stopped you?"

"No one looks at an old man," Victor Zoda said, bitterly.

"But why?" Xavier asked, more stressed at listening to this story than I'd ever seen him. "Why kill Frank? Why kill me? What threat did you imagine I could have been to you if I continued my investigation of Brother Ugo the baker?"

Victor Zoda, the man who liked to talk, shut up like a clam.

Zoda had admitted his involvement in the black-market ransom scheme. He'd acknowledged his work for *Stille Hilfe* smuggling top Nazi war criminals to South America.

He'd even confessed to the murder of a young, innocent Jesuit brother in a case of mistaken identity. But he would say not a word more regarding the old, long-forgotten sin that was tied to the mystery of Brother Ugo.

"It has to do with the encyclical, doesn't it?" I prodded him.

Zoda shook his head violently, facedown on the floor of that dim storeroom.

"Pope Pius XI was planning to deliver an encyclical to the world denouncing anti-Semitism and the Nazis. At the end of nineteen thirty-eight, despite the harm it might have done to the Roman Catholic Church, Pius XI was going to stand up to Hitler and demand respect for all human rights."

"He was crazy!" Zoda said, swearing. "He was insane! He was an old, sick man who was about to bring down the church and then who would he help? Would it have served anyone if he had sacrificed forty million Catholics along with some Jews?"

"I think you were more worried about your own little scam," I said to the back of his head, as I held him tight. "If the Catholic world had turned against Hitler, if the war ended, maybe you wouldn't have found yourself such an influential and wealthy man. What had you ever done to deserve respect? Success? You needed the Nazis to continue making your black-market fortune."

"It wasn't my fault. They made me do it," Zoda yelled, in his old hoarse voice.

I was right. And then I thought the entire plot through. "Oh, God," I said, and I rocked back, realizing the full horror of what Zoda must have done in 1939.

In that instant, the man below me kicked around and tried once more to topple me. I yanked up desperately on his right arm, and for all I know I may have broken it, but the tough old demon kicked again. My short skirt ripped up its side seam as I tumbled off onto the floor. I tried to scramble up to my knees and just saw the lethal heel of his shoe coming down as he stomped it into my face.

I moved my head to the left and I swung at his grinding foot with both hands, hauling him back down to the ground with a desperate tug.

This time he didn't land on his stomach, so I leaned my forearm against his Adam's apple, pressing as hard as I could. His fall had him winded. As I straddled him again, I swiped my free hand into my shoulder bag searching for the phone and came up instead with my leather pack. Before Victor could catch his breath, I flipped open the pack with one hand and pulled out my prize.

Chefs like to keep their favorite tools close. I extracted my boning knife and before the old devil knew what was happening, I held the small stunningly sharp blade up to his throat.

Xavier had been praying. At least that's what I thought he was doing. He was speaking in Latin. But when he saw me grab the knife, he spoke to God in English. "Why doesn't someone come?" Xavier asked, agitated beyond his normal calm and frustrated to distraction by being tethered.

I didn't know if he could handle watching me stick the old man. But I was face to face with a murderer. The last time that had happened I was not prepared to fight. I guess I was learning exactly what I had in me.

"Maddie," Xavier said, pleading. "Maddie, don't hurt him. It's not worth it."

"She won't hurt me, young brother," Victor Zoda hissed, spittle flying from the corner of his mouth. "She doesn't have the stomach for blood."

"I wouldn't bet the house in Encino on that, Victor," I said, huffing a little as my breath became more even. "I was quite a good student when it came to butchering. Best in my class. I want you to know that I won an award for boning a turkey. I removed all the major bones from its carcass, while leaving the meat intact. And I did it with my lucky knife." I pressed slightly on the boning knife at his clavicle and I detected the slightly nauseating smell of urine. Since I was astride his chest, I dared not look back.

"Maddie, please," Xavier pleaded with me. At that exact

moment in time, perhaps he, of all people, could imagine in what high regard I held men. "Madeline," he said as if he were trying to find me again, "leave justice to God."

"God's had sixty years, Xavier. Waiting for God's justice has cost Frank del Valle his life. It almost cost you yours. Or don't you care?"

"Maddie, it's your soul I care about. Forget him."

"Before you plead for mercy for this man," I said to Xavier, "perhaps we should hear the entire story of Brother Ugo. After all, that's the terrible secret he's been trying to protect. To keep the secret of Brother Ugo, he was willing to kill Frank and you and even Monsignor Picca."

"NO!" shouted Zoda, his Adam's apple constricting in fright, almost impaling himself on the knife at his throat. "Never, never did I kill Benny. I won't believe these lies."

"You were there!" I shouted. "You saw him the day he died."

"I did nothing to him. We had a disagreement, nothing more. We have always disagreed about the propriety of Benny publishing his research. He and I both believed the information he had gathered was valuable, but we agreed not to release the data in our lifetimes."

"How convenient for you," I said. "As long as Benny's papers weren't published, no one would know about Pope Pius XI's missing encyclical. Without that, they would never guess your treason." I held the knife steady, looking into Zoda's dark eyes. He must have been wondering if I would really stab him. I wondered the same thing, but went on, "All these years and Monsignor Picca never even knew you were involved."

"Involved in what, for God's sake?" Xavier yelled at me, at the breaking point.

"The murder of Pope Pius XI," I said, still staring at the old man beneath me. He spit up into my face, his saliva hitting my cheek and dripping into my hair. I almost reflexively moved my hand to wipe the foul stuff, but I caught myself, and kept my knife in place.

"We warned Pius he was in the gravest danger. The

Nazis were like serpents. I had inside information, you see? From my contacts. They would never permit the encyclical be delivered. The Holy Father was told the Gestapo would see him dead rather than allow him to denounce Hitler to the world. But he wouldn't listen. The Nazis ordered his assassination."

"Maybe so," I said. "But you're the one who did it, didn't you? You killed the pope."

"You know nothing!"

"Xavier," I said, not taking the chance to look away from Zoda. "What is Jesuit Working Rule Six? In that Book of Rules, the Custom Book of the Society of Jesus." I remembered the day I had flipped through that old book. "The Rules of the Cook."

Xavier took a moment to focus on this new shift in subject. "It has to do with the Infirmarian."

"Tell me," I said.

"Rule Six states: 'He shall allow nobody, except the Infirmarian, to cook and prepare food for any special person, nor do the like himself, without permission.' "

"And would Pope Pius XI be considered a 'special person'?"

"Of course. Do you mean to say that when Pius XI visited the papal villa in the Alban Hills in 1939, his own kitchen was sabotaged?"

"Yes. I believe that's what the old Latin confession we found meant. Brother Ugo Spadero, the mild Jesuit baker at the Castel Gandolfo, was guilty of breaking Rule Six. He must have allowed someone to prepare food or drink for the pope, or witnessed it without thinking to speak up. Certainly he couldn't have imagined the evil intent. I'm convinced he noticed someone tampering with the pope's food, someone who was not the Infirmarian, whatever that is."

"The pope's health specialist. A priest, of course," Xavier said, struggling to understand the enormity of what we, alone on earth, had discovered.

"That's why you were so desperate to get your hands

on all the copies we made of Ugo's confession. Isn't that what you did?'' I asked Zoda, who was pale and was now breathing shallowly beneath me. ''Didn't you poison Pope Pius XI to prevent him from ever issuing the secret encyclical? Didn't you then poison Brother Ugo when he threatened to confess to breaking working Rule Six? Standing in that kitchen, doing his daily routine, Ugo was a witness to the food you tampered with as you carried out the Nazi's plan to assassinate the pope.''

Just when I began to worry that the old man might be passing out, he lunged at me with both hands outstretched, grabbing for my throat with his strong bony fingers. Shocked, I watched as his reckless lunge forced the blade of my boning knife to sink into his flesh up to its short hilt. Too late, I pulled it back, and in so doing, opened a wound that began to pump out blood onto my bronze and black checked designer jacket, onto the old man, and all over the floor.

I hadn't heard myself screaming, but I did suddenly notice the room had gone blazingly bright. I looked up, but the overhead lamps were still not on. It was the sun. The clerestory windows were ablaze now that the sun had broken through the morning's thick haze.

Old Victor Zoda was scrambling to his feet, rushing away from us and out the door. Dripping blood, he stumbled into a pile of empty boxes, knocking them off to the side. We now had a clear view to the open door, with the service hall just beyond. Somewhere down that hall Victor Zoda had disappeared.

''Madeline!'' Xavier shouted, ''Give me the radio!''

I swiveled around on the blood-splattered floor, and finally spotted the Motorola, kicked off to one side. I handed it to Xavier and he grabbed me by the arm. ''Don't go after him, Maddie.''

''But . . .''

He pulled me closer. I closed my eyes and I may have been hallucinating from the stress, but I felt his warm mouth kiss mine. In my exhaustion, I slipped back down to the floor and buried my head in my hands.

From the direction of the door, I heard a faint voice say, "*Scuzi,*" and I looked up.

The light in the room had again become dazzlingly bright after all that gloom. With the passing of a cloud, the interior of the storeroom seemed to glow.

At the door stood a figure.

From my spot on the floor, my gaze first swept across the low red shoes. Astonished, my eyes traveled upward. Above the shoes, the hem of a pure white cassock. Above the cassock, I saw the short hooded red cape, the mozzetta. Beneath was the white wool pallium, the traditional circular collar embroidered with six black crosses. From his shoulders hung the pectoral cross made of gold. On his finger, the fisherman's ring.

Legs splayed, skirt ripped up the side, jacket covered in blood, I was not exactly as I had imagined myself upon being presented to the Holy Father. The pope looked at me kindly.

Xavier bowed his head in deference and made the sign of the cross.

The pope, standing utterly alone in the open doorway, spoke several phrases in Latin.

Xavier answered him. I couldn't understand a word of their exchange except for Xavier injecting the name, "Madeline Bean" in a sea of foreign words.

The pontiff's blue eyes looked at me with real caring and then he turned and disappeared down the hall.

"Xavier," I said, not quite believing what had just happened. I pulled myself up to sit by him on the crate he was still manacled to.

"That may be the most amazing experience I will ever have in my life," Xavier said.

"What did he say?"

"He wandered into the wrong men's room. He's been stuck in the bathroom for the last half hour. Only now did he somehow pull the door open to free himself."

"I think the old me would be laughing now," I said,

feeling feeble. "But, Xavier, did the pope . . . see us?"

"I don't know how long he was standing there," Xavier said, "but it was amazing, Maddie. The Holy Father felt the presence of God in this room. He said it felt like a miracle."

Numb from the combination of fighting a madman, kissing my old love goodbye, and having an impromptu audience with the pope, I said, "It's a miracle I haven't lost it."

Chapter 27

We pulled up to the valet attendant in front of Cucina Paradiso. Stepping out of the Wagoneer, I noticed the night breeze coming off the ocean, clean and cool. The fresh air was the second good reason to drive out to Redondo Beach. The first was the incredible food.

Over the past week, the press dubbed the pope's reception a stunning success. The planning, the menu, the VIPs, the fashions, the décor and even the traffic coordination had been praised on newsprint and on networks, from *People* magazine to the *Society of Jesus Weekly*. Oddly, the juiciest story—how the pope accidentally got stuck in the john—escaped notice from the army of reporters. I put it down to the masterful control the Vatican had over news leaks and the fact that the agencies responsible for the pope's security were too damn embarrassed.

The past week had been one of recognition, congratulation, and mostly recuperation. And now, five days later, Wesley and Holly and I were ready to party the way we like best. We intended to eat, big time.

Jill met us at the door with a warm welcome and showed us immediately to our table. We like to sit in the smaller room on the side, the one lined with mahogany wine racks behind glass. Our table, topped with its fresh off-white cloth, was already set with a bottle of 1985 Sassicaia, perhaps the greatest of the Italian reds. We were expected.

Our celebratory meals were, by tradition, date free,

which was actually a blessing considering the state Holly and I found ourselves in. As we took our seats, Oratzio came to pour our wine and talk about the menu. This process can take the better part of ten minutes, as Wes inquires into the ingredients that are exciting and we swap gossip on our friends in the cooking community. Someone whose restaurant opening has been delayed. Another who has decided to go back to Cannes. The subtle change in the taste of the Sonoma lamb this season. Like that.

Because we love the chef here, Wes suggested to just let Alex decide what to send us. And we finally settled down to talk.

"So," Wes started, "shall we begin with a toast?"

We lifted our glasses.

"To friends," Wes said.

"To enemies," Holly offered.

"L'chaim," I added, surprised to hear myself speaking Yiddish.

"Now," Wes continued, setting down his goblet. "What's a safe subject here, folks?"

"I'll start," Holly said, draining her glass and reaching for the bottle to pour herself another. "Don't everyone blow a gasket, but Donald and I are all patched up. We got it all worked out and everything."

In the past week, Holly had said not a word about what was going on between Donald and herself. Wes and I had been too worried about her hurt feelings to bring it up, but to be honest, we were both dying to know. Each day, Wes would call me and ask if I'd heard anything. Each day, I told Wes, "Let's give her a little more time." It seemed like time was finally up.

"But I've really got to apologize to you two. As you guys know, I left the pope's breakfast before the event was over, which was not a very professional thing to do. I'm really sorry."

"Don't be nuts," I said. "You weren't officially working it."

"Still," Holly said, sipping more wine, "it was our gig and I blew out."

"And you did miss the governor's speech with his amazing joke about the rabbi and the priest and the minister," Wes teased her.

"You guys are so great to me," Holly said. "Anyway, I haven't been talking about what's been going on in my life lately because I had a pretty big shock, as you know."

I thought about the sight of Donald tugging up his zipper while Dottie Moss stood stark naked in the men's room stall. A pretty big shock, indeed.

"But everything is great now, so don't worry."

"I think we're missing a few minor details," Wes prompted her, impatient for the nitty-gritty.

"I wouldn't talk to him, was my problem. I was so damn mad at everyone, I wouldn't even take Donald's calls. Then, this afternoon, he came over to the duplex and kept banging at the door until I couldn't stand it anymore. We talked it all out."

"Wow," I said. I was surprised that Holly had the strength to keep this whole story bottled up inside on the ride out to the restaurant. I was beginning to suspect the young lady was growing up a little. I sighed, proud of her.

"I guess it had to happen sometime. I mean about Donald and his intro to Hollywood. He's been living like this fantasy existence out here, never being shit on, never getting screwed. I mean, who lives like that out here?"

We shook our heads. It is almost impossible to become too jaded about this business. It wreaks its nasty havoc just about everywhere.

"So he gets his first movie made, groovy. And he like rules at the box office. So why should I have expected it all to turn out right?"

"Why shouldn't you, honey?" I asked. "Just because he had a little overnight success, Donald didn't have to go off and start messing around with goddamn Dottie Moss."

"He wasn't messing around, Maddie," Holly said. "He was ambushed."

Our first course arrived—*primi piatti,* an assortment of the chef's best appetizers and a knockout antipasti platter that's not on the menu but is not to be missed.

"Carlos had gotten stuck in the loo. Dottie didn't buy his story, so he showed her where the sticky door was. Then later, Dottie introduced herself to Donald, coming on strong. You know the deal. He's the most talented man making movies today. He's a genius. Blah-blah-friggin'-blah. He tried to excuse himself, so he could pee, and that's when Dottie told him she needed to go, too, and she'd show him where the men's room was. So what could he do? His mamma raised him polite, so he followed her."

"No!" Wes said, following the plot as he forked a startlingly tender morsel of fresh Maryland crab cake, swirled it in the bed of sautéed red onion and basil, and raised it up to his lips.

"Yes! You know, earlier? When Carlos got stuck? He propped the door open with a little notebook, so no one else would get into trouble. But when Dottie got there with Donald, she opened the door and must have kicked that little notebook that was acting like a doorjamb aside, on purpose! Well, you all know what a good boy Donald is. But he was getting himself alarmed. Donald told her she shouldn't come into the john and that's when that witch Dottie let go of the door so the two of them would be trapped inside together."

In seminars advising folks how to break into show business, they often urge you to find creative ways to network. Dottie could teach the advanced class.

"So they couldn't get out. Donald swore to me he tried really hard. Anyway, while they were waiting to be rescued, Dottie began suggesting ideas for movie roles she could play. And at first, that idiot Donald took her seriously, telling her why he wouldn't be interested in updating *Gone with the Wind* to the future, with an intergalactic war and stupid old Dottie playing the part of Scarlett O'Martian. She had millions of ideas. That slut said she was ready to audition. And that she had no objections whatsoever to full frontal nudity.''

''And that's when . . .'' Wes said, eyes widening. He was the only one at that table who had not seen Dottie standing in the nude, so his imagination was getting a workout.

''She pitched him the idea of doing a sci-fi adventure loosely based on the story of Salome and then she began to dance around the bathroom stalls as she stripped to the skin.''

''Oh, man! Where are the security cameras when you really need them?'' Wes asked.

''Oh, Holly,'' I said. ''What did Donald do?''

''Okay, this is the part that really convinced me that he was telling the truth. Donald said he'd never seen a body like hers dancing around like that without a stitch. So he just sort of enjoyed it. I mean there she was. He's a straight guy. He couldn't stop her,'' Holly said, repeating Donald's defense. And then she looked at me and asked straight out, ''Is looking wrong?''

''Nothing wrong with looking,'' I agreed, hoping that was really all that went on.

''Everyone looks,'' concurred Wes. ''That's what this town is about.''

''But here's the real sweet part,'' Holly said, tasting her *carpaccio di pesca spada* for the first time. The house-smoked swordfish was served with cucumbers, lemon, and olive oil and really deserved more attention, but she was almost at the end of her tale. ''Donald never for the world wanted to hurt me, and, well, I believe him.''

Can a man ever be trusted? I found I was pretty unqualified to give any advice, so I just munched the fresh roasted peppers from the antipasto platter.

''I had to make a choice, you know? Like do I believe him and give him another chance? Or do I kick him out of my life like scum?''

''Not every man in the universe is scum,'' Wes asserted.

Both Holly and I looked at him.

"That may not be the strongest argument right now," I said.

"Well, the biggest problem I had with his explanation was how in all of Dottie's surreal dancing about did his fly come to be unzipped?"

This had also been my unspoken question. Inquiring minds want to know.

"See, he had this wicked urge to whiz. When he realized he was stuck inside the men's room with Dottie, he was literally ready to have an accident. Dottie told him not to be silly. Use the next stall."

"Two seconds later, me and Maddie are bursting in and all hell is opening up and swallowing us whole."

"Wild!" I said.

"Maddie, if it was you, would you believe him?"

"It's not about proof, it's about trust," I told her. Wise old Mad Bean. What I didn't say is that trust is like faith—you have to surrender to it, something I seemed incapable of doing. I was prepared to die rather than surrender. Wasn't this the crux of my problems with men? My mind reeled.

"So you and Donald are back together?" Wes asked, finishing the grilled prawns with cannellini beans in fresh tomato and sage on my plate.

"Like Bill and Hillary!" she said, exultant, and not, I'm afraid, picking a faultless comparison. "This afternoon we had the best sex, you know where he's trying to make it up to me for all the suffering he's caused."

"Okay, then! We are finished with the details," Wes said, primly.

"That whore Dottie Moss thinks she can dance? Well, baby, she's got a whole lot more mileage on her than this model, no matter how far she's turned her odometer back. When it comes to dancing without any—"

"Too much information," Wes said, interrupting cheerfully. "What about this baked wild mushrooms soufflé?"

"Oh, wait!" Holly said, remembering something as our plates were cleared and a second bottle of wine appeared.

"Mad, tell us whatever happened with the police."

"They found Victor Zoda's body, eventually. He had run into a locked-up pantry and died there."

"Did they determine the cause of death?" Wes asked, concerned. I had, after all, been holding the knife that Victor fell on.

"They called it a heart attack," I said. "Although he had lost a lot of blood . . ."

"Don't even think it," Wes said, concerned about me. "And Xavier gave them his eyewitness account of what occurred. You were just keeping Zoda from hurting Xavier further. You were holding him until the police came."

"Yeah, yeah, yeah . . ." I was unsure, even now, how far I would have gone. Or how far I actually did go.

"So the cops aren't going to bother you about Zoda, right?" Holly asked.

"It's over," I said, relieved. "Chuck Honnett felt terrible. He had promised me that Zoda would be stopped before he even entered the Mayfield, but that didn't happen. Then when he checked up, he had been told that Zoda was in custody."

"What was up with that?" Wes asked. "Why'd they put you in danger when you warned them about Zoda up front?"

"The security checkpoint was given orders to stop Zoda. And they did. They arrested Beatrice Zoda."

"Wicked B?" Holly asked, shocked.

"They thought she looked suspicious. Her hairstyle is not typical for one invited to a conservative function. And her name was on their list. That's why Honnett was told they had Zoda. Pretty dense, huh?"

"Cops," Wes said, who was not neutral on the subject. "What do you expect?"

"Well," I said, with a glint of a twinkle in my eye, "I may be in for some of the makeup activity about which you cut Holly off before she got to the good part."

"What?" both Holly and Wes shouted.

"Honnett. He wants to take me out to apologize."

"He thinks a dinner is going to make up for almost getting you killed?" Wes asked.

"Order lobster," Holly advised.

"I told him no. But now I'm inspired by Holly's amazing ability to forgive. I'm going to give him a chance."

"You'll see," Holly squealed. "When they're groveling and apologizing they are at their very best!"

Wes shook his head, in silent pain, but allowed us to get our frustrations out by this mild male bashing.

"But I thought Arlo was back in your life," Wes asked.

"Yeah, well . . ."

Arlo was a hothouse flower. He needed careful attention. He could only tolerate limited temperature variations. His food requirements were tricky. In short, Arlo was high maintenance. And it must have occurred to him that without me around, there was no one to water and feed him, to say nothing of pruning his buds. He had second thoughts and wanted back.

"Well, which one do you want?" Holly asked.

"Say," Wes interrupted, "where did you get that necklace?"

The lovely antique cross was covered in tiny diamonds and hung from a very long fine gold chain. Caught in the candlelight from the table, the diamonds sparkled magnificently.

"Oh, this old thing," I said, smiling as I fingered the pavé diamonds, the encrusted surface feeling rough against my thumb. "Xavier gave it to me."

"It's like baseball," Holly muttered. "You strike three men out and then, next thing you know, it's a new inning and it's like back to the top of the batting order."

Wes and I looked at her. Since when did Holly watch baseball? Must be Donald. We were none of us immune to the influences of each relationship.

"Did he really kiss you?" Holly asked.

"I'm not going . . ."

"I told you about Donald's zipper," she cried, indignantly. "You owe me."

"I believe he did," I said. "I believe he would have gone on kissing me if we hadn't been interrupted."

"Ahem," Wes said, wanting to make his point. "Interrupted by *the pope*, for crissakes!"

"Hey, I'd been waiting for that kiss for eight years. It better have been interrupted by someone pretty important." I smiled at him. "Anyway, it released me, in a way. I could finally put some of that old drama to rest."

"And Xavier . . ." Holly asked.

"This necklace belonged to his sister. He gave it to me as a goodbye gift. He's gone back to Pennsylvania. He knows what he wants to do with his life. I always thought he'd made the wrong choice. I'd thought if it had been right for him to join the church he should have been able to keep me in his life, too, as a friend. But, now, I don't think things are as black and white as I like them to be."

"But Madeline Bean does not see gray," Wes joked.

"We'll see," I said. "But I do have some news about Monsignor Picca's journals. Xavier has a friend, another Jesuit brother, who is anxious to finish the monsignor's research."

"But the story of that old pope's assassination! How is Rome handling that bombshell?" Holly asked. "And that missing encyclical. What do they say?"

"No comment," I answered. "They say conspiracy theories are always popular, and nothing more. Can you believe that?"

"Figures," Wes said, closing his eyes in a silent protest. "They will neither confirm nor deny. It's standard."

"It reeks!" Holly said, upset.

"It's the way the real world works. Unless some proof magically appears, my unsubstantiated rambling tale of a story that may or may not have happened sixty years ago doesn't mean spit. Zoda's name will never be connected with his horrible crimes. That old man, Victor Zoda, took a lot of secrets with him to the grave. Only Xavier and I heard him confess the truth. But that is not enough."

"But Xavier's friend. When he goes public with the monsignor's research . . ."

"When Xavier's friend publishes this story in a few years," I said, realistically, "I doubt many will even pay attention."

"Whoa! That's like the end of *Raiders of the Lost Ark*. Big earth-shattering deal, and in the end, it's covered up and tucked away," Holly said. "Amazing!"

"Wait a minute," I said, looking across the main dining room at Cucina Paradiso. "Is that who I think it is?"

Wes said, "Where? Who?"

"Oh my gosh!" Holly said. "It's those two women who were on that diet. The ones from our breakfast who gave the waitress such a hard time."

"They couldn't eat fruit, remember?" Wes said.

"Not until after two," I said, smiling. "They had a list."

"Well don't look now," Holly said, "but their list must say that on Friday night they can scarf four servings of tiramisu. Each."

We howled. Now that was one diet that I could manage.

And then, my buddy Alex Lombardo came out to sit down with us and sample some of his world famous bread pudding. Just for us, this incredible chef brought out a special treat, a tiny castle which had been constructed out of dark and white chocolate, sitting in a puddle of raspberry puree. I felt the walls suddenly close in upon me.

It hit me like a ton of bricks. The last nagging piece of the puzzle dropped into place. I believed I had just discovered one more secret that Victor Zoda had been hiding all these years. And this one could actually bring the bastard's reputation down to hell where it belonged.

Chapter 28

It was almost midnight when Lieutenant Chuck Honnett pulled his old Mustang convertible up in front of the dark home in Encino. Wesley and Holly and I had been waiting outside for over an hour. Almost at once, two patrol cars joined us, and everyone got out of their respective vehicles.

"You've got it?" I asked, nervously.

"I got Judge Edward Randell to leave his cigar night at his club. He signed the search warrant but he reminded me we could've waited until Monday morning, what with the suspect being . . . *dead.*"

"Sorry," I said, as we walked up the narrow sidewalk that led to the entrance of Victor Zoda's home.

The front door sported a lockbox, the kind realtors use when they want to leave the door keys available for showing a property. With Zoda dead, the house and all its contents had been sealed pending probate.

"Has anyone gone through the house yet?" I asked, as Honnett spun the tumblers on the combination lock and opened the strongbox, which held the keys.

"His probate attorney was out here, yesterday, with some family members," Honnett said. "Nobody found anything funny."

"Let's go in," I said. I led the way toward the back of the house, flipping light switches as I went, remembering the evening last week when I'd first visited Victor Zoda.

"Back here," I said. The patrol officers stayed at the

door while Holly and Wesley tried to keep up with Honnett and me.

In the family room, nothing much had changed. The brown Naugahyde furniture. The green shag wall-to-wall. I noticed the cookie crumbs had been vacuumed, but otherwise, the room was very much as I remembered it. On the walls, oak paneling featured bookshelves filled with Reader's Digest versions of the classics.

"In here," I said, trying the handle on a door that was set into the paneling. It was locked.

Honnett stepped forward with the ring of keys he'd extracted from the lockbox. He fitted several narrow keys into the lock, but none of them turned.

"I'll call the officers out front," Honnett said. "They brought axes. I guess we could go at it that way."

"Wait a second," I said. I looked around the room, wondering where an old man would put a key. On the bookshelf, the Reader's Digest novels looked untouched. *Lost Horizon. Great Expectations.* What interest, I wondered, had Zoda shown for literature? And then I saw a volume that interested me. With its creased spine and worn navy leatherette binding, it was the one book that looked like it had been read. I pulled it off the shelf.

"What is it?" Wes asked, moving closer.

"*Treasure Island,*" Holly said, reading the title.

"I think this is it," I said. "There's something tucked inside."

When I opened the book, it appeared normal. I flipped a few chapters until I found a hiding spot carved into the body of the book. A rectangular chunk had been gouged out. In that space lay a small bronze key.

We waited in silence until the door was opened. The room beyond was black. Switching on his flashlight, Honnett led the way.

"Watch it," he advised. There was a step down into the next room, as if this section of the house had been an addition, constructed after the original building was complete.

I felt against the wall to find the light switch, but couldn't find one.

When all four of us had made it safely into that dark room off the family room, our eyes began adjusting to the charcoal gloom. Soon we could make out shapes as we followed the beam of Honnett's lone flashlight. Up above, surrounding the room, I could see blackout curtains hanging over high windows. In the ceiling, the room featured several large concave acrylic skylights that revealed the black of an overcast night.

There wasn't any furniture, but there was a large object in the very center of the room. It was shaped like a box, five feet by ten feet, which was set on a raised platform. The entire unit was completely covered in a shroud of black duvetyn. The beam from Honnett's flashlight disappeared as he circled behind the object and then came around the other side.

"It's not a coffin, is it?" Holly asked.

"Zoda wasn't a vampire," Wes answered, and then said, "Careful, Holly."

Backing up, to get a better look at the entire object, Holly had tripped and caught herself. In gripping the side of the doorframe, she'd found the button that worked the lights.

A blaze of bright floodlights flashed on, and at the same time, the sound of a motor, as the black curtains began to part at the high windows, and the large black duvetyn drape covering the object in the middle of the room began to lift.

"What the . . . ?" Honnett said.

We stared, amazed, as the shroud was lifted. Beneath, in the high-watt glow of the floodlights, the dazzling miniature image of Catherine the Great's Treasure Room began to be exposed.

"I'll be damned," Honnett said, beginning to smile. "Here it is, just like you said. This thing must be worth a fortune. Those jewels are real, you say?"

"I'm sure they are," I said, staring at the perfect replica of Zoda's passion, the fabled Amber Room of Imperial Russia.

"Hot dog, Maddie," Holly said, excited. "Is there a rule about finders keepers?"

"Amazing," Wesley said, walking up and touching the miniature panels inlaid with amber stones. "You said the original room from the tsar's palace outside St. Petersburg was one thousand square feet. So Zoda must have built this thing to a perfect one-twentieth scale."

While they were marveling over the model, standing in the dazzling reflection of thousands of pieces of cut amber, I was searching the rest of the room.

"What now?" Holly asked me. "Isn't this what you thought we would find?"

"I'm looking for another door," I said.

Honnett and Wes looked around. In the new brilliance of the high intensity floodlights, there was clearly no way to hide a door. The walls were constructed of wallboard and plaster, with not a detail of molding with which to hide a door seam.

"Nothing else here," Honnett said.

Holly, who had joined me at the farthest wall, her nose an inch away from the plaster, said, "I think this is all she wrote."

I turned to the center of the room, where the raised platform held the remarkable model of Catherine the Great's stolen treasure room. I walked up to it and tried pushing. Nothing budged.

"You need help?" Wes asked, and was quickly beside me, putting his muscle into the job. Still, nothing moved.

"It's probably bolted to the floor," Honnett said. But he, too, came to my side and started to push.

"Nothing's gonna give," he said.

I peered at the jeweled miniature. The room was duplicated down to the tiniest detail. It was a fairyland castle, with miniature doors and chandeliers.

"Wait a minute," I said. I put my hand carefully into the scaled down model and turned the tiny gold key that was inserted into the exquisite gold lock on the door of the toy jewel room.

We heard a click.

Then, the platform holding the gleaming amber model began to move. Some motorized apparatus rolled the entire structure to the side, leaving a clearing at the center of the room. On the stretch of dark carpet that had been exposed we could all clearly see a large rectangle of mahogany set flush with the floor. It was a hatch with a silver handle.

Now Honnett was bending over, lifting on the hatch. Now Wesley was shouting he had it, as he held the hatch door open so that Honnett and I could look below. They had revealed a secret staircase that led down to a lower level. Beneath our feet was a hidden subterranean room.

Quickly, we charged down the steps. And in an instant, we saw the real treasure that Victor Zoda had been hiding all these years.

In the basement of an ugly green stucco tract home, in a fifties housing development, in a suburb of Los Angeles, stood the jewel-encrusted grand ballroom which the king of Prussia had bestowed upon the Imperial House of Peter the Great in the eighteenth century. Worshipped by the Russians, lusted after by the Nazis, and then, amazingly, missing without a trace for fifty years. The final payoff from some fleeing Nazi criminal to the man who demanded riches in exchange for freedom.

Here, in all its splendor, stood the reconstructed jewel room of the tsars. This twenty-by-fifty-foot rec room, sparkled with dazzling carved amber panels and valued beyond price, would have been the perfect spot, no doubt, to throw a pretty awesome neighborhood Tupperware party.

"You did it," Holly said, whispering in the shadow of the majesty of the room.

"That old bastard," Honnett said, looking at me with something I could have mistaken for respect. "When this hits the fan, Zoda's reputation as a great humanitarian and benefactor will be destroyed."

"You know, Maddie," Wes said, putting his arm around me and leading me to a glittering corner of the room, slightly away from the others, "this means something. It's big. And you're the one who did it. Now can't you see that you are here for a reason?''

"You mean, here in the Treasure Room, or here on this planet?''

Wes smiled at me, raising an eyebrow.

"Are you trying to say that . . . ?''

For one clear moment, I was struck by the thought that there might be a purpose, after all, to the random mayhem of the millions of souls that crash into the rocks of their daily lives. Why did Brother Ugo's plea for forgiveness wait all these decades to slip out into my kitchen? Why did I decide to get involved?

"You mean, it was all preordained? I was supposed to help settle this score? Wesley, you're getting all California cosmic on me,'' I said, trying to push away the overwhelming sense that a universe I'd considered hopeless might be a little less so.

"I mean, can't you open yourself to the possibility that all events, all actions have a purpose? Even those things, Maddie, that make us sick with grief. That beat us down. Even the most horrible pain we are forced to endure?''

"You mean like Xavier breaking my heart years ago? So I could be on my own now, doing what I love to do?''

"I mean like everything,'' Wes said, and hugged me.

"Way too California,'' I said, pulling back from him and laughing.

"What do you make of all this?'' I heard Holly ask Chuck Honnett across the room.

Eavesdropping, I expected a level-headed answer from a predictably jaded source.

He looked around at the shimmering amber panels and said, "Well, maybe some of us better start thanking God she's on our side.''

by
TAMAR MYERS

LARCENY AND OLD LACE
78239-1/$5.99 US/$7.99 Can

As owner of the Den of Antiquity, Abigail Timberlake is accustomed to navigating the cutthroat world of rival dealers at flea markets and auctions. But she never thought she'd be putting her expertise in mayhem and detection to other use—until her aunt was found murdered . . .

GILT BY ASSOCIATION
78237-5/$5.99 US/$7.99 Can

A superb gilt-edged, 18th-century French armoire Abigail purchased for a song at estate auction has just arrived along with something she didn't pay for: a dead body.

THE MING AND I
79255-9/$5.99 US/$7.99 Can

Digging up old family dirt can uncover long buried secrets . . . and a new reason for murder.

SO FAUX, SO GOOD
79254-0/$5.99 US/$7.99 Can

Buy these books at your local bookstore or use this coupon for ordering:

Mail to: Avon Books, Dept BP, Box 767, Rte 2, Dresden, TN 38225 G
Please send me the book(s) I have checked above.
❑ My check or money order—no cash or CODs please—for $__________is enclosed (please add $1.50 per order to cover postage and handling—Canadian residents add 7% GST). U.S. residents make checks payable to Avon Books; Canada residents make checks payable to Hearst Book Group of Canada.
❑ Charge my VISA/MC Acct#____________________Exp Date________
Minimum credit card order is two books or $7.50 (please add postage and handling charge of $1.50 per order—Canadian residents add 7% GST). For faster service, call 1-800-762-0779. Prices and numbers are subject to change without notice. Please allow six to eight weeks for delivery.
Name__________________________________
Address__________________________________
City________________State/Zip________________
Telephone No.________________ TM 1098